Snowy and the Seven Doves

A Twist Upon a Regency Tale
Book 3

By Jude Knight

ARE YOU SIGNED UP FOR DRAGONBLADE'S BLOG?

You'll get the latest news and information on exclusive giveaways, exclusive excerpts, coming releases, sales, free books, cover reveals and more.

Check out our complete list of authors, too!

No spam, no junk. That's a promise!

Sign Up Here

www.dragonbladepublishing.com

Dearest Reader;

Thank you for your support of a small press. At Dragonblade Publishing, we strive to bring you the highest quality Historical Romance from some of the best authors in the business. Without your support, there is no 'us', so we sincerely hope you adore these stories and find some new favorite authors along the way.

Happy Reading!

CEO, Dragonblade Publishing

DEDICATION

To the man who has been my personal romantic hero for five and a half decades (and counting). What I have learned about love and about successful marriages, I learned largely with and from you. Thank you, my love.

May my readers be blessed with a love provides strength to face love's trials, comfort in life's sorrows, joys to warm the heart, memories to treasure, and laughter to lighten the days.

ABOUT THE BOOK

Abandoned in the slums when he was little, Snowy has grown up in the House of Blossoms, a brothel owned by the seven soiled doves who rescued him from the streets. As his twenty-fifth birthday approaches, his foster mothers tell him the truth of his origins, and of the enemy who stole his birthright.

They have a plan for him to take his rightful place in Society, as an escort to a renowned countess whose kindness and courtesy surprisingly overturns all his preconceptions about the selfishness of the aristocracy.

Margaret, Countess Charmain, balances her duties to her estate and her people with practicing the herbal medicine her mother taught her. When an errand of mercy takes her into the slums, and Snowy rescues her from attack, she incurs an obligation to the chivalrous but surly fellow. She will discharge it by letting the arrogant man escort her to a few social functions.

Behind the public identities each wear, they discover a person to love, and a bright tomorrow neither thought possible. But to claim it, they must overcome the villains who destroyed their pasts and would steal their future together.

Chapter One

Seven Dials, London, April 1819

"THAT COUNTESS IS back again," Tommy reported.

Snowy tossed his pen down as he rose. *Pestiferous woman.* If he'd told her once, he'd told her a dozen times that venturing into the slums to visit the residents of a brothel put both her reputation and her life at risk.

The stubborn female's high birth and fancy title would not protect her if some of the slime who polluted the narrow ways behind the building decided to kill her fancy footmen and help themselves to a taste of noble flesh. Had she not learned that the hard way?

To be fair, the front entrance that Tommy guarded was on a tolerable street, right on the edge of the Covent Garden theater district. Her life was probably not at risk during the daytime, though if she was seen entering, her good name would be history. He didn't save her to see her ruined.

Snowy's anger rose again at the recollection of their first meeting. He would never forget his first sight of the lovely young woman standing over her footman's body and swinging a weighted reticule to keep six armed men at bay.

"Go back to your post," Snowy growled at Tommy. "I'll see

to the lady." He left his account books and locked the door of his office. He would escort Lady Charmain home—*again*—once she had finished whatever errand of mercy brought her back to the House of Blossoms.

He sighed. If he had not brought the lady here for refuge after he'd rescued her, she would never have met the women who lived here, and never have begun bringing them herbal remedies from her still room. *How did a countess become a gifted herbalist?*

No. He did not want to know. His only interest was in seeing the lady returned to her own world.

Or, at least, that was the only interest that he would be satisfying. His desire for the lady was out of place, ridiculous, and impossible. *She is a noble lady, and you are a slum brat raised in a brothel.* Fortified by the reminder, he slowed his steps. No need to hurry through the place as if anxious to see her.

Blue, whose nickname was an ironic comment on his flaming red hair, guarded the flight of stairs to the floor with the private apartments. He stood as Snowy approached. "Where is the countess?" Snowy asked.

Blue jerked a finger up the stairs. "Wiv Mistress Lily," he grunted, which took some of the wind out of Snowy's sails. If Lily herself had invited the aristocrat to visit, then Snowy's objections were on shaky ground. Lily would not have brought the countess here on a whim.

At his knock, Lily called for him to enter. "Snowy," she said. "I am pleased you are here. You know Lady Charmain, of course."

Snowy gave the lady his best court bow. "My lady." Not only did Lily expect him to display the impeccable manners she had paid his tutors to beat into him, but it discomposed Countess Charmain, which was turnabout and fair play, for she had been discomposing him since the day he'd looked into her vivid blue eyes.

"Good afternoon, Mr. White." The lift to her chin hinted that she knew he disapproved of her presence and was ready to challenge him on it.

Lily ignored the tension, though Snowy had no doubt she was aware of it. No one could read people better than Mistress Lily. "Lady Charmain has brought over the herbs and other ingredients for the poultice she recommended to Jasmine. Will you take her down to the kitchen, Snowy, so she can show Poppy how to make it?"

"I was busy," Snowy grumbled. That fetched him the glare that, when he was younger, would have presaged a clip across the ear. He had received a few, because he'd been a cheeky young brat, full of his own importance. In the House of Blossoms, Lily's word was law. Even those who owned the house with her seldom argued with her decisions. Those who wished to live under her benign protection did as they were told or suffered the consequences.

Snowy grinned at the memory of a few trespasses she had not discovered, and gave the countess another extravagant bow. "If you will allow me to show you the way, Lady Charmain."

She moved to pick up her basket from a table, but Snowy got to it first. "I will carry it," he insisted. It wasn't heavy, but it was the principle of the thing. Ladies had servants to carry their packages. He needed to act the servant to emphasize the distance between her class and his. Not that it made any difference to the troubling physical reaction that plagued him in her presence.

She led the way down the passage toward the stairs, past the private bedchambers of the girls who worked in the house.

It was mid-afternoon, and most of them were still asleep. Not all.

Orchid leaned against the doorway of her room buffing her fingernails, her brightly colored robe draped to show her cleavage and her long, bare legs. Orchid was probably not her real name, but it had become tradition in the House of Blossoms to adopt a flower name in imitation of the seven founders, the original Blossoms, who were all either named for flowers at their christening or had adopted the name of a flower as a working name.

Daphne, in a short chemise that barely skimmed the top of her thighs, leaned out of her door to see who was passing, the neck tie loose so her ample breasts nearly tumbled out.

The pair of them had a bet on, which Snowy had heard about from Poppy, the cook. A guinea was at stake over which of them would be the first to take Snowy as a lover. Both of them were going to lose. Snowy had long since lost interest in casual encounters but was not in the market for anything more serious.

Flaunting their assets wasn't going to change his mind. In fact, he and Poppy had a side bet on which would give up the chase first and, in the meantime, he locked his bed chamber door and the door at the top of the stairs leading to his attic apartment.

Neither of the girls looked directly at the countess. They had even less idea than Snowy how to interact with a female of her class.

Since the House was not currently open for business, he conducted Lady Charmain down the main stairs, and then through the reception rooms on the ground floor to the kitchen stairs. She said nothing, her face a mask of amiable interest.

If the girls upstairs knew how his body reacted to the primly dressed, imperious, waspish countess, they would laugh themselves silly.

Mr. White was his usual surly self. He disapproved of a lady like Margaret visiting the slums, and particularly a house like this, or that's what he'd said, though his mocking bows hinted it was Margaret herself to whom he took exception.

Or perhaps he was like this with everyone. Certainly, he walked past the two scantily clad women upstairs as if they did not exist, though they were clearly displaying themselves in the hopes of attracting his attention.

Her deepest scars came from men like that in her own world. Arrogant, conceited men convinced that everyone else—and especially every female—was inferior. Men who paid attention to others only when it served their purposes.

Men like her deceased father and brothers. Like the officer who'd courted her in her dismal first Season so her father would pay him to go away, which he did, out of Margaret's dowry. Like the suitors who had clustered about her since she'd become an heiress, eagerly in lust with her title, her lands, and her bank account.

Mr. White was like the rest of them, and her fascination with him was ridiculous.

Perhaps it was a by-product of his rescue, which had admittedly been spectacular. If she closed her eyes, she could see him again, as she saw him in dreams that replayed that terrible evening.

She is walking through a narrow alley in the dusk, her mind still on the patient, a badly beaten woman, whom she had visited in a tumble-down building in the stews.

Without warning, men appear out of the darkness. Her footman goes down before either of them can react, felled by a cosh to the head. She shrinks back against a wall, and they gather around her, hooting and laughing, enjoying her fear. She understands little of their thieves cant, but she is not a fool. She knows what they have in mind.

She stands over the footman's unconscious body, jabbing at her attackers with her umbrella, vowing to inflict as much pain as possible before they take her.

Suddenly, another man is there. An incredibly handsome man, with close-cropped dark hair and the build of a Greek god. Two of her five attackers go down under his assault, out of the fight.

She fights the other three at his side until they flee. He turns to her, and she looks into his grey eyes and prepares to thank him. He speaks first.

"What the hell is a lady like you doing here? This is not Mayfair, princess. You cannot walk around the slums as if you own them." A

well-educated voice. The tones of a gentleman of her own class. An indignant reply is on the tip of her tongue, but before she can say a word, her mind disappears down a spiral of darkness.

The dreams ended there, but in real life she woke up in the House of Blossoms, being treated for a cut to the arm that had bled profusely and several blows to the head. Her footman, too. And the driver and groom who had been waiting in the street, and whom her assailants must have attacked before they came after her.

Mr. White, she was told, had loaded them all into her carriage and driven them to the brothel. When she tried to thank him, he berated her again for stepping out of her place. "I should never have had to bring you and the men you endangered here," he complained.

Mr. White was a conundrum. Educated, as she had noted from the first. He bowed like a courtier but worked in a brothel as their bookkeeper. Apart from those two scolds in the heated aftermath of the attack, he was always exceptionally polite, but he made his disapproval clear with every overly ornate bow, every frown, every quirk of a sardonic eyebrow.

She did not know the source of his objection. Was it because he thought Margaret should not be in a disorderly house, or because it was his home?

What would he think of Mistress Lily's proposal? He would refuse it, of course. She should have refused herself, except that Mistress Lily said allowing Snowy to escort her to three ton events would repay her debt to the House of Blossoms and Mr. White for preventing her rape and murder. That's what she said. Rape and murder. Harsh words for a harsh reality.

Honest words, shocking to the ears of one who lived in the Polite World, where truths were unspoken or decorated to the point of invisibility, and where lies were told with sincere conviction.

"Say nothing of this," Mistress Lily had said. "Now that I have your agreement, I will speak with Snowy."

Which left Margaret with nothing at all to talk about, and Mr. White was uncommunicative at the best of times. They descended to the kitchen in silence.

Poppy, the cook, was alone in the kitchen. She was a statuesque redhead in her forties, much the same age as Mistress Lily. Unlike the brothel owner, Poppy was a friendly soul with a warm smile, which she turned to Margaret as she and Mr. White entered the kitchen.

"It is the countess! What can I do for you today, my lady? Have you come to sample my apple tarts?"

"Lily says her ladyship is to show you how to make a poultice for Jasmine," Mr. White grumbled.

Poppy spared him a glance. "Is that right?" She beckoned to Margaret. "Come over here, my duck. You can spread your doings out on the table and tell me what they all are."

Mr. White put the basket on the table and stepped out of the way.

Margaret began to take the ingredients out packet by jar by bundle, opening each one and explaining its place in the poultice.

The cloth—finely woven muslin—would have boiling water poured on it to heat it. The prepared herbs would be boiled, too, then wrapped in the cloth. Margaret had chamomile flowers, licorice and ginger root, both to be grated, and cinnamon bark. Some swore by mustard seed, and others used the fruit of the fennel plant, but Margaret's mother had good results from those four items, and Margaret continued using her recipe.

The last item was a bottle of almond oil.

"When the cloth and its contents are cool enough not to burn, spread a palmful of the oil on the patient's abdomen, and then place the poultice over it. When the pain is particularly bad, I find it effective to put a wrapped, heated brick against the poultice to keep it warm, so it will work for longer."

Poppy nodded. "I understand. Now go ahead and make one, and I shall watch." Without looking away or changing her tone, she picked up a wooden spoon and cracked it down, almost catching Mr. White's fingers as he attempted to take an apple tart that was cooling on a rack at the end of the table. "Snowy. No pinching."

"You offered one to the countess," he complained.

"You haven't earned it," the cook retorted.

Mr. White put his head on one side, and his eyes pleading, his mouth drooping. "Awwww. Poppy."

The boyish begging tugged at Margaret's heart. He might be a conceited pompous ass, but he clearly loved the brothel's cook.

The smile he sent Margaret was almost shy. "Poppy makes the finest apple tarts in the world," he said.

Poppy blushed with pleasure. "Get along with you. He'd sell his soul for an apple tart, Lady Charmain. Even one made with dried apple."

"Or a pie," Mr. White added. "Poppy's pies are even better than her tarts."

"Make yourself useful, my duck," Poppy commanded Mr. White. "Once her ladyship has the water she needs, bring the kettle back to the boil and make a cup of tea. We'll all three have a drink and an apple tart while we wait for the poultice to cool. Carry on, Lady Charmain."

Snowy had to admit that the countess sounded as if she knew her herbs. Besides, Jasmine could do with the help. She was the oldest of the seven soiled doves who had pooled their resources to start the House of Blossoms. ("Soiled doves" was one of the politer terms the gentlemen visitors used for the women who serviced them.) Jasmine had been having unpleasant cramps during her woman's inconvenience for as long as Snowy could remember, and they had become worse in the past three years. He hoped Lady Charmain's remedy would give her some relief.

Like Poppy and Lily, Jasmine no longer accommodated the gentlemen visitors. Her piano playing, though, was a favorite entertainment for those who were waiting for the girl of their choice, recovering from a bout of mattress thrashing, or just spending an evening out.

A surprising number of gentlemen came to the House of Blossoms merely to play cards, listen to the music, enjoy Poppy's cooking, and talk. Lily, who had been one of the most sought-after courtesans of her generation, taught the girls that listening to their clients with every sign of fascination was an even more important skill than those they exercised upstairs.

Other residents of the house were also troubled each month by the same complaint, if not as badly. If the poultice proved successful, it would make a difference to them, too.

Snowy relaxed once he saw how Lady Charmain addressed Poppy. He knew she was polite to Lily, but Lily had a presence about her that demanded respect. Even the most drunken and arrogant of lordings spoke respectfully to Lily's face, whatever they might say behind her back.

Poppy was a different matter. She had no such air of command, though she certainly demanded perfection from the girls who worked in the kitchen. She still spoke with more than a trace of the accent of the county from which she hailed. And she was a cook—a lesser being in the eyes of the likes of the countess.

But Poppy had a kind heart and a happy outlook on life. Of the seven women who had raised Snowy, she was the one he had gone to with a scraped knee or hurt feelings. She had always had an encouraging word, a hug or a kiss, and something delicious to eat. So even though Snowy was protective of all the original Blossoms, Poppy had a special place in his heart.

Lady Charmain had greeted her with courtesy. The countess was now paying serious attention to Poppy's questions and answering them politely. She even laughed when Poppy made a joke. Perhaps, she was not that bad, after all.

That was a dangerous line of thought. He needed to continue regarding her as the enemy, lest he act on his attraction and get his face slapped—or worse. What could an actual countess do to a man who offended her?

Then again, he'd seen the way she looked at him when she

thought his attention was elsewhere. Perhaps she would be amenable to his advances. He'd found out at Oxford that many fine ladies liked a romp with a peasant, as long as nobody knew about it. His first aristocratic lover had explained that to him, when he had wanted to take her driving.

"One can enjoy a bit of the rough in private, sweet boy," she had told him. "However, one is never seen in public with the help."

Snowy was no longer a boy, and he was certainly not sweet. He had sworn off aristocratic ladies (though only after putting aside enough from their gifts to fund his first investment). In any case, he never dallied with married women. Lady Charmain was a countess, so therefore she must have an earl. Whoever or whatever she had, Snowy considered him a useless waste of space who did not take proper care of his lady. Why else would she be visiting the slums?

In any case, she was off limits on both counts. He would not be making any advances, however much the countess disturbed his dreams.

"There," she said, folding the muslin into a parcel. "Now, we wait for it to cool."

Snowy moved over to the tray with the tea pot snug in its cozy, a jug of milk and a bowl of sugar lumps, and three cups. "Now," he said, "we can eat apple tarts."

Chapter Two

TODAY BEING A Thursday, Margaret was not able to linger at the House of Blossoms. As soon as the poultice was cool enough to use, she and Poppy took it up to the suffering Jasmine, and then Margaret called for her carriage. Mr. White materialized from somewhere to escort her, insisting on riding with her driver to the edge of Mayfair.

She opened the carriage door to call her thanks as he walked away. He turned back and tossed her a smile and a wave. Perhaps he was not always a sour grouch.

She arrived with a full hour to change and get ready for her afternoon at home to visitors, then needed to spend twenty minutes soothing Aunt Aurelia. Unfortunately, she had been unable to keep the assault in the slums from her great aunt's ears, since Mr. White had still been lecturing her about her foolhardy behavior when he'd brought her and her servants home, bruised, cut, and shaken.

Now, every time Margaret left the house, Aunt Aurelia was convinced that she was in the most dangerous parts of London, being murdered.

Or, worse, embarrassing the family. Aunt Aurelia was sure Margaret was on the brink of scandal at every moment, with only Aunt Aurelia's constant advice and criticisms keeping her from making another, and more public, mistake like the one that had ruined her first Season.

"You need not worry, Aunt. Mr. White makes sure that no harm comes to me."

Aunt Aurelia sniffed. "It will do your prospects no good, Margaret, if you are known to consort with that brute." The sniff was followed by a sigh. "If only you would accept one of your suitors and get married. Heaven knows, you are not getting any younger."

As Margaret entered the drawing room forty minutes later with her social smile pasted firmly in place, she reflected that, while she might not be getting any younger, her suitors were. The latest had just turned twenty-two and was the son of a man who had been courting her himself for the past two years.

She had refused the father in 1817, when he was plain Mr. Snowden. He was back paying court to her again last year, after his uncle died, making him a viscount. Apparently, he thought the new title might make him more acceptable to her. She refused him again.

Had he sent his son to court her this year? Margaret had a nasty feeling that was the case.

Margaret wanted to bar both Snowdens from her house after what happened to a friend of hers the year before. Aunt Aurelia would not hear of it.

"Lord Snowden was not involved in the attack on Mr. and Mrs. Ashby, Margaret. The magistrate was quite clear. And you know perfectly well that Mr. Snowden was led astray by villains. He was let off with a warning and was very sorry for his mistake."

All of which was true, but not the whole story. Lord Snowden was friend to the Deffew brothers, who had kidnapped Margaret's friend Regina with the help of a group of young men, including the son of one of them and Snowden's own son. Young Deffew was now Lord Snowden's ward, after his father and uncle died in the midst of their crimes.

Margaret did not believe Lord Snowden was entirely innocent of involvement in the affair. Still, it was true that the magistrate had released the young men. And it was easier to let Aunt Aurelia have her way, so here was young Mr. Snowden, in her drawing room again.

"You look delightful today, my lady," said Mr. Snowden, with a courtly bow. At least he had more charm than his father, though she had no doubt he was firmly under his father's thumb, and so would she be if she was foolish enough to take his suit seriously.

His eyes, with dark rings around the pale grey iris, reminded her of another man. His dark hair was similar, too, apart from the flash of white at one temple. "The Snowden streak", he'd called it. "Most men of my family have it. Not my father, but my great-uncle had it, certainly, and so did Father's cousin, I am told."

Margaret wondered if the current Lord Snowden or his cousin had left a souvenir of Town night life to be raised in the House of Blossoms. It was the most likely explanation of the resemblance between Mr. Snowden and Mr. White.

The room, already filled with flowers sent in anticipation of their donors' arrival, soon filled with the bouquet-senders themselves.

The suitors could be divided into four groups. The most obvious were the fortune hunters, for Margaret and her great aunt were the last of their family, and Margaret had inherited everything. Including Aunt Aurelia.

The fortune hunters were usually easy to recognize. If Margaret was in any doubt, her solicitor and the husbands of her closest friends would investigate to find out whether the man in question saw her only as a fat purse to keep him in idle luxury or to feed a gambling habit.

The title hunters were after a more subtle kind of wealth. The deaths of her brothers had left Margaret as the last surviving heir, and her title was one that could descend through a female if only a daughter remained in the direct line. Her sons, if she had sons, would inherit the earldom. Margaret suspected the Snowdens of lusting after her oak leaves.

The Snowdens also wanted Margaret's land. Lord Snowden had been buying up property between her estate and his for years, ever since he'd taken over the management of the Snowden lands from his uncle. He waxed lyrical at every opportunity about the mining opportunities and the benefits of a canal.

No doubt there were others with a yen for her land.

By far the largest group simply gathered around Margaret because she was fashionable, though how that had come about, Margaret wasn't certain. Her looks were nothing special, though they had certainly improved since she was seventeen, a shy debutante hiding in the corner, too tall and sturdy to be overlooked, but with a splodgy complexion, boringly straight hair that refused to take a curl, and no conversation.

Back then, she'd had only a small dowry and no particular connections—her father at that time being a wastrel younger son. Furthermore, her mother was suffering from the illness that later killed her, and for much of the Season, Margaret had been left to the dubious oversight of her father or one of her brothers.

Margaret had been ripe for exploitation then. Now, six years later, she was not only better dressed and better groomed but she had learned to project confidence, and not to give her trust easily. And to be as polite as necessary to the pack—or rather, the gaggle—of suitors, without giving any of them reason to believe she favored one more than any other.

None of Margaret's special friends were in town to leaven the mix. So she was forced to amuse herself, as she usually did, by assigning points for compliments—or removing points for particularly inappropriate ones.

"More glorious than the sun," was not applicable to any human woman, and not even original. In fact, it lost more points for being stolen from the Bible, a misappropriation that bordered on blasphemy.

The *"deep pools of your eyes"* had her wondering whether the would-be charmer had ever seen water.

She'd nearly lost all composure at references to her *"angelic temper"*. It was probably just as well Arial had not been present, for she could just imagine how amused her friend would be at such fudge.

Then there were the would-be poets, who'd insisted on reading her their effusions.

The sonnet that cast her as the fairy queen, and her suitors as her adoring court had nothing in its favor, apart from a rhyme at the end of each line.

Likewise, an ode to her dainty foot completely ignored the size of said appendage and had undoubtedly been repurposed. The author had probably written it for an actress.

Did they honestly believe she appreciated such fustian?

Mr. Snowden won two points. One for the laughing eyes he had turned on her at the "dainty foot" reference, and one for the good manners that prevented him from speaking his critique out loud. She would not appreciate a scuffle in her drawing room, and the poet was sensitive about his verses.

They came and they went, none staying longer than the customary thirty minutes, but the queue of new arrivals seeming endless. By the time the clock struck five and she could turn them all out, she had a headache from all the smiling.

Aunt Aurelia was convinced Margaret would not be happy until she had a husband. Margaret knew she would be miserable married to anyone who didn't want to understand her or who tried to control her.

Which took all of her current suitors off the list of possibilities.

LOTUS, HOLLY, AND Petunia arrived from the farm at mid-morning several days after Lady Charmain's visit. It wasn't often that all six of the surviving founders of the House of Blossoms got together, and it had been seven years since the last time all the founders, even Petunia, met here in London.

Snowy had been touching up the dye he used on his hair—a weekly task since he first went away to school; he didn't find out they were coming until they were already upstairs in Lily's private sitting room, with the door shut, and everyone else told they were not to be disturbed.

Fortunately, not many were awake in the house. The last of the gentlemen who stayed overnight had breakfasted and departed, and the girls and serving staff had gone to bed. But Snowy found a few kitchen servants excitedly discussing the instruction to prepare trays to be taken up to Mistress Lily's rooms. He hovered just outside the door listening to them gossip.

"Place settings for seven," the assistant cook commented.

One of the scullery maids whimpered, "Do you think Mistress Iris will be there? I don't want to carry up a tray if Mistress Iris will be there."

"Don't be more of a fool than you can help," the assistant cook snapped. "Mistress Iris has gone to her maker. She has no need for plates and cutlery. The seventh place will be for Mr. Snowy, of course. Now lift that carefully. The sooner we get these upstairs, the sooner we can all go to bed."

Snowy retreated to his office, wondering what was going on. He was interrupted not five minutes later when the assistant cook knocked on the door. "Mistress Lily wishes you to join the ladies upstairs, Snowy."

Snowy gulped. Was he in trouble? He suppressed the reaction. He was no longer a boy to tremble at a summons to Lily's room. He hoped he showed none of his inward reaction to the assistant cook. "Thank you for bringing the message. Sleep well."

Her eyes were alight with curiosity, but she asked no questions. He couldn't have answered them if she had. He might be a man, but he would be devastated if he had done something to upset the women who had been his family since he was a small child.

Their meeting seven years ago had been because of him. He had finished his one year at Winchester College with excellent marks and a deep resentment of the upper-class boys who had done their best to put him back into the place they thought he belonged.

He had flatly refused to take up the scholarship to Oxford he'd earned, and the ladies gathered to persuade him to change his mind. Even Iris, so sick that she had to be carried from the carriage, made the trip from the farm where she had gone to die.

She told him that university would extend his horizons, showing him a way of life he had not experienced. Lily said it would win him valuable contacts. Jasmine waxed lyrical about the books he would read and the ideas he would encounter. Lotus suggested that a university-educated man would find a better job; one with greater prospects.

Poppy declared it was time he enjoyed himself with other young men, since he lived with women, had been educated by private tutors and knew few people his own age. Holly said that he would not be alone, as he had been at school, for people from many different walks of life went to Oxford. Even Petunia said he should try, "–for you are gentleman, Snowy, and gentlemen go to university."

Snowy had not been able to stand against the seven of them combined. He couldn't bear to disappoint them. They had been right, too, as they always were when they all agreed on something. He had loved Oxford. He had enjoyed being a student, both the life of scholarship and that outside of the books. His opinion of arrogant upper-class idiots had not changed, but he'd made friends among the serious scholars, and kept many of them to this day. One or two of them were even gentry, though neither arrogant nor idiots.

No doubt the ladies had some new plan for his life, but this time, he was an adult, with a plan and a set path. This time, they would not have their way. He mounted the stairs and knocked on the door to be admitted into Lily's sitting room, where the six women sat around a table laid for seven.

Petunia jumped up to give him a hug and a smacking kiss on the cheek. "Snowy! Hello, Snowy! I love you, Snowy."

Snowy returned the hug. "I love you too, Aunt Petunia." When he was a child, he'd called them all "aunt", but he had abandoned the affectionate title after that memorable meeting before he went off to university. He had demanded to know his family origins and Lily had outright refused to discuss the matter, but only after Lotus disclosed he was not related to any of them.

For Petunia, who was confused by change, he made an exception.

"Hello, Lotus," he said now. "Hello, Holly. Did you have a good trip up from the country?"

"The roads are worse than ever," Lotus grumbled.

Holly, who talked more to her plants than to people, just smiled.

"Sit down, love," Poppy told him. "Load your plate, duckie. Eat first, talk later."

Talk about what, Snowy wondered, though he wasn't going to ask. Indeed, they did talk around the table as they ate. Jasmine, who managed the House, did most of the talking.

The news went the other way, too. Lotus, who managed the people at the farm, and Holly, who only ever became voluble when talking about her garden, had plenty to tell their friends and business partners about the market garden and associated barnyard they called the farm.

The farm had been the ladies' first investment outside of the House of Blossoms. Lotus had proposed buying the farm as a refuge for Petunia, who had been badly beaten by a client and had never been quite the same since, Holly, whose shy nature made the work abhorrent to her, and Snowy, because—Lotus said—boys did better with fresh air and lots of space.

"And others," Lotus had said. "It will be a place for us and the girls to go for a break from the work." From the beginning, the House of Blossoms had only employed the willing.

In the fifteen years since they purchased the place, girls had gone there to have babies, to recover from an illness or injury, or to retrain for other work. The farm also made a profit. It not only supplied produce for Poppy's kitchen, but also a number of other commercial eateries in London. Brothels and gambling dens, initially, but now it supplied other places, including a gentleman's club.

When everyone had eaten their fill, Poppy and Petunia cleared the table and set the loaded trays outside the door. Still, no one had mentioned the reason for this gathering.

"Let us move to the comfortable chairs," Poppy suggested.

Lily, the acknowledged leader of them all, had left most of the talking to everyone else, but, as Snowy took his seat, all the others turned their gaze on her.

"Snowy," she said. "If you are wondering whether this meeting is about you, the answer is *yes*. It is." She looked around at her friends as if to garner strength—an unusual sign of vulnerability.

Snowy stayed silent. He could not think of anything he had done to offend or upset any of them. Perhaps—the sudden thought had him gazing uncertainly at each of the six women— one of them was ill? They didn't look any different than usual. Even Jasmine, who was delicately sneezing into a small square of linen, was probably just reacting to the large bunch of flowers that Holly must've brought with her from the country.

Lily cleared her throat. "Seven years ago, you asked me about your parents and your family. I promised your mother that I would tell nobody about you, including you, until the man who tried to kill you was dead or imprisoned, or until you were past the impulsiveness of youth."

Snowy could not have spoken if he tried. This was beyond anything he had expected.

"We—" she gestured to include the other ladies—"decided to wait until you were twenty-five. Next week is your twenty-fifth birthday. I believe your mother would be very proud of you. We—" again the inclusive gesture—"certainly are. You are entirely capable of taking on the villain who stole your future from you, if that is what you decide to do. The decision will be entirely up to you. Once you have all the facts, and have made your choice, we will help in any way we can."

Jasmine smiled as she said, "We have been collecting information to help you for the past nineteen years, Moses." That was the name they had given him, for they'd found him cast adrift from his family and surrounded by human crocodiles. Until they'd dubbed him Snowy, instead. Only Jasmine still called him Moses.

They seemed to be jumping ahead. Snowy needed to know more about what Lily had said already. "Who is my family? Is my mother still alive? Who tried to kill me?"

"Tell him the story in order, Lily," Poppy suggested. "Start with how you found him."

"It was February, and colder than the hearts of men," Lily began. "I was mistress to a nobleman in those days. Had a nice little house in St John's Wood, and no good reason to be in London town, except it was just after Petunia..." she broke off what she had been about to say. "Iris and I were going to visit the herbwoman who was looking after her."

After Aunt Petunia had been beaten to within an inch of her life by a customer, is what Lily did not say. Snowy knew the story. The Madam at the brothel where Petunia had worked wanted to dispose of the evidence by dropping Petunia's battered body into the Thames, even while she was still breathing.

Holly, Lotus, and Jasmine, who'd worked in the same place, stole the injured woman, and Jasmine and Lotus had taken her to a Chinese herbwoman while Holly crossed London to tell Lily and Iris, who were Petunia's sisters.

"You were in the alley where the herbwoman lived, a terrified little boy, all bruised and bloody, naked, and near dead of the cold. I couldn't leave you there. I took you with me to the herbwoman. After she'd patched you up, I was going to drop you off to the orphan asylum. But in the end, I took you home with me. You see, we—my friends and I—guessed whose child you must be."

And you didn't take me back? Snowy wondered. But no. What Lily had said about his mother meant she had tried to return him.

"You spoke like a swell," Lily explained. "And Iris and I recognized the white streak at your temple."

Snowy touched his left temple; the dye he'd been applying a short while before was still damp, and when he pulled his fingers away, they glistened with a thin layer of dark brown. He grimaced but he'd promised Lily he'd always hide it, and she made him repeat that promise every year around this time. The reason for it was suddenly—awfully—clear. He leaned forward.

"I looked like one of your customers?" he asked.

"Like a family from near our home," Lily corrected. "That white streak was in the family. The viscount and his brother had it, and so did the viscount's son. Not the brother's son, though."

Snowy blinked at that. "I am related to a viscount?"

"My dearest duck," said Poppy, "you *are* a viscount."

Chapter Three

MARGARET WAS IN her herb garden. She could not cultivate the full range of culinary or medicinal herbs in unprotected beds beset by the coal dust-laden atmosphere of London, but she grew the species impervious to the conditions.

Other plants, those more sensitive to their environment, she could coax along in her little greenhouse. And still others came down by cart or canal from her estate in North Leicestershire, carefully packed and protected from the sun.

This morning was a fine clear spring day, warm enough that some of the pall of smoke had lifted from the leafy streets surrounding her London home and she'd decided to spend it clipping the rosemary to shape the bushes and encourage growth. The rosemary had finished flowering and the lavender had not started, but the rich spicy scent of the leaves made her work a pleasure, and she was humming to herself when she heard a familiar female voice on the terrace outside the French doors from the drawing room.

"No need to announce me, Bowen. I can see Lady Charmain among her plants."

Margaret straightened and hurried toward the visitor. "Arial! I did not expect you in Town for another two weeks! When did you arrive? Is everyone well? How are the babies?"

She remembered the clippers in her hand just in time to put them down before she hugged her friend in greeting. She and Arial, Countess of Stancroft, had been friends since the day Margaret's mother took her to visit the neighboring estate.

Lady Charmain had been supplying ointment from her still room to soothe Arial's terrible burns since the poor little girl had arrived at Greenmount, near Margaret's home. Arial and her grieving father had escaped a terrible fire that took a large part of their family seat and half of their family, but not before she'd suffered from burns on her face and body that had caused her to hide from Society for most of her life, until she'd married and emerged from her cocoon like a rare, fabulous butterfly.

Margaret had been one of Arial's only childhood friends; when her pain had subsided enough for distraction to make her more comfortable, Lord and Lady Charmain brought along their daughter as a playmate. That first meeting had been followed by many more. After Margaret's own mother died on the heels of the disaster of her first season, Margaret spent more time at Greenmount than she did in her own home.

Arial laughed as she put up four fingers and counted off one. "Let me see. Peter had to come up to town early for a meeting of the Privileges Committee, so we came with him, to save him a four-day journey there and back to get us. He is quite certain only *he* can ensure our safety on the road." She looked up to heaven with her one eye. The ruins of the other were hidden behind the beautifully painted mask that covered half her face from just above the mouth.

Margaret laughed, as she was meant to.

Arial counted off the second finger. "We arrived last night, and I came over as soon as I was certain I could make the short carriage ride without..." She trailed off, and patted her belly, from within which another little Stancroft was disrupting his or her mother's mornings.

Folding down the third finger, she said, "Apart from the tentative start to the day, I am marvelously well, as are all the rest of

our household. I shall leave it at that, or I will talk your ear off."
She smiled.

"At least tell me about the children," Margaret begged. "How
is our darling little Harry?" John Henry, Arial's son, was Lord
Ransome to the wider world, but remained *Harry* to his doting
relatives and their friends.

Arial laughed again, this time for sheer delight. "I cannot
remember why we thought it would be a good idea for him to
walk. He is never still, he climbs everything in sight, and we've
had to appoint a nursery maid whose sole responsibility is to fish
him out of trouble."

Her beaming smile spoke of her pride, and Margaret scolded
herself for her frisson of envy. If anyone deserved happiness, it
was Arial, after her many years of pain and social isolation.

"The little girls?" Margaret asked. Arial and Peter had filled
their house with female relatives—his sisters and her cousins—
most of them still in the nursery or schoolroom.

"Flourishing, and excited to be in Town, for Peter has rashly
promised to take them to Astley's and Gunter's and a dozen other
places. As to this one—" Arial's hands once more went posses-
sively over her belly—"the midwife says all is proceeding as it
should. We expect to give Harry a brother or a sister in Septem-
ber."

Margaret remembered her manners. "Come and sit in the
summerhouse, and I shall send for something to drink. Would
you prefer tea? Hot chocolate? A small ale? I believe Cook still has
some lemons, if you would like lemonade."

Arial wrinkled her brow as she considered. "Lemonade can be
very good or very bad. I take it yours is good, Margaret?"

Margaret nodded. "Very good. Cook squeezes the lemons
over a block of sugar, then heats the mix until the sugar melts,
and cools it by pouring it through a sieve onto ice cubes. She uses
filtered water, for the ice cubes, of course. She adds slices of
ginger root and sprigs of mint to the glass." Margaret smacked
her lips at the thought. She was certainly having the lemonade.

Soon, the two ladies were sipping their cold drinks and sharing anecdotes from their time apart, adding detail to snippets that had peppered the weekly letters they exchanged.

"Has Lord Snowden taken the hint and stopped bothering you?" Arial asked.

Three refused proposals over two years followed by a visit from the husbands of her friends made a fairly strong hint, Margaret had to agree. "He has, but I don't believe he has given up hope of acquiring me and my delightful coal seams. His son has been a regular visitor since I returned to London."

Arial's eye widened at that. "The same son who was instrumental in Regina's abduction last year? I cannot believe it!"

Margaret had thought that might be her friend's reaction. Their friend Regina and her husband, Elijah Ashby, had not pressed charges. With both of the instigators dead, the Ashbys saw no point in opening Regina's reputation up to public comment.

Goodness only knew what Regina would say if she knew young Mr. Snowden and his father had brushed the whole thing off as a youthful error of judgement. Mr. Snowden seemed to think his apology was penance enough.

Margaret doubted the Ashbys took the same view.

"Aunt Aurelia would not hear of me turning them away. She seems to think that, since neither of them were prosecuted, they are both innocent."

Arial was frowning. "Do you wish Peter to—"

Margaret shook her head. "Snowden is no more trouble than any of the other immature young men. Less than some. He has a fair share of charm and is perfectly willing to take no for an answer, whether it is to drive or to dance at a ball. I only see him when he attends my afternoons at home, or when we come across one another at entertainments."

In fact, he and his father were far more of a nuisance in the country, where there were fewer other people to dilute their presence. She was nostalgic for the days when the men in the district, including her own family, had disregarded her as negligible.

Arial sipped the last of her drink and put the glass down. "That's good, then. But if things change, be sure to let me know." She folded her hands together in her lap and leaned forward. "Now, Margaret. You said in your letters that you had had an adventure and met an interesting man. Tell your best friend all about it."

Margaret smiled. She was so pleased that Arial had come up to London early. "Would you believe I was attacked in the slums, and rescued by the bookkeeper of a *brothel*? Arial, he is the most gorgeous man you have ever seen, at least until he opens his mouth, when he makes it clear he thinks I am a frivolous, useless aristocrat. Oh, and he is enough like young Snowden to be a brother."

Her friend stared at her with her mouth open. When Margaret said no more, she shut it, and said, "You cannot stop there, Margaret. Start at the beginning and leave nothing out."

❈

ONCE A WEEK, Snowy had lunch with a group of fellow investors—a working meal, during which they reported on existing projects and discussed new opportunities.

Today's vigorous discussion was about reinvesting the profits now flowing in from their very first joint project, a canal in the north of England. Several of the investors backed another canal project, promoted by Gary—Gaheris Fullerton—whom Snowy had known since Oxford.

Drew Winderfield argued that the days of canals were limited, and they should be putting their money into projects to create a steam locomotive that would be commercially-feasible beyond the short lines that served the collieries. The discussion continued even after the meeting was over and the other investors had left, the decision still on the table.

"Locomotives are unreliable," Gary declared. Gary was the first real friend Snowy had ever had, another scholarship student and one of the smartest men he knew. The second son of a poor working family in the Midlands, he'd read law at Oxford and overcome the disadvantages of his origins to complete his four years at an Inn of Court and be accepted to the Bar.

"If Murray and his ilk can overcome the difficulties with the steam locomotive, the canals are not going to be able to compete," Drew countered. The fourth son of a duke, Lord Andrew Winderfield had been brought into the group by another investor because his family owned a prosperous shipping company, but he'd soon become another friend. He was one of the few aristocrats Snowy trusted. An outsider, despite his lofty connections, for his mother had been a Persian princess.

Snowy thought about his own problem while his friends argued on, each raising the same points and counter-points he'd heard before. He had no idea what particular argument they'd reached when Drew asked, "What do you think, Snowy?"

"I'll consider it between now and the next meeting," he said, reluctant to admit that he hadn't been listening.

His friends exchanged glances. "I don't think he asked us to stay on after the meeting to debate the merits of locomotives," Drew surmised.

"Out with it then," Gary commanded. "The witness at the bar will present his testimony."

Where to start? "I have learned something... unsettling." Which was a hell of an understatement. Snowy's world had been rocked on its axis. He focused on Drew. "You know a bit about where I came from, and what the Blossoms mean to me."

Drew nodded. "Your foster mothers," he said.

It was as good a description as any. "They gave me a present for my birthday—the true story of my origins. If it *is* true. The thing is, they would never lie to me, so they believe it. But to me, it is just too fantastic." He batted one hand at the air, as if he could knock away his own confusion.

"Go on," Drew prompted, when Snowy remained silent.

"No," Gary protested. "Elucidate. If you are not Moses White, brothel bookkeeper and investor extraordinaire, *who* are you?"

Snowy's huff of amusement was genuine. "I am Moses White, of course. At least, now, and for most of my life. But apparently, I started out as Henry Snowden, the only son of Edmund Snowden, who was the third son of Arthur, Viscount Snowden."

His friend looked startled, though not as flabbergasted as Snowy himself had been, at least initially.

"Lily and her sister Iris found me in an alley when I was six years old. I'd been stripped and beaten. They figured out who I was, and tried to return me, but my mother asked them to keep me, and especially, to keep me hidden."

Gary lifted his eyebrows. "The lady suspected someone of trying to do away with you?"

Snowy nodded. "Edmund Snowden's cousin, Richard. Mrs. Snowden—my mother—married Richard Snowden after Edmund died. The son of Mrs. Snowden's first marriage was kidnapped from his family's garden when he was little more than an infant, along with his nurse. You may recall hearing about the story. You would only have been children, but it was in all the papers at the time, and people still bring it up whenever a child goes missing. There was a ransom note, but no instructions for how to pay it. The nurse's body was recovered from the Thames. Mr. Snowden, my stepfather, insisted I must be dead, as well, and the authorities closed the case."

"What made his wife think Snowden was the villain?" Gary wanted to know.

Snowy had asked the same question. "The way he looked at me, apparently. Several unexplained accidents that failed to kill me. A rash of deaths in the family that made Richard the heir presumptive if I was dead. Also, she told Lily she'd overheard a snippet of conversation with a close crony. He was cross with his friend for failing to make sure they were rid of the brat."

Gary was clearly not convinced. "Women can get odd ideas. A pity, if her hysteria has kept you from your birth right all these years."

Anyone, male or female, could get odd ideas, but Snowy didn't think that was the explanation. "The thing is, Gary, no one has a harder head than a successful courtesan, and my foster-mothers—*it was an apt description*—"were convinced I was in real danger. Lily and Iris—Petunia too—grew up in the village on Viscount Snowden's estate. Apparently, the viscount's nephew had a reputation as a ruthless man who would do anything to get his own way. And this friend of his, a fellow called Deffew, was poured from the same mold."

Drew acknowledged the point with an inclination of his head, but said, "Indicative, but not conclusive."

"The thing is—there was a rash of deaths in the family in the six years before I was kidnapped. Both of my uncles and my father. Also, my one male cousin, the remaining heir apparent, was abducted six months before I was and later found dead. That made me heir apparent. After my supposed death, the family tragedies stopped. But my abduction was considered part of a pattern and since others had already died, no one considered that I might, in fact, still be alive."

"More strongly indicative," Gary said. "I take it your foster mothers remained in contact with your mother?"

"Through a trusted maid, Lily said. Until the maid was dismissed and, as far as Lily could discover, my mother disappeared off the face of the earth. Living retired, her husband said. No funeral. No mourning. She was just gone." Like everyone else involved with Richard. The more Snowy thought about it, the more determined he was to find out what had really happened.

"Years ago," Drew noted. "Hard to investigate after all this time."

"If all this is true, someone must know something," Gary

pointed out. "Someone always does. Was there a proper investigation at the time? Or just the local constable?"

Snowy nodded. "They had the Bow Street runners on it. I don't know if Bow Street would still have a record after twenty-three years."

"They will. I'll ask for it," Gary offered. Write me a note of appointment in case my esteemed master wants to know what I'm up to." He was currently working for a King's Counsel who, according to Gary, thought he was God.

Snowy nodded his agreement and went on to his main point. "My foster mothers," he said, "want me to claim my birth right. Apparently, my grandfather died eighteen months ago, which means I should be the current viscount. Lily laid information with a solicitor, who has put in a claim to the Lord Chancellor, so Snowden is still not confirmed in his title. If the solicitor can't come up with a claimant before the end of this session of Parliament, Snowden wins. But if he is responsible for the deaths of half my family, I don't want that."

The other two were nodding, but it wasn't as simple as that. He continued, "On the other hand, I don't know that I want to be a viscount, either. You know my opinion of the nobility—saving your presence, of course, Drew. Besides, what do I know about being a viscount?"

"I can't see there is any point if you cannot prove your case," Gary said. "Even if you are Henry Snowden, can you prove it? You need more information. That much is clear."

Drew agreed. "As much history as we can find for the men involved and your family. What other people think of them. What they're doing now. Anything that might help you to make your decision."

"I can ask around in the law fraternity," Gary offered.

"I can talk to my father and ask my sisters and cousins what is known about the Snowden family in the ton," said Drew.

It was precisely what Snowy had been going to ask his friends. "And I have asked the Blossoms to find out what they can. You would not believe some of the things that customers tell a good-time girl."

"Give me forty-eight hours," said Drew.

"I am in court that day," Gary noted. "I have to be in chambers by ten, all ready to worship my esteemed master. Let's meet here for breakfast. Eight o'clock? Snowy won't have gone to bed yet, and it'll do Drew good to get up early."

Chapter Four

S EVERAL DAYS LATER, armed with the information his friends had gathered, Snowy decided his next step would be to see his solicitor. He had one, apparently, chosen years ago by Lily and his mother. The firm held signed depositions from both women, and Lily had been sending them yearly reports on Snowy's wellbeing.

Gary told him the firm had a reputation for integrity, which would stand him in good stead if he decided to make a claim for the title.

So Snowy asked for an appointment, using the *Henry Snowden* to sign the request so that the solicitors would be more likely to see him. It made his skin crawl to sign in the name of that long ago boy, even though he understood that he was that boy, grown up. He was not the same person he would have been if he had grown up in privilege. Claiming the name felt like a commitment he was not ready to make.

A message was returned within the hour, naming a time the following afternoon. Lily and Gary agreed to accompany him.

The outer office, with its paneled walls, its discretely luxurious carpet, and its matching furnishings quietly announced that the firm was old but successful. Glass-fronted bookcases full of large books, all bound in identical red leather with gold lettering, suggested the library of a gentlemen's club.

It had the hush of a library, too, or a church—broken only by the scratch of quill pens used by clerks who sat at the neat desks and stood at work stands lined up behind a waist-high balustrade that separated the room in two. It didn't smell of cigars or brandy. Instead, the dry scent of parchment, leather, and ink met Snowy's nostrils like incense in a church. Apart from the man at the desk outside of the balustrade, none of the industrious clerks looked up from their work.

Snowy placed a card showing his new-found name on the desk in front of the man who had noticed their entry. He stood, immediately. "If you and your party will come this way, my lord. Mr. Fortescue will be with you shortly."

Snowy offered Lily his arm, and Gary followed along behind.

The clerk bowed them into a comfortable parlor, tastefully furnished and decorated. Gary whistled when the man left the room. "This is a bit of all right, isn't it? Shouts 'Trust us. We know what we're doing.'"

Lily smiled. "Appearances set the scene," she agreed. "Appear as if you are well-rewarded for what you do, and you will be." She had achieved the same message, if in a very different style, with the House of Blossoms.

Snowy ignored the byplay. His muscles twitched with the need to run as far and as fast as possible. "My lord," the clerk had called him, as if he had already decided to take the title and had won it from his father's thieving cousin. For now, Snowy's battle was to stay where he was and to keep his face impassive. He was finding it a difficult one to win.

Being here is committing to nothing.

The clerk returned with a tray containing tea makings and the appropriate crockery, followed by another clerk carrying plates of small savories and cakes. No apple pies, Snowy was disappointed to note. They offloaded their trays onto the table in front of Lily, then the first clerk took both trays and the second went to sit behind the desk.

The first clerk's exit from the room was interrupted by the entrance of a gentleman who brought such a sense of presence with him he could only be a principal of the firm, and that impression was cemented when he stepped forward with his hand out, saying to Lily, "Mistress Larissa Halcombe, I assume. It is a pleasure to meet you at long last, madam."

His salutation reminded Snowy that he wasn't the only one in the House of Blossoms with a made-up name.

The solicitor bowed over Lily's hand, then turned to Snowy. "You are Snowden's son. You look very much as Ned did when we were in Brasenose together. It is a pleasure to meet you, my lord. I am Fortescue."

Snowy shook the man's proffered hand, but protested, "'My lord' is a little premature, Mr. Fortescue. I have yet to be resurrected from the dead and, if I decide to take that step, I will still need to prove I am who I say I am."

"There are difficulties, I do not deny it." Mr. Fortescue tossed his hand as if throwing them over his shoulder, a broad grin suggesting he was eager to overcome any challenges. He turned his attention to Gary.

"This is my friend and adviser," Snowy began.

"Gaheris Fullerton," Fortescue said. "One of the smartest young barristers in the Inns of Court. Your principal asked me to read the opinion he had you write on the Hadfield case, young Fullerton. Cogently argued." He shook Gary's hand, then gestured to the nearby chairs. "Please, all of you, sit down. Mistress Halcombe, would you be kind enough to preside over the teapot?" Once everyone was comfortably seated, he said, "Now, what do you want from me, young man, if you do not wish to—as you say—be resurrected from the dead?"

Snowy knew the answer to that. "Information," he replied. "I know that my father's cousin was my mother's second husband. That my mother believed her husband had paid for my kidnapping and murder. That he has benefited from deaths in his family and among business rivals and associates. That he has a reputation as a hard man, and that his servants fear him."

Fortescue inclined his head in acknowledgement but said nothing.

Snowy continued. "I know my mother was last seen in Society shortly after I disappeared, and that no one has heard of or seen her in at least a decade. Snowden has acted as proxy for his uncle for the past eight years, and no one had seen my grandfather for five of those years, until a doctor was summoned eighteen months ago when he died. Snowden has claimed the viscountcy, but it cannot be confirmed nor can he be called to Lords until I have been declared dead."

"These are all facts," Fortescue agreed.

Snowy took a cup from Lily, not because he wanted tea but because he wanted something to do with his hands. "What can you add to that, Mr. Fortescue? What happened to my mother? Why has Snowden escaped responsibility for his crimes for so long? If I chose to take up my name and my heritage, what barriers will I face?"

TEN DAYS HAD passed since Mistress Lily had asked Margaret to be ready to do Mr. White a favor if he asked. She had given up expecting to hear from him. On the two occasions she had brought herbal remedies to the House of Blossoms, she'd looked for his stern face but he did not put in an appearance. Perhaps he was in his office poring over his books. Wasn't that what bookkeepers did?

No doubt he was aware of her visits—the man seemed to have his finger on the pulse of the place. He was, she was convinced, far more than a mere bookkeeper. She refused to think about the man and yet she thought about him all the time. She was far too fascinated for her own comfort—and by a man from a completely different world. One who despised her, at that.

Then, one morning, in with her mail but showing the signs of being hand-delivered, was a note from Mr. White. It was very short. Written in a neat but attractive hand, it said simply:

Dear Madam,

The undersigned begs the privilege of calling on you at a convenient time to discuss the matter proposed by Mistress L. My messenger awaits your reply.

It was signed with a large flourishing S, but it could be from no one else.

Margaret appointed the time of one o'clock that afternoon, when Aunt Aurelia would almost certainly be having what she called, "a little lie down, just to rest my eyes."

She wanted to hear whatever Mr. White had to say before she decided whether to tell her great aunt, who was sure to disapprove of being seen with a man from a brothel.

As one o'clock approached, she hovered on the half-way landing, watching out the window for a carriage. A couple of minutes before the appointed time, an umbrella swerved from the scattered trickle of pedestrians and mounted the steps to disappear under the porch. She heard the door knocker and retreated back up to the drawing room to wait.

She had told her butler to bring Mr. White straight up, and Bowen announced him as the clock on the mantel chimed the hour. He was nothing if not punctual, Margaret decided.

"I will fetch the tea, my lady," Bowen said, with a bow.

"Thank you, Bowen."

The butler departed, leaving the door ajar.

"Mr. White, please be seated." Margaret had chosen chairs on the far side of the room from the door so their conversation would be private while propriety was observed at the same time.

Today, Mr. White was dressed like a Society gentleman, his coat a piece of sartorial magnificence, his cravat perfectly tied. Margaret could not take her eyes off his hair, where a streak of white adorned one temple. Had that been there before? She couldn't remember, though surely such a distinctive trait would have stood out and be easily recalled.

He took the indicated chair. "Thank you for receiving me, my lady."

"You've dyed your hair," she blurted. *Good Lord. I just said that out loud. How rude.* Her cheeks heated. "I beg your pardon. That was a very personal remark. It is just—I know another person with a streak of white in the same place." The resemblance to Mr. Snowden was remarkable.

They were interrupted by the arrival of the tea tray, which Bowen put on the table next to Margaret. He hovered for a moment.

"Thank you, Bowen. That will be all."

Bowen appeared embarrassed but spoke anyway. "Should I send a maid to sit with you, my lady, since Miss Denning is not awake?"

"Leave the door open," Margaret told him, touched at his concern. "I shall be perfectly well."

The creases at the outside edges of Mr. White's gray eyes deepened. He showed no other signs, but clearly the exchange with the butler had amused him. He waited until Bowen had left the room, pausing on the threshold to glare at Mr. White, before pushing the door slightly wider than it had been.

Margaret expected Mr. White to comment on the butler's concern or her insistence on seeing her visitor alone. Instead, he addressed her previous comment. "I have been dyeing my white streak to hide it every week since I was a boy," he told her. "I stopped a fortnight ago. The roots are coming through white, but I had one of the girls bleach out the dye on the ends."

She wanted to ask him if he was a Snowden by-blow and, if so, why he'd felt the need to hide the evidence, but she swallowed the impertinent question and instead asked him how he took his tea.

He accepted the prepared cup before he said, "Lily says she

asked you if you will allow me to escort you to a few Society engagements. She said you agreed." The same crinkles lightened his expression, and this time his lips quirked at the corners. "Knowing Lily, she probably coerced you by saying you owe me a favor. Please, put that out of your mind. If there was any debt at all, you have repaid it with your herbal knowledge."

Margaret was unaccountably disappointed. Or perhaps, not so unaccountably. She would not at all mind being seen on the arm of such a specimen of manhood, with or without the Snowden streak. If nothing else, it would definitely be entertaining. "Is that your way of telling me you do not want my help to enter Society?"

"I *would* like your help. May I escort you? Just to a few events?"

She took a sip of her own tea to give herself time to compose a response. "What sort of events? Whom do you wish to meet, and with what goal? If I am to help you, I would like to know what it is I am helping you toward."

Mr. White considered that, gravely. "You are not at all as I expected, Lady Charmain. I have been told I am too quick to judge those of the upper classes. In your case, I believe my initial prejudice to have been wrong, and I apologize if I've given any offense."

That was unexpected. Margaret inclined her head. "Apology accepted."

His smile this time was full and genuine. *Gracious.* He was handsome when he was stern. When he smiled, he was devastating. Perhaps this was a bad idea.

But before Margaret could back away from her semicommitment, he answered her questions.

"I will let you choose the events, my lady. Just give me a list of when I am to be at your door and the sort of event for which I am to dress. I wish to be seen by as many of your class as possible. And I would particularly like to meet the gentleman you referred to earlier. That is, I believe you meant Edmund Snowden? I should also like to meet his father. My goal is to be noticed. Aunt Lily believes, and I agree with her, that my resemblance to the Snowden family will prompt a reaction." He frowned, just a little. "If I may continue to speak frankly?"

"I think you should," Margaret said.

He was grave as he availed himself of the invitation. "Rumor has it that the Snowden men have aspirations for your hand, my lady, though it is unclear whether the father or the son is the would-be groom. However, that being the case, my advisors and I think they will be wary of offending you. If there are negative consequences to this game of charades, that should keep you free of them."

Margaret felt her eyebrows shoot up as her eyes widened. "Goodness. What sort of negative consequences are you expecting?"

"One can only speculate. You know the two men. How do you think they will react to my foray into Society, looking as I do?"

Margaret thought about that. Lord Snowden seldom showed much of a reaction, but she did not think he would be pleased if a base-born relative suddenly turned up under his nose in front of all of his peers. He had no reason to blame Margaret, however. His son Edmund was less predictable. Margaret suspected he might think it a bit of a lark.

Mr. White clearly didn't share the younger man's irresponsible attitude to life, and the wry sense of humor Mr. White occasionally displayed had little in common with Mr. Snowden's enjoyment of pranks and escapades. The half-brothers, if they were half-brothers and not merely cousins, were not much alike.

"Are they your family?" she asked Mr. White.

He looked down into his cup, the first time he had avoided her eyes. "My family are the ladies at the House of Blossoms," he replied, firmly.

Which was not a 'no'. Margaret contemplated the stir he would make, not just with the Snowdens but with all her suitors.

And, in fact, with every participant in the aptly-named marriage mart. A mysterious and handsome young man with the body of a god and the eyes of a wolf?

Could he play the part, though? She waved a hand to indicate his clothes. "I see you have appropriate dress for afternoon visiting and the like. What of evenings?"

Something about that amused him, but he answered promptly. "I can be suitably costumed for any event you choose Lady Charmain. Also, if it concerns you, I am competent on the dance floor, can ride a horse, and have been schooled in appropriate table manners."

Those wolf eyes twinkled.

She refused to rise to his baiting. She had been wondering precisely that, and her doubts had more to do with his behavior since she met him than his origins. "Very well, then. We have a bargain. Shall we look at the invitations I currently possess and decide on which to accept?"

⟫⟫⟫⟫⟪⟪⟪⟪

GARY AND DREW had come to witness his transformation and, as Snowy dressed for his grand entrance at a ton ball with Lady Charmain on his arm, his conscience was bothering him.

"I believe the countess thinks of this as a merry prank," he announced to the room, when the valet that Lily insisted he needed had gone off to find another stack of cravats. "Perhaps I should have told her that I have made a claim for the viscountcy."

"We discussed this after we met with your grandfather's solicitor," Gary pointed out. "I said then, and I say now, that your plan to provoke Snowden into illegal behavior requires him to be unsure about your identity and your intentions."

Drew shook his head. "I still don't think the lady would repeat anything you told her in confidence."

He was probably right, but that wasn't Snowy's chief reason

for keeping her at arms' length. He had almost backed away from Lily's plan for him to enter Society in her company when he discovered that Lady Charmain was unwed. Without a husband to act as a brake on his attraction to the lady, he really could not afford to get to close to her.

Besides, Drew might be wrong. Snowy hadn't been raised in the lady's class, and Snowden had. Perhaps, like many of her kind, she would not count a promise to a slum-raised brat as having any significance. He could not have her running straight to Snowden with anything Snowy told her, and gossiping to the rest of Society about it, besides.

Gossip, of course, was one of Snowy's aims, but all his advisers agreed that uninformed speculation would serve better this early in the game, rather than the facts. The less polite Society knew, the more they would wonder.

Fortescue had confirmed what Gary had already told them. "The evidential gap is the issue. Snowden's legal advisers will argue that the boy kidnapped from the garden was not the boy Mistress Lily found in the alley. Unless we can find your mother's maid, who saw you before and after the abduction, we have no one who can confirm that you are one and the same."

"If you're worrying about the risk," Drew said, "do not. This might be dangerous for you, yes. From what we've discovered so far, Snowden does not take kindly to being crossed. But I agree that you're not making a target out of Lady Charmain. She is not involved, except that she is doing a favor for a friend."

"Making a target out of me is precisely the point," Snowy commented. Snowden had repeatedly used his position, first as heir to a viscount and more recently as viscount, to avoid investigation, and had smoothly talked his way out of prosecution when he was implicated in a crime. As he had been last year, of conspiracy to kidnap.

There had never been any direct evidence. Even the fate of Snowy's mother, poor lady, had brought him commiseration for his tragic loss rather than suspicion.

The valet returned to make yet another attempt at achieving perfection, and the discussion ended. This time, Snowy managed to remain perfectly still except when moving precisely as directed by the valet. He could not, himself, detect any difference between the creation the valet approved and the earlier ones he'd rejected. Perhaps the man was merely making a point about how capable he was.

The precise placement of a cravat pin took several more minutes fussing, and then at last Snowy was permitted to put his arms into his waistcoat. The coat came next. No wonder nobleman strutted and strolled. They could do nothing else in coats that stretched so tightly across their shoulders.

"You may inspect yourself in the mirror, sir," the valet commanded.

Snowy did as he was told. He certainly looked the part—elegant and frivolous.

Some of his thoughts must have been showing on his face, because Drew said, "It serves its purpose, Snowy. Even for those of us who want more out of life than the next ball or carriage race and our quarterly allowance. It will serve *your* purpose. Who is going to look at you and doubt you were born in the purple?"

Gary grinned. "Certainly not Snowden, one hopes."

Chapter Five

MARGARET WAS MORE excited about the ball than any in the past three seasons. Mr. White had asked her to select the event for the greatest possible impact. He wanted his first appearance in Society to be notable. He wanted the Snowdens, father and son, to be present, although he would prefer not to be introduced to them just yet.

They had settled on the Duchess of Winshire's annual ball for those of her goddaughters who were making their debut this Season. It was one of the highlights of the social calendar. Everybody who received one of the highly-prized invitations would attend if humanly possible, even, possibly, the Prince Regent.

Mr. Snowden had already told Regina how thrilled he was to be honored with an invitation. Mr. White had only commented that he had only ever been to public assemblies, such as those at Vauxhall Gardens. "Unless you count Cyprian Balls," he added, watching her closely for a reaction.

She refused to dignify that remark with an answer and managed to hide her amusement at his teasing.

For both men, it would be their first Winshire Debut Ball. They would certainly find it memorable.

Aunt Aurelia had refused to attend the ball. She disapproved of Margaret allowing Mr. White to be her escort and had said so loudly and repeatedly. She had been suddenly smitten with what she said was a cold when she discovered Margaret would not be moved.

Perhaps Aunt Aurelia might have made the effort if she realized how much more Margaret expected to enjoy the evening with her maid to lend propriety rather than her carping great aunt.

Margaret was going in a new gown. It was a crisp apricot silk that shimmered in the light, the bodice and puffed short sleeves decorated with leaf shapes in autumn colors of red, yellow, orange and brown, with a knee-high band of such leaves around the base of the skirt, spaced apart at the top and increasing to a thick cluster at the hem. Each leaf had been individually edged, stiffened and sewn in place down the center with a stem of clear glass beads that sparkled in the candle light.

Her maid had tonged and pinned her hair into a cascade of curls then added more of the leaves with their glimmering beads.

The jewelry she wore had a floral theme—six diamonds in a silver setting forming the petals of a daisy or a forget-me-not, with a seventh in the center. Each earring was a single forget-me-not, and the necklace was a string of them, curving neatly around the base of her neck, with a teardrop diamond descending from the middle three flowers.

Long white gloves, apricot-colored dancing shoes, and her ensemble was complete. She was pleased with her reflection in her mirror. What would Mr. White think?

He was already in the drawing room and rose as she entered, his eyes widening. For a moment, before he collected himself, there was hunger in his gaze. And then it was gone, so quickly she wondered if she had imagined it.

"Lady Charmain, I shall be the most envied man at the ball," he said. "You look amazing."

Which was very gratifying, but did he mean it? And why should she care whether he did or not? She did not even like the man. She was merely repaying a favor.

They delayed their arrival, timing it so the reception line would still be there but most of the guests would have arrived. Still, they stood for some time in the queue. Margaret's escort garnered a lot of stares and comments whispered too low for Margaret to hear but, since they did not happen to be standing near any of Margaret's acquaintances, no one demanded to meet Mr. White or to be told who he was.

Those around her and Mr. White were all too busy shouting greetings and comments on the weather, the event, and one another's clothes. The noise was incredible.

Her escort was easily the best-looking man in the queue. She found him compelling in his usual day attire. In evening costume, he was stunning. He seemed content to look around him, which Margaret appreciated, since any conversation would have to be conducted in a yell to be heard, or with their heads so close together they'd have no option but to call the banns.

The noisy crowd made its way fairly quickly up the stairs, and Margaret and Mr. White were soon showing their invitations to a pair of footmen who stood guard over the doors through which those ahead of them in the queue had been admitted.

One footman opened the doors, and the other announced them in a loud voice. "Lady Charmain. Mr. White."

They stepped forward into a large room, where dozens of people interrupted their conversations and turned to look at them. All of Her Grace's debuting goddaughters and their parents or other sponsors lined up with the duke and the duchess, which meant a lot of introductions and exchanges of the courtesies.

The doors behind them must have closed again, for the sound of the waiting guests was suddenly muted. Ahead of them, the Duke and Duchess of Winshire smiled to welcome her and Mr. White. The rest of the receiving line was spread across the room behind them, almost to the double doors at the far end, which opened as Margaret watched, so that guests who had met the hosts and their protégées could pass into the ballroom.

Mr. White conducted her to the ducal couple and performed a creditable bow before them. No one looking at his dress, his manners, or his conduct would believe he was raised, as he had told her and she knew to be true, in a brothel.

The duchess greeted Margaret and passed her on to the duke, then surprised Margaret by taking both of Mr. White's hands. "Mr. White! James, darling, this is Drew's friend, Mr. White."

The duke smiled, warmly. "Mr. White. My son tells me he owes his not inconsiderable investment success to your advice. I am pleased to meet you at last."

Mr. White's bow was precisely right for a gentleman meeting a duke. Respectful, but not subservient. "Lord Andrew gives me too much credit, Your Grace. We decide on our investments together, and he is at least as responsible for our success as any of the group."

"Perhaps you would have tea with me one afternoon, Mr. White," the duchess suggested. "I suspect I know what you are about, and I may be able to help."

Mr. White's mask of polite interest slipped. "Drew didn't...?"

Her Grace chuckled. "My stepson said nothing beyond wishing for you to be invited to this ball, Mr. White, but your features speak for themselves. As I am sure you know. Shall we say three in the afternoon next Monday?"

Mr. White bowed again. "Your Grace."

The duchess turned her bright smile to Margaret. "Lady Charmain, I hope you enjoy the ball." She beckoned them to follow her the two or three paces to an older couple who hovered protectively over their pretty daughter. "Have you met the Countess of Mertonbridge? Her daughter, Lady Elizabeth, is making her debut this Season. Constance, darling, Countess Charmain and her escort, Mr. White."

With those words, she passed Margaret and Mr. White to the next group in the line. Lady Mertonbridge presented her husband and daughter to Margaret, and Mr. White to them all. A compliment or two to the debutante and an exchange of remarks about the weather, and the lady took them to be introduced to the next group. In this manner, they progressed along the room from debutante's family to debutante's family.

Finally, it was their turn to pass through the double doors, which led on to a long flight of stairs down to the floor of the ballroom. They stood at the top and passed their invitations to the butler.

"Is the duchess always like that?" Mr. White asked in a whisper as the butler announced them, his voice ringing out through the enormous space.

"I barely know her," Margaret admitted, "but she is a truly kind lady. She has been wonderful to my friends Regina and Arial."

Mr. White held up his hand, and Margaret laid her fingers on it, as if they were about to dance. As he conducted her down the stairs, he commented, "I am sure she is, but she is also scarily prescient. And blunt. I expected people to notice I look like a Snowden, but I did not expect them to comment to my face."

Margaret pursed her lips. "Very few will. But Her Grace walks her own path. She is, after all, a duchess."

Mr. White's face lightened as his own lips quirked into a smile. "That explains it."

She picked a few familiar faces from the sea of those looking up at the couple on the stairs. Arial and Peter, the Earl and Countess of Stancroft. Regina and Elijah Ashby. The Marquess of Deerhaven and his countess, Cordelia. And, making his way through the crowded center of the room, Mr. Snowden.

"Will you go to afternoon tea with the duchess?" Margaret wondered aloud, and immediately realized that she had overstepped. "I am sorry. It is none of my affair."

This time, he managed a smile. "Do not start watching your words with me, Lady Charmain. I like that you leave me in no doubt about your thoughts. Yes, I will attend the duchess on Monday afternoon." He grinned as he repeated her words, "She is, after all, a duchess."

Dear heavens, the man was devastating when he smiled.

"Mr. Edmund Snowden is coming this way," she told Mr. White, as they reached the foot of the stairs.

"Yes, I saw. At least, I saw a boy with a streak of white heading this way. Do you see his father?"

Margaret shook her head.

He grinned again. "Let's not make this easy for him," he said. He put her hand in the crook of his elbow and led her away along the side of the room.

⁂

LADY CHARMAIN WAS willing enough to slip anonymously through the crowd, but the crowd didn't co-operate. Person after person stopped them, some to petition Lady Charmain for a dance and others with a polite greeting to the lady and a curious stare at Snowy.

Lady Charmain presented him to them all as Moses White, without comment, which was all to the good. The more people he was introduced to before he came face-to-face with the Snowdens, the better. He shook hands, praised the duchess's hospitality, and politely deflected comments that were, in truth, oblique questions about his origins, such as, "Would that be the Shropshire Whites?"

Before they were a quarter of the way around the room, Lady Charmain had given away her last dance. Snowy was pleased he had claimed two when they first arranged to attend the ball together, for, if he'd left it until now, he might have missed out. *Dancing with Lady Charmain is not the point of the evening,* he scolded himself. But even so...

He, too, had asked a number of ladies to dance. On the dance floor, he would be seen but could not be approached, which was ideal for his purposes. He would dance all night if he had to. He just hoped he could remember what the ladies looked like, their names, and which dance he had requested.

Drew was a familiar port in the sea of strangers; he shook hands with Snowy and bowed over Lady Charmain's hand. "We have danced together a time or two, my lady. Have you met my sister, Rosemary?"

The ladies acknowledged they had met. Something about a committee to raise funds for the widows and orphans of soldiers. Lady Charmain kept going up in Snowy's estimation. Then it was his turn to be presented to Lady Rosemary. Like her brother, she did not stand on her dignity as a duke's daughter.

"I'm delighted to meet you, Mr. White. My brother thinks very highly of you. Am I meant to comment on how much you look like Chalky Snowden?"

"Families are complicated things," Snowy offered. Lily had suggested that as a response to anyone who was bold enough or honest enough to question the resemblance.

Another couple joined them. Intriguingly, the lady wore a mask covering one side of her face from just above the lips. It was painted and trimmed to match her gown, but the lack of an eyehole declared that the aim was concealment rather than adornment.

"Arial, Peter, may I present my escort this evening?" Lady Charmain asked the newcomers. "This is Mr. Moses White, a friend of mine. Mr. White, Lord and Lady Stancroft are my dear friends. Arial and I have been as close as sisters since we were children."

"We were neighbors," Lady Stancroft explained. "Or near enough. Lord Snowden owns the intermediate estate, but we were only thirty minutes from one another by the country lanes."

The mention of Lord Snowden was deliberate. Lady Stancroft's eye was alive with curiosity, but she did not ask the questions that clearly hovered on her mind.

Lord Stancroft changed the subject. "Lord Andrew tells me you have an interest in railways, Mr. White."

Drew and Snowy both laughed.

"Drew has an interest in railways," Snowy corrected, "and his friends are obliged to keep up with developments in the interests of self-preservation."

In moments, they were deep in discussion. Lord Stancroft was part owner of a coal mine in Leicestershire and used a steam engine to pull wagons from the colliery to a nearby river for transport. "What about wrought iron to surface the rails?" he said.

"My brother Barnaby says Birkinshaw of Bedlington is experimenting with an I-beam in wrought iron. He predicts a tripling or more of the lifespan." Rosemary added.

"Is your brother here this evening?" Snowy wondered. "Your brother has quoted him so often I almost feel I know him."

"Oh yes," Drew assured him. "Our stepmother commanded the presence of any of us in London, both Father's family and her own. I'll make sure to introduce you and Barney before the evening is over."

The orchestra, which had been playing quietly in the background, produced a crescendo of sound, and the assembled gentry turned obediently to the stairs. The Duke and Duchess of Winshire stood on the top landing, a debutante and her father or uncle behind them. His Grace spoke into the sudden silence.

"My ladies, my lords, and gentlemen, welcome to Four Winds House. Thank you for being with us this evening to welcome to Society six lovely young ladies, goddaughters to my dear wife."

The duchess took her cue. "Our debutantes will lead off the dancing. Dear friends, Lady Diana Parrish."

The older man escorted the young lady down the stairs and onto the dancing floor, which had miraculously cleared of its cluster of chattering people.

One by one, the duchess announced each girl, who descended the stairs to the dancing floor on the arm of whomever had been appointed to lead her out in this first dance, and then the duke led the duchess onto the floor, another couple made up the set of eight, and the orchestra began to play.

"I had better find my own partner," Drew murmured. "Aunt Eleanor expects us all on the floor after they complete the first full pattern, to signal to the rest of the company it is time to join in. Come on, Rosie."

They didn't go far. Another couple, also brother and sister by the look, greeted them with smiles and split up, the gentleman to escort Lady Rosemary, and the lady on Drew's arm. They took to the floor, as did several other couples.

"May I have the pleasure, Lady Charmain?" Snowy asked. She took his offered hand. The dance instructor that Lily had hired years ago had insisted that dancing was courtship. "Fix your gaze on your partner, Mr. White. A lovely lithesome lady, swaying in time to the music, deserves every ounce of your attention. With the right partner, a dance can be an expression of love."

Snowy thought that a piece of poetic nonsense. Love in the romantic sense, as far as he could tell, was a polite word for lust. In any case, in the dancing he'd done since those long-ago lessons, he'd never had a partner who captured his full attention. Nor to be fair, had he ever had a partner more interested in gazing at him than in conversing with everyone around them.

He led Lady Charmain out into a round dance with a pattern of eight, and when she began to sway in time to the music, he could not look away. His gaze was well and truly fixed, and she, that lovely lithesome lady, gazed back.

Around him she went in the pattern of the dance, her eyes lingering on his until she passed behind his back. He turned his face to hers as she came around to the front again, crossed the other lady in the pattern and turned around the other gentleman.

He watched her all the way, until she was going around him again and then stepping to his side to take his hand as another lady took his other and they circled in their group of eight.

Snowy did not take his eyes off her, nor did she stop looking at him, as they stepped through all the patterns, circling, turning, stepping forward and back, promenading down behind the rows and up between them.

When the music drew to a close, they stood for a moment more, hands linked. It was a comfort to him that she looked as dazed as he felt.

She took a deep breath and the wonder on her face transformed into her usual social smile. "You did not overstate your ability, Mr. White," she said, her voice quavering slightly. "The dance was very enjoyable."

He'd have been disheartened at her understated description if her breathlessness and the slight shake in her voice had not belied her words. The dance had been as unsettling for her as it had for him. What would it be like if they kissed?

"The dance was incredible," he corrected her. "I have never enjoyed a dance more. May I escort you to your next partner?"

Lady Charmain looked around her and blushed. "We are still standing in the middle of the floor."

Had she only just noticed? The thought was deeply satisfying. He winged his elbow at her, and she took it. Just her fingers gently resting on his arm, and the sensation swept through his core to the basest part of him.

He had desired her from the first, but convinced himself that she would never look at a man from the slums. In fact, though, he wasn't, was he? He was a viscount, a man whose breeding she need not despise. Beyond that, he now knew she was in no way the stuck-up countess of his imagination.

A kiss seemed more and more likely, more and more inevitable, by the minute. She still hadn't taken her eyes from him, and he smiled down into them.

Then their moment was over. A gentleman of about his own height, but slender with the weediness of youth, placed himself in front of them. He spoke to Lady Charmain, but his eyes were on Snowy. "Lady Charmain, we have the next dance."

The streak of white among the dark curls recalled Snowy to his purpose and identified the boy. Edmund Snowden. His half-brother. And his enemy? That remained to be seen.

"Mr. White," Lady Charmain asked, "have you met Mr. Snowden?"

Snowy gave the slight bow with which gentlemen acknowledged an introduction. "Snowden."

"White?" the young man's response was a question.

Snowy ignored it. "If you will excuse me, my lady, I must find my partner for the next dance."

"Of course, Mr. White. Have a pleasant evening."

He lifted her hand to his lips, in part to tweak young Snowden but mostly because he could not resist touching her. "Until the supper dance, my lady." He would have preferred to kiss her fingers, but he was not here to make a scandal, just an impression. He contented himself with miming a kiss in the air while he imagined stripping off her glove and kissing each bare finger and then her palm.

Perhaps not the best visual image in the current circumstances. His tight silk breeches would soon reveal the direction of his thoughts.

"Until the supper dance," she agreed.

He let go of her hand with reluctance, nodded again to young Snowden, and left to find his way through the crowd to the young lady who had favored him with the next dance.

Chapter Six

"WHO IS HE," Mr. Snowden demanded as soon as they were out on the floor. "Who are his people? Dear Lord, did you see his streak? Is he a Snowden by-blow, Lady Charmain?"

"Mr. Snowden!" Margaret managed to imbue the name with righteous indignation.

They were separated by the patterns of the dance, and when he was back at her side again, he had clearly had time to get over the shock and recall his manners as a gentleman. "I beg your pardon, Lady Charmain, for my unfortunate language."

Margaret was prepared to be generous. "You had a surprise, Mr. Snowden. He certainly looks as if he might be a member of your family, but I'm afraid I know no more about his origins than you do."

"I have not seen him before," Snowden commented. "I am sure my father has not, either. He would have said something. Is Mr. White new to London?"

Another question Margaret was not prepared to answer. "He is a friend of Lord Andrew Winderfield," she offered.

"And of yours," Snowden accused, before he had to dance off to meet the other lady in their square.

"Did Lord Andrew introduce you?" he asked when he returned.

"He did not," she replied. "Mr. White is involved in some of the charitable causes that I also support." Which was true, in its own way. Providing medical herbs to the women in the brothel was a charitable cause, and Mr. White was bookkeeper there.

The dance continued in the same way, with young Snowden attempting to question her about Mr. White whenever the dance brought them together, and Margaret doing her best to answer honestly and sound as if she was answering completely and yet fulfil her role in this mission, as promised.

It was exhausting to be so deceptive. Margaret was pleased when the music finally came to a close.

Mr. Snowden offered her his arm. "Surely you know more," he said.

"Enough, Mr. Snowden," Margaret scolded. "I have told you everything I can, and I must say, if I had known you intended an interrogation, I would never have agreed to a dance."

He had the grace to look abashed.

Margaret was relieved to see another of her court, even if it did happen to be one of the hungriest of the title hunters. "Here comes my next partner, Mr. Snowden. I will not thank you for the dance. I trust you will amend your manners before you ask me again."

Which was a little unfair since Mr. White's presence was clearly having the intended impact on at least one Snowden. On both Snowdens, in fact. As the music started again for the next set, she noticed the viscount making his way through the crowd toward them, his face grim.

Margaret promptly abandoned Mr. Snowden to his father. "Mr. Thrisden, let us take our places," she said, and he eagerly escorted her onto the floor.

By dancing every dance and spending short breaks between sets with her friends Regina and Elijah Ashby, Margaret managed to stay clear of Lord Snowden. As expected, Lord Snowden did not approach her while she was with them. The Ashbys and the

Snowdens had been ignoring one another in the year since young Snowden joined in the attacks on the Ashbys.

Not that she feared Lord Snowden, precisely. In their part of the county, he had a reputation for a vicious temper, but her status as a lady and a countess surely protected her. Besides, he would control himself in such company.

However, he had a way of looking at her that made her uncomfortable, and she feared he would be able to tell she had deliberately brought Mr. White here to annoy him as a sort of petty revenge for continuing to pursue her after she refused him.

SNOWY RECOGNIZED THE supposed Lord Snowden, if for no other reason than the way the man berated young Snowden. Only a relative would have ranted in such a fashion, and only for a relative would the brash young man have crumpled in on himself so abjectly.

There was also something of a family resemblance between the two men, though not as great as the one between Snowy's half-brother and the face Snowy saw every day in the mirror.

The older man had kept a trim figure, but his hair had receded to leave his pate bald, except where he had combed hair over it. The grim lines to his face spoke of a person who seldom laughed or even smiled. He was richly-dressed, and in the latest style, which was interesting.

Both Gary and Drew had heard rumors that Lord Snowden's income had been curtailed by the ongoing question about whether or not he was the heir to the estate he had managed for so long while his uncle was alive.

"According to one of the clerks who works for his solicitor, he still gets his salary as steward and his allowance as heir, but he has always overspent and borrowed from his uncle, or sold off something that belongs to the estate to cover his debts," Gary had said. "The solicitor ordered an inventory and won't make him a loan or allow anything to be sold. Apparently, they have argued about it several times, and loudly."

Snowy avoided the man by staying on the dance floor as much as possible.

At last, it was time for the supper dance. It was, he was delighted to discover, a waltz. He would have Lady Charmain to himself for the whole dance.

It was everything he had hoped and more. He forgot Lord Snowden, the mystery of his mother's disappearance, the decisions he needed to make about his future, all the other people in the ballroom. Only Lady Charmain existed. He wished he could dance with her forever.

The sentimentality of the thought almost snapped him out of the dream, but her eyes, as entranced as he was, dragged him back under. Just this one dance then. He would enjoy every moment, then never dance with her again. He could not risk dragging her into the trouble his every instinct said was coming.

At least no more than he had done already by persuading her to consent to his escort.

"Is there something wrong, Mr. White?" she murmured.

Lovely, caring, and insightful. *I will protect her. With my life, if need be.* "A passing thought, my lady. Not worth spoiling the finest dance I have ever had."

He floated through the rest of the dance on the benediction of her smile.

At supper, they sat with her friends, Lord and Lady Deerhaven, Lord and Lady Stancroft, Mr. and Mrs. Ashby, and Lord and Lady Arthur Versey. The Ashbys had been mentioned in reports on Snowden. Rumors only.

It was certain that Lord Snowden's closest friend had died while attempting an attack on the couple, and Snowden's son and the son of that best friend had been involved. Details were sketchy and no prosecution had followed, but the two young men spent the rest of the year rusticating at Snowden's country seat.

My country seat, if I claim it.

Perhaps the Ashbys kept the Snowdens away, for neither of them approached the group, though the son was sitting with a group several tables away, and kept sneaking peeks at Snowy, as did a dark-browed young man who sat next to him. Snowden senior was less subtle. He stood glowering at Snowy from the other side of the room.

"Lord Snowden is glaring at you, Mr. White," Mr. Ashby said. "Have you had a falling out?"

"I have no memory of ever meeting the gentleman," Snowy told him.

Those around the table looked surprised. "I thought…" Mr. Ashby began, and then trailed off.

"You have the Snowden streak," said his wife. "Although I suppose Snowdens do not hold all rights to a tuft of white hair."

Perhaps this was an opportunity for the next step of his plan. He had been seen in public. Now to begin hinting at his real identity. The ton, Lily had said, could be trusted to gossip and speculate. The step after that was to see what Snowden did when he heard what was being said.

"I have been told my father had it," he said. "I do not remember my father, but I recently met a man who was at university with him, and who says I look very much like him." He looked deliberately at Snowden senior and smiled. "Perhaps the fellow glaring at me has noticed the same resemblance?"

"I have good reason not to trust him," Ashby said. "And I am reserving judgement about whether I should trust you."

Snowy was charmed. His experience with the gentry, gained mostly at Oxford, was that they covered what they actually intended to do with polite nothings that implied something quite different. But Lady Charmain had proved the exception and been honest with him from the beginning; her friends were apparently of the same ilk.

"Properly so," he told Ashby. "You do not know me. It is true that I mean Lady Charmain no harm, but you have no reason to believe me. I am glad she has friends to support and protect her."

"I am perfectly capable of protecting myself," Lady Charmain insisted.

"You are a formidable woman, my lady," Snowy agreed. "But it is always good to have the support of friends."

Ashby lifted his glass in a salute. "I cannot argue with that."

"Try the oyster tarts, Elijah," said Mrs. Ashby. "They are particularly fine."

The conversation moved to food and then to politics. Lord Arthur, whose brother was a duke, said the Prime Minister was predicting a general election. Snowy was impressed when he saw that all the ladies had a view on the key issues that would shape the election, and especially that the gentlemen listened to them.

Spending time with Lady Charmain's friends was knocking gaping holes in his prejudices.

Chapter Seven

A CANDLE ON either side of the ornate mirror on the study wall lit Snowden's face and upper body without relieving the gloom behind him. The black of his evening wear merged with the darkness, leaving the planes of his face and the folds of his white cravat to swim against the shadows.

"It cannot be him," he told his reflection. "He's dead. He died more than two decades ago. A boy of that age? A soft, spoiled brat like that? And a pretty one? He could never have survived."

The dark eyes of the reflection stared back. He thought he saw an ironic twitch of the eyebrow.

"Curse Matt. He was meant to kill the little horror and throw the body somewhere it would be found."

Snowden scowled and the reflection scowled back. The plan should have succeeded. It had worked once. And with a body to grieve over, Madeline would have recovered. Snowden could have charmed her into believing in him again. Instead, she'd insisted that the boy was still alive.

"She was meant to be mine." He nodded his head once, decisively, and his reflection nodded back, agreeing with him. He had seen the pretty girl first, begun to court her. Then she'd met cursed Edmund. The man with everything. His uncle's favorite. The golden boy.

Tonight's imposter had looked just like Edmund. "It cannot be the boy. He's a by-blow; that must be it. Perfect Edmund's base-born brat."

How he would like to tell Madeline that Edmund had been diddling someone else. His teeth flashed white in the candle light at the thought of her likely reaction.

His own pain, though, was greater. He had won her for such a short time, and then lost her. She blamed him for the boy's disappearance, and in the end, he'd had to put her away where she could do no harm.

It wasn't fair. Matt Deffew had ruined everything. The boy had ruined everything by biting his abductor's hand, wriggling from his grasp, and running away to die anonymously in the mean streets.

Matt was dead and could not pay for his mistake. The boy, too, was dead. He must be. And Madeline, to his everlasting sorrow. There was no one alive to punish.

In the reflection, Richard raised an eyebrow. Of course. There was only one recourse. Richard was right. Snowden must take his revenge on the imposter.

Chapter Eight

A S SHE SAT over breakfast the following morning, Margaret received a note from Arial asking if she could call. She returned an affirmative, knowing her friend would be full of questions about Mr. White.

By the time Arial arrived, with Regina in tow, Aunt Aurelia was up. Margaret had not expected to see her, since she normally breakfasted in bed, and she was still sulking about Mr. White. However, her maid must have mentioned that Margaret's friend was expected, and so the four of them sat down for a polite cup of tea.

As Margaret poured the tea, Regina said, "I trust your cold is improved."

Aunt Aurelia had the grace to look a little shame faced. "I am perfectly well today, thank you."

Margaret could not resist a small poke of revenge. "Her Grace was pleased to meet Mr. White. She invited him to call on her." She passed her aunt a cup of tea, made the way she preferred it.

Aunt Aurelia sniffed. "The Duchess of Winshire raised her first husband's base-born daughters and married a Persian. One must respect her position and her breeding, of course, but not necessarily her judgement."

A glance at Arial and Regina showed they were trying not to

laugh. Margaret gave Arial her cup.

Margaret could argue that the Duke of Winshire was as English as Aunt Aurelia, but it would be of no use. His first wife, the mother of his children, had been a Persian princess, which damned him forever in Aunt Aurelia's eyes. Her great aunt's views on the class system and the superiority of the English nobility were rigid and lofty, as she proved with her next remark.

"Mr. White is not of our kind. Add to that, one suspects, from his appearance, that he is an irregular connection of the house of Snowden, and I am disappointed in Margaret for lowering herself to encourage him. As I told her, Lady Stancroft, it will not do her any good with her worthy suitors to be seen in that man's company."

As Margaret served Regina, she decided it was time to assert herself. "Thank you, Aunt Aurelia. You have made your opinion perfectly clear. However, if any of my suitors were worthy of my attention, they would not be offended by my doing a favor for the man who saved my life."

"Which he would not have had to do, Margaret, if you had not been in a place you should never have gone. But there. I do not know why I bother. You were a rebellious child and a foolish girl. You have become a stubborn woman. I am going to my rooms. Good day, Lady Stancroft, Mrs. Ashby." She clattered her cup back into her saucer and flounced out of the room.

She was getting worse. She had always been perfectly pleasant in front of guests, saving her criticisms and complaints until she and Margaret were alone. Margaret was going to have to retire her to the country and hire a companion.

"I apologize for that scene," she said to her friends. She managed to keep her voice level, though her hand trembled as she lifted her cup.

"No apology needed," Regina assured her. "You behaved with dignity, Margaret."

"We are not responsible for the misbehavior of our relatives," Arial agreed. "Do not worry about it, Margaret."

Regina frowned. "Is it common for her to speak to you like that in front of guests? Or is it just that she knows we can be trusted?"

Margaret had to admit that Regina had put into words Margaret's own concerns. "She has been becoming more querulous. I think it is time for her to retire. I hate to hurt her feelings, but such scolds in front of the wrong audience could..." She trailed off, quailing at the thought of such public embarrassment.

"She could damage your reputation with a misplaced word," Arial agreed. "People will believe she has cause for her comments."

Margaret nodded. After a moment's silence, she said, "I do not suppose that is why you called."

Regina grinned at Margaret over her own cup. "We were both very impressed by your Mr. White. He is..." she appeared to be searching the ceiling for a word.

"Delectable," Arial offered. "You have been holding out on us, Margaret. You told us that he was stern and borderline rude. You did not tell us that he was almost as beautiful as Peter."

To Arial, no one was as handsome as her husband, and she had a point. Margaret had become accustomed to his appearance since she met him two years ago, but if considered dispassionately, he was breath-taking. A completely different type, though. A blond Apollo to Mr. White's dark Hermes.

"Mr. White is certainly easy on the eyes," she conceded. *At the least.*

"That is *all* you have to say?" Regina asked. "Margaret, darling, we watched you dance with him. Twice. You cannot tell me you are not attracted to him, and he to you. He could hardly take his eyes off you all night."

Really?

"She is blushing," Arial told Regina.

"It is not like that," Margaret insisted, in spite of the way her face burned. "Yes, he is an attractive man, especially when he is not acting like a bear with a sore paw, but he is not interested in me in *that* way, and even if he was, I could not possibly consider him as a suitor."

Regina raised an eyebrow. "Because he is from the slums and perhaps base-born?" she asked.

"Those things matter, Regina," Arial said. "You know they do, even if we all agree they shouldn't. Margaret needs to think of her future children."

"I have no idea where Mr. White is truly from or what his intentions are in confronting the Snowdens," Margaret told them. "That is why I cannot see him as anything more than a temporary escort. I cannot trust a man who keeps secrets from me. Not that he owes me an explanation. I am merely returning favor for favor."

Arial sipped her tea while she considered that remark. "He is still delectable," she said, decisively. "If nothing else, he makes a very attractive accessory to a lady in a ball gown."

Regina chuckled. "True. And it may be spiteful of me, but I enjoyed Lord Snowden's consternation last night."

"Lord Snowden's reaction, if I understand Mr. White correctly, was rather the point of last night," Margaret observed.

"You have two more outings with him, you said," Arial noted.

Margaret agreed. "We are riding in Hyde Park this afternoon, and tomorrow evening, he is to escort me to Lady Hamner's garden party." Another of Lord Andrew's invitations. Lady Hamner was a sort of sister-in-law, a former ward of the Duchess of Winshire, and rumored to be a base-born child of that lady's first husband.

"After that," she added, "he tells me he will seek an introduction to Lord Snowden. I am not to be involved in his further plans, he says."

Regina leaned forward to touch Margaret's knee. "Be careful, Margaret. I do not trust Lord Snowden, and Mr. White is intent on some end of his own. I do not want you caught in the middle."

A knock on the door was followed by the entrance of her

butler. "My lady, Lord Snowden has called. I have said I would ascertain whether you were at home."

Before Margaret could reply, Lord Snowden pushed her poor servant out of the way so he could enter the room. "Lady Charmain, I must speak with you. That man you were with last night. How well do you know him? How did you come to be escorted by him, with your chaperone nowhere in sight?"

Margaret would have answered the first two questions, if vaguely, but the third annoyed her. She stood, adopting her father's chilliest manner. "You will explain to me what business it is of yours, Lord Snowden."

"What business?" he spluttered, and then repeated the words. "What *business*?" He drew himself up and tucked his thumbs into the pockets of his waistcoat. "It is the business of any sober and responsible gentleman, to defend and protect misguided young women of their acquaintance."

He removed one hand to wave a finger in her face. "Particularly those without male relatives to perform that office."

"Lord Snowden, you overstate your right to that office," Regina informed the man. "Lady Charmain has many male advisers and friends, including her maternal uncle who is her trustee, my husband, Lord Stancroft and Lord Deerhaven. But even if she did not, you would not have any right to question her behavior."

Lord Snowden's mouth curved in a placatory smile, but it did not reach his eyes. Grey eyes, but not silver grey like his son's and Snowy's. No, his eyes were more the color of slate, with a corona of gold around the pupil. It was more the expression than the color, though, that made them like snakes' eyes, cold and pitiless.

"It is good to know the lady has friends to look out for her, Mrs. Ashby," he said. "Perhaps I should be addressing my concerns to those gentlemen, for I fear she has been poorly advised."

He turned back to Margaret and widened his smile and his hands. "Indeed, I was precipitate, dear Lady Charmain, for I am not yet your father-in-law, though I know my dear Edmund has hopes."

His chilly eyes narrowed as he watched her for a reaction.

"Precipitate indeed," Arial commented. "Since, as I understand it, Lady Charmain has given no special signs of favor to Mr. Edmund Snowden."

Lord Snowden fought a visible struggle to control his tongue and his temper, before he said, "I see I was mistaken to think I would be able to have a sensible conversation with you, Lady Charmain, especially in the company of your friends." He managed to make the word 'friends' sound like a word from the gutter.

"If you came here merely to insult me, Lord Snowden," Margaret told him, "I think you should leave."

He took two paces toward the door, then spun around and shook his finger at her once more. "The man is a dangerous charlatan. Do not be seen with him again, Lady Charmain. For the sake of your reputation *and* especially your good health."

He stormed out of the room, and a moment later, they heard the front door bang behind him.

Pompous bully.

"Well," said Regina. "If Mr. White was looking for a reaction from Lord Snowden, I would say he has succeeded."

⟫⟫⟫⟪⟪⟪

LADY CHARMAIN'S HORSE was being walked back and forth in front of her house when Snowy arrived. He tied his hired gelding to a tethering ring on the street and was mounting the stairs when her front door opened, and she exited.

He stepped back to admire her riding habit. Or, rather, the curves displayed in the jacket and skirt that hugged her torso. "My lady, I trust I did not keep you waiting."

"I suspect you are a few minutes early, Mr. White. I confess, I was watching for you out of the window."

He raised his eyebrows. "You were eager to ride today?"

She paused as she waited for the groom to bring her horse over. "My great aunt is in fine form today, Mr. White. I had no wish to be embarrassed by whatever she chooses to say to you."

Her honesty should be expected by now, but it always astonished him. Aroused him, too, which was perverse. "She objects to you riding with a low life from the slums," he suggested, though whether he sought to spark her temper or to show understanding, he could not have said.

"Her opinion," Lady Charmain retorted. "Not mine." Not for this lady a polite and civil answer. The truth about her aunt, unvarnished. *And about her own thoughts on the matter, too?*

"May I toss you up into the saddle, my lady?" he asked, bending to make a stirrup of his hand.

She put one neatly booted foot into his care, grasped the pommel, and leapt, so all he needed to do was continue the impetus upward. With a graceful twist in the air, she landed in the saddle, then busied herself arranging her legs and skirts. "Thank you, Mr. White."

"A pleasure, my lady." And a truer word was never spoken.

He mounted his own horse, and they paced off in the direction of the park.

"Were you satisfied with the stir you made last night, Mr. White?" she asked.

"I was," he confirmed. He was even more satisfied with this morning's work. He and his friends had been moving around town, seeding the news that the delay in confirming Snowden in the title of viscount was because of the existence of a rival claimant. One in the direct line.

If that and his public appearances didn't draw Snowden into a confrontation, he'd start using his true legal name.

"Lord Snowden visited me this morning," Lady Charmain said, in a conversational tone. "He ordered me not to go out with you any more, Mr. White."

She nudged her horse into a narrow gap between a parked carriage and a slow-moving dray, and Snowy had to drop back to follow her.

When he caught up, he noted, "And yet, here you are."

"Lord Snowden has no authority over me. From what he said, he will next visit my maternal uncle, to demand I am reined in. For my own good, of course. Apparently, you are a dangerous man, Mr. White."

Snowy was disconcerted. "I apologize, my lady. I did not want to bring trouble on you."

"You have not," she assured him. "My uncle has no authority over me and is far too lazy to exert himself if he had. He will undoubtedly listen politely to Lord Snowden and have his butler show the man out, then go back to sleep in his favorite chair."

Snowy had found out a little about the lady before he decided to follow Lily's stratagem for putting himself in Snowden's way. She was an orphan and the last of the Charmain direct line. Her mother, father, and two brothers had all died in the past six years. Due to the wording of the Writ of Summons that endowed an ancestor with the title, she had inherited the title. She was rich, and wealth and title made her a marital prize. Her great aunt was a crabbed old stick and now he found that her maternal uncle was careless of her wellbeing.

"Have you other family?" he asked.

She looked straight ahead through her horse's ears, her eyes growing suspiciously wet. "My uncle never married, and my father was an only child," she replied.

So, whom did she have to defend her from Snowden and his machinations? Snowy pulled up his horse. "This was a bad idea. Lady Charmain, let me escort you home."

She stared at him. "Why?"

"I did not intend to put you in a predicament. Snowden is a dangerous man, my lady. I thought your position in Society would protect you, but I did not realize that you and your great aunt are, to all intents and purposes, alone. I release you from your promise, Lady Charmain. Let me escort you home."

Lady Charmain snorted. "You are being ridiculous. What do you imagine that Lord Snowden can do to me? As I said to him, he has no authority over me. I am of age. I am in control of my own estate and all of my holdings. I am continuing on to the Park. You may accompany me or not, as you wish." She shifted her weight on the horse and loosened the reins. "Move on, Bess."

Snowy was left gaping at the lady's back and her horse's rear end.

He set his own horse hurrying to catch up. "I meant no offense, Lady Charmain."

She glanced at him and away again. "If it will ease your conscience, Mr. White, I have powerful friends. You have met some of them." Another glance. "I will not go on any errands in the middle of the night with complete strangers. Will that make you feel better?"

A reference to the incident last year, when Snowden's son abducted the lady who was now Mrs. Ashby by purporting to bring a message from her injured son. It was a trap—a plot to force the lady into marriage with a rejected suitor. The lady had been rescued, and the suitor, a man called Deffew, had died with his brother trying to kill her and her betrothed.

The Ashbys were, he assumed, among the friends she mentioned. Elijah Ashby was a formidable man, as was the Earl of Stancroft, who had also been at last night's ball. He was a former military officer and a force to be reckoned with.

"It will help," he told her. *But barely.* "Please be cautious. You do not know what Snowden is capable of."

They turned through a gate into Hyde Park, and there were both Ashby and Stancroft, waiting just inside the gate.

"I see," Snowy commented. "You have already arranged your protection."

Lady Charmain rolled her eyes as the two riders raised their hats to acknowledge her, then fell in behind her and Snowy. "I had no idea they would be here, Mr. White, but at a guess, I expect they feel they need to protect me from you!"

Snowy sent a wry grin to the men following. He couldn't blame them for their suspicions, and he appreciated their concern for the lovely lady he had come to like far too much.

"Oh look," Lady Charmain said, indicating with an inclination of her head. "Lord and Lady Deerhaven, Lady Stancroft, and Mrs. Ashby are in that carriage over there."

Her mare bounded in that direction, and a moment later Snowy followed, their two escorts behind.

Soon, Lady Charmain was leaning over the side of the carriage in conversation with her friends. Mr. Ashby came up on one side of Snowy, and Lord Stancroft on the other.

"Gentlemen," Snowy greeted them.

"White," they both said.

Snowy decided to take the bull by the horns. "I was delighted to see you both waiting for us. Snowden called on Lady Charmain this morning, to tell her to have nothing to do with me. She told me of this on the way here and refused to allow me to escort her home. Stay as suspicious of me as you wish, but please continue to watch out for the lady. That man is far more dangerous than she will believe."

The men exchanged glances as if communicating something between them.

"I heard an interesting rumor today," Lord Stancroft mused. "It seems Snowden might not be the viscount after all. A claimant in the direct line has turned up, or so they say."

"Is that what they say?" Snowy asked, with an attempt at disinterest. Gary and Drew had done a good job, then.

"You wouldn't know anything about that, would you, White?" Ashby asked outright.

The Marquess of Deerhaven leaned over from the coach. "The only person not entirely accounted for in the direct line is the grandson of the previous viscount. Snowden is a nephew—he married the son's widow after the son died, and Edmund Snowden is her son, but she already had a son from her previous marriage; he was the heir apparent at the time he disappeared."

His words attracted the attention of the ladies. "That's right," Lady Deerhaven said. "I remember reading about it in the newspapers. It was several years before our first Season, Regina."

"Yes," Mrs. Ashby agreed. "He was abducted when he was not quite three years of age, and never found again. He is believed to be dead, but they never found the body."

Should he tell them? They would know soon enough. He rather wanted Lady Charmain to know, in any case. "1797," Snowy said. "He was stolen from his mother's garden one day in 1797. Those who found him assumed he escaped from those who were trying to beat him to death in the slums. Or perhaps they thought they had already killed him. The child doesn't remember much apart from fear and blows."

A stillness spread over the group. Even the horses seemed to be holding their breaths.

Lady Charmain broke the silence. "Did those who found him not take him back to his mother? Or could he not tell them where he was from?"

Snowy took off his hat and brushed his hand over the streak. "This identified him. Those who found him knew the mark. But when they contacted his mother, she asked them to keep him hidden, for he had escaped death by a whisker twice before, and she feared a fourth attempt would succeed. And too, there were other suspicious deaths of prominent family members in the line of succession."

"It is like a horrid novel," Lady Stancroft declared. "The Lost Heir. Returned to claim his own from the wicked stepfather."

Deerhaven pointed out the very problem Snowy and his friend were trying to solve. "Proving such a claim might present difficulties."

"Provoking said wicked stepfather might present opportunities," Snowy said. "Things may be said—or tried—to the man who was that child."

The gentlemen nodded, thoughtfully.

"However, the stepfather is proving to be both more erratic and more arrogant than expected." He turned to Lady Charmain. "I will leave you with your friends, my lady. I do not wish you to put yourself in harm's way."

"I see," said Lady Stancroft. "Margaret has told you that Snowden threatened her, correct?"

"I have no intention of allowing anyone to bully me," Lady Charmain said. "Mr. White, or Lord Snowden, or whatever your name is, you promised me your escort on a ride in Hyde Park, and again to a garden party tomorrow, and I am holding you to that promise. I am sure that Lord Snowden—oh dear, how awkward it is not knowing what to call people—I am sure that *man* will not dare to confront me when I am out with my friends, and I shall instruct that he is never again to be permitted into my house."

"Call me Snowy, as my friends do," Snowy offered. "Very well, my lady. I will keep my promise. But may we please ride with your friends?" He had just noticed young Snowden gaping at him from across an expanse of grass. He was with another young man—the same slender youth with fair hair and dark eyebrows who had been with him last night—and both were obviously observing the group.

"Deffew and Snowden," Ashby murmured. "To our right. Margaret, for the sake of my peace of mind, would you please ride with us?"

To Snowy's relief, the lady made no further demur.

He expected the inquisition on his origins to continue, but apparently, Lady Charmain's friends had decided to leave the topic. He found himself riding with first one of the men and then the other, then with Lady Charmain again, and then called alongside the carriage to exchange courtesies with the marquess and the ladies.

The conversation ranged over politics, philosophy, industry, and literature. He would have scoffed if anyone had told him a fortnight ago that he would go riding in the fashionable hour in

Hyde Park with seven aristocrats—for apparently Mrs. Ashby was the daughter of a viscount and Mr. Ashby was also the scion, if distantly, of a noble house. At any rate, Snowy would certainly not have expected to enjoy himself as much as he did.

From time to time, they stopped to greet other people, and Snowy was always presented. "Our friend, Mr. White," they said, which was clever. He appreciated how they were giving him the exposure he needed to tweak Snowden's tail while at the same time protecting Lady Charmain by making her the only one among a group of highly-connected people.

By the time they had driven around the carriageway of the park and approached the gate again, Ashby, Stancroft and Deerhaven had all separately assured him they would be at the garden party tomorrow, and he need not fear for Lady Charmain's safety.

It did not escape his notice that Snowden and his fair-haired companion followed them all the way, never approaching, but always within sight, and always watching.

"LET'S GO TO the garden party together," Cordelia suggested. "Margaret, we will pick you up at noon. Snowy, shall we meet you here, or is there somewhere else you would like us to collect you?"

Her friends had insisted on escorting her home from the Park, bringing Mr. White—no, *Snowy*—along with them. And now, they were insisting on forming a protective cordon around her for the garden party.

"Here will work perfectly," Snowy said, smiling at Cordelia.

Margaret surrendered. Their overreaction was irritating, but she understood everyone had her best interests at heart. "Very well, Cordelia. Aunt Aurelia has cried off, and it will be nice to have your company."

Her friends were too polite to scoff at the fiction that Aunt Aurelia was "company", but Regina said, "She disapproves of Lady Hamner, I suppose."

Margaret sighed. Her great aunt was putting her in an impossible situation, with her prejudices and poor judgement. Lady Hamner might be the daughter of an Irish actress, but her father *had* been a duke, and Lady Hamner had been raised by his duchess in her household. Furthermore, she was acknowledged and loved by her half-brother, the current duke, and had married a wealthy and respectable earl. Her younger sister had also married well.

If Aunt Aurelia mentioned her opinion of Lady Hamner in public, she would annoy several powerful families. Just as well, then, she had refused the invitation to the garden party.

A few minutes later, after she had said her farewells and gone inside, her butler told her that Aunt Aurelia was entertaining guests in the drawing room. Margaret was not pleased to find young Mr. Snowden and his friend Mr. Deffew drinking tea and listening to Aunt Aurelia complain about Mr. White's origins, character, manners, and possible intentions.

The two gentlemen stood when she entered the room. "I did not realize you had guests, Aunt," she said.

Aunt Aurelia tittered. "Do not be frivolous, Margaret. Mr. Snowden and Mr. Deffew have come to visit *you*, of course." She frowned. "They enter entirely into my feelings on that dreadful man, Margaret. Mark my words, you are asking for trouble allowing him to be so familiar."

Margaret was not going to allow the woman to goad her into a response in front of the two too-interested young men. "Will you step into the hall with me, please, Aunt Aurelia?"

Aunt Aurelia smirked. "To have private conversation with me when you have visitors, my dear, would be poor manners."

The smirk tipped the balance. Margaret's voice was cold even to her own ears when she turned to the gentleman. "It would not be my choice, gentlemen, to have this discussion in front of an audience, but when my aunt freely discusses my private business with other people, I suppose my scruples are unnecessary."

"Now, Margaret. Losing your temper is not ladylike," Aunt Aurelia prodded.

Margaret managed to keep her voice calm. "Aunt Aurelia, you are my companion, not my keeper, and surely *not* my governess. Furthermore, it would appear that you no longer feel able to keep me company when I go out, which puts me in a difficult spot. I cannot have a companion who picks and chooses when to carry out her duties, or who criticizes me in front of—and to—other people. It is time we discussed your retirement, Aunt. For now, please go to your room. You may send a maid to sit with us while the gentlemen are present."

Aunt Aurelia's eyes were nearly popping out of her head. "But you cannot send me away. I am your only living relative. I helped to raise you."

Two out of three were untrue. Sadly, she and Aunt Aurelia were the last surviving members of her family. But Aunt Aurelia had shown no interest in her at all until Margaret's father died, shortly after her brothers. Given what she knew of the lady now, Margaret suspected that her father had refused to give house room to his mother's aunt. He never did anything that might diminish his own comfort.

Then Margaret inherited the title and the estates for the benefit of her first son. Suddenly dependent upon the young woman she had ignored for more than twenty years, Aunt Aurelia had appointed herself as companion, instructor, and commentator.

And Margaret certainly *could* send her away. It was only pity and maybe the hope that their relationship would become warmer and more familiar—as well as the fact that Aunt Aurelia was totally dependent on Margaret—that had prevented her from doing so months ago.

Mr. Deffew shifted uneasily. "We should go," he whispered to Mr. Snowden. Fortunately, Margaret had excellent hearing.

"I have to talk to her," Mr. Snowden replied, equally quietly.

"Or do you want to tell Father that we left without saying anything?"

Margaret did not take her eyes off Aunt Aurelia, nor acknowledge in any way that she had heard the whispers. Aunt Aurelia glared back, but Margaret could see uncertainty in her eyes. Perhaps even a bit of fear.

For heaven's sake. She was going to set the woman up in the dower house with servants and an allowance, not throw her out into the street. Aunt Aurelia did not wait for her to say so. She sniffed loudly. "You always were a difficult child," she said. "Willful like your mother." With her nose in the air, she stormed off, slamming the door behind her.

Margaret opened it again and asked the butler to send in a maid.

"I apologize for washing our family linen in public, gentlemen." They looked much more cheerful now that her aunt was gone and the scene was over. Undoubtedly, it would make a fine story for them to spread wherever they went. "She is growing old. I intend to settle her in the dower house at my estate." She sighed. "And I will need to find another companion, which is a nuisance. But there, you did not visit me today to discuss my domestic troubles."

Mr. Snowden looked at Deffew who returned the look with a panicked one of his own. Clearly, Snowden was on his own with whatever task his father had given him.

The maid entered the room and took a seat in the corner.

Mr. Snowden looked at her, and grimaced. Then he took a breath, clearly nerving himself for what he was about to say. "Lady Charmain, I need to warn you, and also ask you a favor."

"Carry on," Margaret said. Nothing in her tone could be interpreted as encouraging.

"First," he said, "I was pleased to see that you had your friends with you in the park. That man you were with at the ball—he is dangerous, my lady. I was worried about you." He fluttered his eyelashes and sent her a warm smile before continuing. She was grateful she wasn't easily swayed by his charms and could read his true intent.

"He is a fraud and a charlatan. My father has found out that he claims to be Henry Snowden, my half-brother, who died when I was a baby. He can't be, of course. It is just a trick. Father thinks he wants us to pay him to go away, for he won't get the viscountcy. My father is the *true* viscount."

Margaret inclined her head. "And the favor?" she asked.

Mr. Snowden leaned forward in his seat, his eyes wide and earnest. "You could be of great assistance to us. If you told us what he was about, and what he plans to do..." He raised his eyebrows in a hopeful question, then added. "But only if you can do so safely."

"You want me to spy on him," Margaret said.

"I wouldn't put it like that," Snowden protested. "Not spying; more just passing things on. As a friend, of course."

"I see." Margaret began packing the empty tea cups back onto the tray. "Well, then, gentlemen. You have delivered your message and asked your question. I am going to have to ask you to leave. I have unfinished business with my aunt."

"Will you do it?" Mr. Snowden asked.

In response, Margaret went to the door and called to the butler. "Please escort Mr. Snowden and Mr. Deffew to the door." She turned back into the room, and said, "Thank you for calling, gentlemen." She then continued walking out the door and up the stairs, leaving them no alternative but to go away.

She felt grimy, as if covered in a slick of grease that was in turn coated in dirt and dust. Between the confrontation with Aunt Aurelia and the machinations of Snowden and his son, the happy mood in which she had returned from the afternoon's outing was completely gone.

On the other hand, tomorrow she was meeting Snowy again. It would be nice to think that the lift in her heart at the thought of their next meeting was because she wanted to help his cause by telling him about the untimely visit of the two young men. The attraction, though, was Snowy himself. She was in danger of developing a tendre for the main, despite the warnings of her friends, and her own concerns. Despite Snowy's own disinterest in her except as a means to an end. *Ah, Margaret, you are in a sad case.*

Chapter Nine

T HAT EVENING, LILY shocked Snowy by telling him it was time to hand over his bookkeeping responsibilities. "Orchid is ready to retire from the trade, and she has always been good with numbers," she said.

Snowy knew Lily would not have to recruit to fill Orchid's place, either. Not only did the House of Blossoms have a record of keeping their girls safe from the worst kind of clients, but the girls kept most of their earnings and were encouraged to invest them. The house charged a fee on which it made a profit after providing accommodation, medical care, and a clothing allowance, but made most of its considerable income on drink, food, and games of chance.

Added to that, Lily and her friends offered their workers advice on saving and investing, and on retraining to anyone who wanted to leave the lucrative trade and take up one that was less physically and emotionally demanding.

"I am your bookkeeper," Snowy complained. "Find something else for Orchid to do."

"You can't be a viscount and the bookkeeper in a brothel," Lily told him.

"I haven't made up my mind to claim my title," Snowy pointed out. Which wasn't altogether true. The more he learned about

Snowden, the more revolting he found the idea of the man benefitting from his crime. *Crimes, probably.* The deaths in the Snowden family needed some explaining, and Snowy had not yet been able to discover what happened to his mother. He didn't remember the woman, but the urge to protect her even in death was strong in him, as strong as it was for any of his foster mothers.

Lily rolled her eyes. She had always been able to see right through him.

He grumbled anyway. "Besides, there's no guarantee I'll succeed, even if I do make a claim."

"You will win, Snowy," Lily insisted, shaking her head at his pessimism. "You are the rightful heir, and we have proof."

The sworn testimony of women, particularly women who earned their living on their backs, would not have much weight in a court of law, especially against a titled gentleman. Snowy didn't bother to point that out. Lily already knew it.

"Teach Orchid, Snowy," she ordered. "Whatever happens to your claim, you cannot remain our bookkeeper. You are an educated gentleman. If something happens to prevent you from taking your title, then you will need to find employment doing something worthy of your education and status. Orchid and the other girls don't have many choices. You do. *You* can be anything, my boy."

Not quite anything, but Snowy, with his university training and his investment wealth, certainly had more opportunities than a retired harlot. He sighed. "Very well, Lily. I will show Orchid how I keep the books, and we'll see how she gets on."

The training got off to a bad start when Orchid tried some of her seductive tactics on her tutor. Even if Snowy's mind had not been full of a certain countess, and even if he was not aware that Orchid was just trying to win the bet with Daphne, he would not have been interested.

"Stop that, Orchid," he told her, when she placed a hand on his thigh as if by accident, then ran it up toward his groin on purpose. "You know I don't bed any of the House's girls."

She would scoff if he told her he'd sworn off sex altogether. The encounters of his randy adolescence had soured when he'd first come to understand the inequalities between those who purchased sex and those who provided the service. His knowledge came from first-hand experience; he'd funded his first investments by selling his body to bored widows and matrons.

Never again. He would never allow himself to be so used, nor would he ever use another human being for his own pleasure. As for mutual encounters, in that direction lay romance and commitment. The thought of either scared him witless. *Unless the commitment was to Lady Charmain.* The thought surfaced, and he shoved it down, again.

Orchid didn't need to know any of his thoughts. "Keep it up, and I will send you back upstairs. If you want to learn what I have to teach, behave yourself."

After that, the lesson proceeded well. Despite what Lily said about Orchid's skill, Snowy was surprised at how much she already knew. "I used to help my father with his books," she told Snowy when he praised her. "He owned a shop."

Her eyes were far away and moist for a moment. Pleasant memories, clearly, but painful to her because of what came after. She never spoke about her past, but Snowy knew Lily bought her contract from a much worse brothel into which she'd been sold by the creditors of her shopkeeper father after both her parents died of a fever when she was only a girl.

He arranged to meet her again the following morning and went to get ready for his outing into Lady Charmain's world.

The others were approaching her ladyship's house as he walked within sight of it. The Deerhaven's elegant landau carried the marchioness, Mrs. Ashby and Lady Stancroft. Their husbands rode together behind the carriage, leading a spare horse.

Lady Charmain came down the steps from her house, and all of a sudden, she was all he could see. He must have hurried his steps, for there he was, handing her up into the landau before

Deerhaven's groom could perform that office. He managed to recover his senses sufficiently to greet the rest of the company as he mounted the horse they'd brought for him and followed the carriage with the rest of the gentlemen.

The Hamners had a property in the country, just thirty minutes from town. They made good time until close to the Hamner estate, when they found themselves caught in a snarl. A dray had collided with another wagon carrying produce. The road was covered with cabbages and the drivers were attempting to untangle their horses. If it had been up to Snowy, they would have walked from that point, and left the grooms to bring the vehicle and the horses.

He supposed the ladies did not wish to put their gowns at risk on the road verge. Or perhaps people of their kind simply took it for granted that fifteen minutes sitting in a slow-moving carriage was better than a ten-minute walk.

He made no comment, but simply followed along until it was their turn to hand their horses over to the grooms brought for the purpose and assist the ladies from the vehicle.

He did his best to suppress his contemptuous amusement, but must have let some of it leak into his expression, for the Marquess of Deerhaven said, out of the corner of his mouth, "Ridiculous, isn't it? We could have walked faster."

His marchioness overheard him, and her eyes twinkled with humor as she said, "We obey Society's expectations in the little things so we can ignore them in the matters that are important."

A good precept. If Snowy was going to be a viscount, it was one worth remembering.

MARGARET SAT WITH her friends in the shade, sipping fruit juice and watching Peter, Ash, Deerhaven, and Snowy on the large artificial lake with half a dozen other men, rowing two to a boat in a series of races. The ladies had been out on the water, but when the men challenged one another to a race, they had asked to be set ashore on the island, where refreshments were set out in the temple-like folly.

"You like him, don't you?" Regina asked Margaret.

"Which him?" Margaret asked, though she knew perfectly well that Regina was referring to Snowy.

"I do," Arial said. "Peter does, too. He is not what we expected when you told us about allowing him to escort you, Margaret."

Margaret dropped the pretense to pursue this more interesting topic.

"What did you think he would be like?"

Arial thought about it. "A lot rougher. Less concerned about your safety and your reputation."

"After all," Cordelia pointed out, "you did meet him in a slum alley not far from the brothel where he works. It was not a recommendation of good character."

Regina agreed. "We were concerned but are reassured now we have met him."

"He has been raised as a gentleman," Margaret said. "In my experience, he is more of a gentleman than many you meet in Society."

The other ladies nodded. "Lord Snowden for one," Regina agreed and tilted her head toward the man himself, watching them from the far shore. His son and young Deffew, his ward, were out racing on the lake, but Snowden did not turn his stare away from the four ladies.

"The rumors say Snowden is not the viscount, that there is a lost heir. It is Snowy, isn't it? That's what he was telling us at the Park. Arial commented. "Did he start the rumors, Margaret?"

"said he has not told me," Margaret answered, suppressing the slight hurt that she had been used in his plan but not told what it was. "But consider the way these rumors have appeared just when he chooses to go into Society—it is too unlikely a coincidence. I think he must be behind them. Lord Snowden must be rattled, given he sent his son to repeat what he called to tell me himself: Snowy is a charlatan, a fraud, and that I must cease seeing him immediately."

Regina's reaction was the same as Margaret's. "The cheek!"

"Interesting, though," Cordelia mused. "Have you told Snowy?"

A face on the other shore had caught Margaret's eye. It could not be... At this distance, it was impossible to be sure, but somehow, she was. She squinted in a subtle attempt to block the sun's reflection on the waters of the lake.

"Margaret?" Arial asked.

"Hmmm?" She turned her head to peer at them. What had they been talking about? "No, I haven't had the opportunity, yet."

Her friends were looking at her with concern. "You have gone pale, darling," Arial said. "Is something the matter?"

"Nothing," she assured them. "I thought I saw someone I knew long ago, but I am sure I must be wrong. He was some distance away, and I could not see his face clearly. Just the hair color and the uniform."

"Not the odious officer!" Arial exclaimed.

"The odious officer?" asked Cordelia.

Arial was the only one who knew quite how odious Martin had been, but the rest was not a secret. "A man who trifled with my affections during my first Season. I was too young to realize his compliments were lies and his promises so much empty air. I am sure it cannot be him. As far as I know, his regiment is still posted overseas." For years she had been checking the listings in the newspapers, hoping he never sold out.

Not that he would. He was an impecunious younger son, and his army career was one of the few things he genuinely loved.

She didn't want to talk about it anymore. "Look, they are lining up the winners of the heats for the final race."

It was a successful distraction, for Ash and Peter were on the little jetty, preparing to clamber back into a boat. They must be in the final. Not Deerhaven and Snowy. They were rowing straight across the lake toward the island, presumably to join the ladies.

She looked across the lake to where she thought she had seen Martin. She couldn't see him now.

Dear Heavens, she hoped it wasn't him. She'd thought— she'd hoped—he was safely off in the Far East, which was where his regiment had been posted after peace had been signed with the United States.

Of course, she'd known he would probably come back to England one day, if he survived the hazards of his profession. She'd expected he would, for he had the devil's own luck. But she certainly did not want him appearing in England, in London no less, before she had found herself a husband.

"Did you see?" Deerhaven called as he and Snowy approached. "Stancroft and Ashby are in the final."

"We saw!" Cordelia agreed. "Come and sit by me, Deerhaven, and we shall cheer for them to win."

"White and I came second in our heat," Deerhaven told them, as he obeyed his wife. "We almost had them, did we not, White? White rowed at Oxford, my love."

Margaret moved over so Snowy could sit beside her.

"They are off!" Deerhaven announced, unnecessarily, as the flag dropped, and the rowers bent to their oars.

"Is something wrong, my lady?" Snowy murmured under cover of the enthusiastic cheers and shouts of the others. "Has something happened? Is it Snowden?"

Margaret pasted on a cheerful smile and answered the final question. "I am perfectly well. Snowden cannot hurt me with his staring."

"Glaring, more like," Snowy commented, his eyes on the subject of their conversation, who stood opposite them, ignoring the race and scowling at Margaret.

"Walk with me," Margaret said, scrambling to her feet.

Snowy leapt to his own but demurred. "Is it wise? You have redeemed your pledge to Lily. If you step back now, Snowden will leave you alone."

Margaret snorted. "Unlikely. He has not done so since my father died, leaving me in possession of the land and the title."

"He wants your land?" Snowy asked.

She put her hand on the arm he offered, and they began to stroll along the shore in the direction the rowers would appear when they rounded the island in their final pull to the finish, which was an imaginary line across the lake to the island just beyond the jetty.

"He wants access over the land for a canal to carry his coal, also any coal that might be beneath the land. I doubt he wants the actual land, but he bothered my father for years, seeking access. He neglects his own tenants, and I will never let him get his hands on mine."

Snowy nodded. "I suppose the title is the sauce on the pudding," he said.

"He wants it for a son or a grandson," Margaret agreed. "Or so I believe. He will not get it. Young Mr. Snowden does not behave as if his suit is in earnest, however. He flirts, but he flirts with everyone, even Aunt Aurelia. Otherwise, he treats me more like a maiden aunt than an object of his attraction. When I refuse his entreaties to go walking or driving, I see relief in his eyes. He is, after all, a very young man."

Snowy put his hand over Margaret's, sending tingles up her arm and down to her core, but his attention was directed along the path ahead of them. "He and his even younger friend are coming this way," he said.

Sure enough, Snowden and Deffew were walking up from the island's jetty.

Chapter Ten

THE DISTRACTION WAS welcome. Snowy was wearing tight moleskins that his valet had assured him were suitable for both riding and a garden party. His physical reaction to Lady Charmain's attractions was at risk of becoming visible.

Deffew saw them first and nudged Snowden, who looked up and grinned. "Lady Charmain! I was looking for you and your escort." He held out a hand as he approached. "Mr. White, is it not? I am Edmund Snowden, but everyone calls me Chalky."

The boy had cheek, Snowy would give him that. He shook the offered hand. "Everyone calls me Snowy."

Chalky waved a casual hand toward his friend. "My friend, Dickon Deffew."

Deffew gave a shallow bow. "My lady. Mr. White." Deffew lacked his friend's charm; his whole demeanor was sulky.

"You and the marquess made an impressive showing on the water, Snowy," Chalky said.

"You left us well in your wake," Deffew grumbled. He added, reluctantly, "You row well."

They were going to play the civil courtesies game, were they? Snowy could do that. "We were left in our turn, when the winners nosed us out at the line."

"Yes, bad luck," Chalky sympathized.

Snowy shrugged. "It was more lack of practice. I haven't rowed since Oxford."

"I coxed at Cambridge," Chalky offered. "I wanted to row, but they said I didn't have the shoulders for it."

Snowy eyed him. "You have the build," he said. "You'd bulk up if you did the right exercise." He grinned. "Haying is good. Uses many of the same muscles."

"Gentlemen don't do haying," Deffew sneered.

Lady Charmain sneered back, if one could call her look of ladylike contempt a sneer. "I disagree, Mr. Deffew. My father and my brothers used to help to bring in the hay. And the corn harvest. And the barley. The Marquess of Deerhaven also works the fields in harvest season."

Chalky's eyes lit up. "The proof of the pudding is in the eating, Dickon. We got beaten by two gentlemen who do harvesting work."

Deffew's sullen expression intensified, but he said nothing more. It crossed Snowy's mind that he might be shy. He'd had a friend at university with very similar eyebrows who looked more and more angry the more embarrassed he got. Either that, or Deffew was determined to see Snowy as an enemy.

Chalky shot his friend a doubtful look, then turned anxious eyes on Snowy. "May I speak to you in private for a moment, Mr. White?"

Snowy frowned. "I am escorting the lady," he said.

"If we just step apart a little?" the young man pleaded. "You do not mind, do you, my lady?"

Snowy lifted his brows. He was curious about what Chalky wanted, and Lady Charmain should be safe enough on the island with him in sight and her friends in shouting distance, but the decision must be hers.

"I will wait here, Snowy," she said, decisively. "Go and talk to your br... to Mr. Snowden."

Chalky's eyes widened so far, the whites showed around them, and Snowy, too, picked up the near slip, but he said nothing.

He led Chalky fifteen paces away. "Here I am, then. What did you want us to talk about?"

"Are you?" The young man asked. "My brother?"

"Half-brother," Snowy confirmed.

"My father's bastard." It was not a question, but Chalky did not sound certain.

"Try again," Snowy suggested.

"It's impossible," Chalky insisted. "You cannot be my brother Hal. He died when I was a baby."

Snowy raised an eyebrow. He had one argument Chalky might find convincing. *Not Chalky. Eddie. Didn't Poppy tell the tale of how I called every little baby Eddie when I was a wee lad? Was that a memory of my own baby brother?.* "Remember this, Eddie?" Snowy began to sing:

> *Sleep my baby, warm and cozy;*
> *In your mother's loving arms.*
> *Nestle close and safely slumber*
> *Let my love your worries calm.*

Eddie joined in on the second part of the verse.

> *No one will disturb your resting;*
> *Harm will ever pass you by.*
> *Child beloved, on my bosom*
> *Sleep to mother's lullaby.*

"Mama's lullaby," they said together.

Eddie shook his head as if to clear it. "You *are* Hal. But how? What happened to you? Where have you been?"

Before Snowy could open his mouth to suggest they should meet to talk about it where they would not be interrupted, Eddie held up his hands in a halt gesture. "My father mustn't find out. He'll lose his nut! It's wonderful, Hal, don't get me wrong. But I'm afraid of what Father might do."

Snowy managed not to snort. What could the man do that was worse than he'd already tried? "He'll find I'm much harder to kill now that I'm grown, Eddie. And he didn't succeed when I was two."

"He wouldn't..." Eddie trailed off and grimaced. "I can't quite believe it, Hal. But I can't deny it either."

If Eddie was acting, he was better than anyone Snowy had ever seen on the stage. "We need to talk, you and me. Will you meet me for dinner? Perhaps at Fourniers? I'll book a private room, Eddie. Shall we say at seven tonight?"

The young man's smile was tremulous. "Ned. Only Dickon— my friend Deffew—calls me Ned, but I've always imagined that Mama might have done so if she had lived until I was grown. Hal."

"Hal." Snowy nodded once. "I like it. Meet me, Ned, just the two of us. I'll tell you what I know, and we'll see where that leaves us. Your friend is getting restless."

Deffew had taken a step toward them and then back and repeated the action several times. "I'll meet you there, Hal. Don't worry. I won't say a word to anyone." He lifted his voice. "Come on, Deffers. I'm done here. Let's go and see if we can find a card game."

He left Snowy with a beaming smile bright enough to make the blindest person suspicious.

His friend was pestering him as they walked away. "What happened? What did he say? Did you find out—"

Ned interrupted. "Leave off, Deffers. I'm bored with the whole thing. In fact, I'm bored with this party. Let's slip out without telling anyone."

"Uncle Richard won't be happy," Deffew was saying, as they rounded the corner and their voices faded.

"Well?" Lady Charmain asked. "Am I to be told what any of that means? A lovely song, by the way. You and your brother bonding over a lullaby?"

Snowy had to smile. "You, my lady, are far too smart for my

peace of mind, yet I find I enjoy it. Keeps me on my toes."

"I suppose," she said, "that is all the answer I am going to get."

"See? I knew you were smart." He took her hand and placed it on her arm. "I promise I will tell you everything soon. Will that satisfy?"

She made the snorting sound with which she signified disbelief and disapproval. Finding it endearing was proof he was far gone indeed. "It will have to, Snowy. For the present."

⋙⋘

AUNT AURELIA REFUSED to come down to dinner, sending word she had been gravely insulted by Margaret's words and required an apology before she would speak to Margaret again.

Margaret decided that dealing with her aunt could wait for the next day. Or perhaps she should first send a message to her estate to have the dower house prepared.

Yes. That was the best path forward. Set the whole thing up, perhaps even find a replacement companion. Then tell Aunt Aurelia about her retirement and send her to the country on the same day.

Margaret was not afraid of her aunt's reaction, precisely. She was tired of the constant carping and criticism, certainly. She would do a great deal to avoid more of it than necessary.

But Margaret had better things to think about over her dinner than her aunt's abrasive personality. Snowy was not finished with her. He had said it would just be the three events, and it was better if she knew nothing. But just today, he said he would explain everything when he could. Soon, he said.

That meant he planned to see her again, and she smiled at the thought, for it made her all the more certain her attraction to him was returned.

The following morning, Aunt Aurelia refused to come down

again, even for church. Margaret went on her own.

"No Snowy today?" Arial asked, when they stopped to greet one another after the service.

"It was not one of our agreed events," Margaret told her. "I do not know when he might call again."

"He will," Arial assured her. "A man doesn't look at a woman the way Snowy looks at you and then just walk away."

Margaret hoped she was right. "He said he will explain what is going on. Soon, he said. So, I know he intends to see me again."

"What was his view about what Mr. Snowden said about you not seeing him again?"

"He said he thought Lord Snowden was a threat, but that he is ready for it. He believes Mr. Snowden is just doing his father's bidding, which I think is true." The surly Mr. Deffew was more Margaret's idea of a villain. "Mr. Snowden always seems so cheerful and eager to please."

Arial quoted Shakespeare's Hamlet, "One may smile and smile and be a villain."

Not an uplifting thought, for how was a person to know whom to trust?

"The 'odious officer' smiled a lot, as I remember," Margaret observed.

⟫⟫⟫⟩⟨⟨⟨⟨

WHEN SHE ARRIVED home, it was to find that Aunt Aurelia had ordered the gig Margaret kept for household shopping, and gone out. To complain to her sour circle, probably. Still, it would only be for a short time more.

"You also had a visitor, my lady," the butler said. "Lord Snowden. As you instructed, I told him you were not at home. Miss Denning had gone out before he arrived."

"Thank you, Bowen," Margaret said. She settled at her desk to write a letter to her steward at Malmsworth Towers, her principal estate. The dower house had to be prepared and staffed. It should already be clean and sound, at least. Servants went down from the main house once a month to take off the dust covers and give the place a thorough clean, and to report any necessary maintenance.

That being the case, she told the steward the dower house must be habitable by Wednesday afternoon, even if that meant sending in servants from the main house until new servants could be hired.

Aunt Aurelia arrived home and went straight up to her room, and thirty minutes later, a note arrived from Uncle Eustace. Before she opened it, Margaret guessed where her aunt had been, and sure enough, Uncle Eustace complained of her visit, opening his letter in typical fashion, without a salutation or any of the usual courtesies.

"I had a call from that sour old besom you insisted on letting into your house after your father died. Says you're dallying with the hired help or next to it. I don't believe a bit of it. And if it was true, it's none of my business. You're a grown woman and a countess in your own right. Get rid of the meddlesome baggage. That's my advice. Come and see your old uncle some time, but don't tell me what you're doing. What I do not know will not hurt me. E. Webster."

SNOWY'S HALF-BROTHER DIDN'T arrive at their meeting. Snowy waited for an hour in the private room he'd hired at Fournier's before giving up and ordering a solitary meal. Putting together Ned's failure to turn up with his visit to Lady Charmain and his implied threats, Snowy had to wonder whether the change of mind he'd thought he'd witnessed was just an act.

Or perhaps Ned just lost his nerve. Pity. Snowy regretted it more than he expected, which just went to show that it didn't do to place trust in people.

He stayed away from the haunts of the ton on Sunday. Lady Charmain had performed superbly, and the rumors about the true heir were also doing their job. The next move was up to the lawyers, unless Snowden took the bait and went on the attack.

On Monday, ten minutes before the appointed time and dressed in his finest, he presented himself at the London home of the Duke and Duchess of Winshire. His early arrival was fortuitous as it took most of that time to be passed from the footman who opened the door, to the butler who sent a message for yet another footman to conduct him up the opulent stairs and along elegant passages to Her Grace's private sitting room. He was announced just as the clock struck the hour.

"I do appreciate punctuality," said the duchess. "Come in, my dear." Snowy observed immediately that the room was like the lady herself: elegant and beautifully presented, but with a warmth about it that drew a person in.

Snowy took the chair she indicated, on the other side of a low table from the duchess herself. She busied herself with the tea makings and then dismissed all the servants, leaving the two of them alone.

"Being closeted with a young man without facing untoward accusations is one of the benefits of advancing age and high social position, Lord Snowden," she said. "They are fewer than you might think." She handed him his cup of tea.

"Your Grace is a beautiful woman," Snowy told her, ignoring the way she had addressed him. He had a feeling she used the title to unsettle him and was determined not to show how well it was working.

"For an old lady." The duchess's eyes twinkled. "I have grandchildren, Snowden. You wince. If you plan to take the title, you had better get used to it." With the precision of a needle, she added, "Do not think of it as your stepfather's title, my dear. Think of it as your father's, God rest his soul."

The woman read his mind like a witch. *Or like Lily.* How his foster mother would laugh at being compared to a duchess!

"I will try, Your Grace."

"Good. I knew your mother. You take your coloring from your father, but you and your brother share the shape of your mother's eyes. You have a way of holding your head to once side just as she did, too."

Every word seemed to slip into a hole in his heart of which he had not been aware, warming the space, making it seem less empty. He looked like his mother! *I should tell Ned.* No. Ned had not turned up. He was not on Snowy's side.

The duchess took a sip of her own tea. "I owe you a debt, Snowden. When your mother disappeared from Society, I took your grandfather's word that her mind was turned by your death, and she was living retired while she recovered. I obeyed my husband's command to stay out of your family's private business. I should have insisted on visiting. Perhaps there is something I could have done." She shook her head, sadly.

The duchess had previously been married to the Duke of Haverford, of whom Snowy had heard nothing good. "You could not have helped her, Your Grace."

"I can help you, Snowden," the duchess retorted. "What is it you need?"

"I appreciate the thought, ma'am. I am not sure that anyone can give me what I really need."

The duchess tipped her head to one side. "Tell me what that is, and we shall see."

"Information, mostly. I believe we'll find most of it. Lord Andrew has put me on to an enquiry agent. A man called Wakefield. He is apparently very good."

"I can vouch for him," Her Grace agreed. "He and his wife are connections of my family, and excellent at their work. But tell me what information you are looking for, my dear. I have sources of my own."

"I want the whole truth, Your Grace. I want to know if Snowden was behind my kidnapping; whether it was attempted murder, as my mother and my foster mothers believed. I want to know whether my father was murdered, what happened to my mother, everything about my past I should have grown up knowing.

"I will settle for evidence of two things. That the boy—me—Aunt Lily found in that alley is the same boy who was stolen from a garden in Mayfair two days earlier. And that my mother's second husband was responsible for my abduction and attempted murder."

"I see." The duchess proved she did see by adding, "The first will make it easier for you to claim the viscountcy. The second will allow you to seek justice."

In truth, Snowy would settle for the first. He would have an opportunity to seek justice when Snowden tried to kill him again.

Chapter Eleven

O N MONDAY, MARGARET had a busy day.
       She told her grooms to have her traveling coach ready
to depart the next morning and sent a courier to arrange
accommodation at the halfway point between London and
Malmsworth Towers.

She visited her solicitor and her bank to set up an allowance,
to be paid quarterly from a bank in Birmingham that had a branch
in the market town closest to Malmsworth Towers.

She went to lunch with her friends and accepted Arial's offer
of Pauline Turner as a companion. She was a stepsister of Peter's,
who lived with Peter and Arial. She'd agreed to help Margaret
just until other arrangements could be made.

By afternoon, Margaret had made all the necessary arrangements to send her aunt into retirement. It was time to tell Aurelia
to get ready and go.

Margaret dropped by Arial's first, so Pauline could pack a bag
with a few essentials, and then the two of them made their way
onward. She braced herself for the coming conflict. As they
entered the house, Margaret introduced Bowen to her new
companion.

"Bowen, this is Miss Turner. She will be staying with us. Will
you ensure a room is prepared for her, please? Is Miss Denning

in?"

"She is in the drawing room, my lady, with the gentleman who called to see you."

Something in Bowen's voice caused Margaret to pause in the entry hall. "Does this gentleman have a name?"

"A Major Lord Hungerford-Fox, my lady."

The odious officer—Martin!—was here? "Has he been waiting long?"

"He and Miss Denning have been talking for over an hour, my lady." Bowen, that consummate professional, came as close as he ever had to a disapproving tone.

Very well. All that meant was that Margaret had yet another cockroach to evict from the house before she gave Aunt Aurelia her marching orders. "Tell Miss Denning's dresser that I wish to see her as soon as Major Hungerford-Fox takes his leave."

"Very good, my lady. Should I serve tea, my lady?"

"Not until after Major Hungerford-Fox has left. In fact, wait until I ask for it. Bowen, I may need a couple of stout footmen to ensure the gentleman takes his dismissal. Pauline, will you stay with me?"

Pauline, bless her, asked no questions but set her shoulders. "You can count on me, Margaret."

"I speak for all the servants, my lady," said Bowen, "when I say you can count on us."

Aunt Aurelia and Martin were sitting with their heads together, talking quietly. When Margaret and Pauline entered the room, Aunt Aurelia started back, guilt written all over her face.

Martin leapt to his feet and advanced with both hands out, a broad grin on his face. "Margaret! Darling! You look wonderful! I cannot tell you how pleased I am to see you," he exclaimed.

Margaret ignored his outstretched hands, putting her hands behind her back and steeled her tone of voice. "Major Lord Hungerford-Fox. What a surprise."

His smile faltered at her cold tone, then came back even broader. "Ah. You are rightly angry with me, my dear love. Just so. Yet I meant my disappearance for the best, Margaret."

She raised an eyebrow but did not give the man the satisfaction of a response, though the words were a tumult in her brain.

Grief was what she had felt at first, when her seducer had taken her father's offer of half her dowry to leave England and keep his mouth shut about what he had done. Grief and shame, reinforced by her father and his aunt who blamed her for the whole.

Anger came later, when she began to realize how well a cunning man had played on the emotions of a lonely, neglected girl whose mother was dying during his assault on her virtue.

She had wondered, from time to time, which of those emotions would be uppermost should she ever come face to face with Martin again. She had not expected to feel only contempt.

"The good major left for your own sake, Margaret," Aunt Aurelia proclaimed. "He could not take a gently bred woman into a war, to live on nothing more than a captain's pittance."

Others had.

Martin extended his hands again, his smile coaxing. "It is true, dearest love. It broke my heart to leave you, but I am back again now, and there are no further impediments to our union."

"Except that I would not have you if you were the only man left living upon the face of the earth, Major Lord Hungerford-Fox," Margaret told him. After all the violent emotions of the past six years, with those words she at last sailed free into the calm beyond the storm.

"You do not mean that, Margaret," Martin told her, his voice kindly.

Aunt Aurelia had her own mite to add. "Don't be a fool, girl. You've already given him your virtue. You owe him your hand."

Margaret ignored her aunt and addressed Martin. "You are not welcome here, sir. You will leave now, and do not return."

"Margaret!" His tone was a masterpiece of amused affront. As if she were a child. But she was not and never would be again the foolish girl he'd left behind. She was a strong woman of independent means now, with a character forged like steel in the flames of misguided passion.

"Shall I fetch the footmen to escort this person to the door, Margaret?" Pauline asked.

Martin, who had taken no notice of Pauline since she entered the room, looked at her, incredulous. "Who is this female?" At the same moment, Aunt Aurelia snapped, "You forget your place, Miss Turner."

Margaret ignored them both, as two footmen entered the room, Bowen behind them. He must have been listening. "The officer is leaving. Please ensure he is not permitted into this house again. I am never at home to him."

"It is my house, too," Aunt Aurelia ejected. "I will always be at home to Major Lord Hungerford-Fox."

Martin smirked.

"You will not be living here, Aunt Aurelia," Margaret told her. "I have made arrangements for you to retire to the dower house."

Aunt Aurelia lifted her chin. "I have no intention of retiring to the dower house. And leave you here alone? I know my duty, however unpleasant you make it."

Margaret glared at Martin. "Out, major. Now. Aunt Aurelia, we will continue this conversation when we no longer have an audience."

The two footmen stepped one each side of Martin and the butler came up behind him, hustling him out of the house.

"I am going up to my room," Aunt Aurelia declared.

"No." Margaret stepped in front of her, and Pauline came up to her side. "Not until I have had my say, Aunt. You have disrespected me in my own house for the last time."

Aunt Aurelia tried to speak, but Margaret spoke over her. "I will no longer pay for you to live in my house, abusing me to my face and speaking ill of me behind it. You leave this house tomorrow morning. Where you go is your choice, but I have ordered the dower house to be prepared for you, and my solicitor has been instructed to pay you a quarterly allowance. If you chose to go elsewhere, you will still receive the allowance, but I will not fund your housing. Do I make myself clear?"

"Ungrateful, unnatural girl. You were a disappointment to your father, with your sluttish ways and your meagre looks. And now you would turn me out after all I have done for you?"

Margaret ignored her to speak to her dresser, who had come into the room while Aunt Aurelia was speaking. "Miss Denning is leaving my house tomorrow morning. Please make certain her things are packed. Anything she does not wish to take with her can be forwarded once she gives me an address to send them to."

"You would turn your own great-aunt out into the street?" Aunt Aurelia asked. "Wicked girl." She flounced out of the room.

The butler appeared in the doorway as soon as she vacated it. "My lady, you have another visitor."

Margaret sighed. She really could not cope with much more today. "I am not at home for callers, Bowen."

"He insists on speaking to you, my lady. He says it is a matter of life and death." The butler handed over a card.

Deffew? What on earth did he want?

"I had better see him. Pauline, would you mind?"

They went down together. Deffew was pacing the entry hall, his eyes wide and worried, his hair mussed as if he had brushed his hand through it in distress. Even as they descended the stairs, he did it again.

"Mr. Deffew?" Margaret said.

"My lady, I need Mr. White. Ned needs him. Please, can you tell me where I might find him?"

⋙⋘

"MR. WHITE?" TOMMY, the doorman, stopped Snowy as he walked in the House of Blossoms. "Her upstairs wants to see ya soonest. Tell 'im to come up immeejit, she said."

Snowy nodded and headed for the stairs. It was late in the afternoon, and the house was buzzing with preparations for the evening. On the first and second floors, servants made ready the rooms that would receive guests—dusting, cleaning, and polishing, putting out fresh flowers and filling decanters in the reception areas, laying out cards and dice, changing linen on the beds, ensuring that any equipment that might be needed was clean and checked for damage.

Below stairs, he knew, the kitchen staff would be preparing delectable dish after dish to tempt appetites, and footmen under the supervision of the butler would be bringing up wine and spirits from the cellar.

On the third floor, the women who were the primary draw-card of the House were also ensuring the merchandise was in top condition. Mistress Lily demanded meticulous attention to personal hygiene, cosmetics and jewelry that enhanced beauty without overwhelming, and clothing that hinted at more than it revealed.

Customers came to the House of Blossoms to feel at home, surrounded by the appurtenances of their upper-class lives, but with an available (if shared) harem of willing and skilled courtesans.

It had been a recipe for success. If the remaining six of the original seven Blossoms closed the House tomorrow, they could live comfortably on their savings and investments for the remainder of their days.

Lily's door was open, so Snowy went straight in. She, Poppy, and Jasmine were gathered around a table sorting through fabric swatches, but looked up when Snowy entered the room.

He bowed. "Ladies. Lily, Blue said I was to come straight up."

Lily moved a stack of fabrics and then another until she found a folded and sealed sheet of paper, which she passed to him. "You have an urgent message from your countess. One of her footmen delivered it half an hour ago."

Jasmine held up a rich brocade in a ruby red. "What think

you of this for the chairs in the red room?"

Snowy broke the seal and unfolded the paper but answered her query absently before he began to read, "Whatever you decide on the refurbishment is fine by me." Then he quickly scanned Lady Charmain's few sentences:

> *Snowy, Dickon Deffew is here. He begs you to meet with him. He will not tell me what it is about, except that your brother is in grave danger. He will wait here until five o'clock.*

Snowy handed the page to Lily, who read it and passed it on to the other two.

"The lady wrote this," she said. "I recognized her hand. Whether under duress or not..."

"It could be a trap," Jasmine said.

Poppy shook her head. "Lady Charmain would not be party to a trap."

Snowy checked his pocket watch. He had a little over thirty minutes. He could easily get there in time if nothing happened to delay him.

Lily was examining his expression. "You are going, aren't you? Please be careful, Snowy. This Deffew is your cousin's creature, as is the brother he is using as bait."

She was probably right, but if Ned, whom his mother had loved, was truly in grave danger, then Snowy had to save him.

Chapter Twelve

THE TOWNHOUSE LOOKED quiet enough. It was still a few minutes before five o'clock, so Snowy felt it safe to send Tommy, the doorman from the House of Blossoms, around to the rear of the building with one of the other men Lily had insisted on him bringing. They would check for an ambush while Blue, the guard, and the two remaining men surveyed the street.

Snowy waited out the front with Blue until Tommy ran back to the corner and signaled the all's clear.

"Wait here," Snowy said to Blue. "I'm going in. I'll yell if anything seems suspicious. I'll wave from the window if it is safe, and you can all go home. If you don't see my signal within fifteen minutes, come in after me."

He was just in time, it seemed, for as the butler let him in the door, Dickon Deffew was descending the internal stairs, talking over his shoulder to Lady Charmain.

Her eyes lit up when she saw Snowy. "Mr. Deffew, Mr. White has come. Snowy, please come up."

"Thank God," said Mr. Deffew, his voice shaking with some sort of an emotion. "Mr. White, you have to help me."

Her ladyship didn't look as if she was under duress.

As for the young man, if he was not frightened and anxious, he was a brilliant actor.

Snowy mounted the stairs and followed the two of them into the drawing room, alert for a possible ambush. The only other person in the room was a woman he had seen with Lady Stancroft at the ball he'd attended. He bowed. "Miss Turner."

Deffew didn't wait on polite niceties. "Mr. White. Thank God. I thought I was going to have to leave without seeing you. If I'm not home by six, Uncle Richard—my guardian, Ned's father—will want to know where I've been." He shuddered. "You don't know how bad that would be."

"We will leave you to talk," Lady Charmain said. "Mr. White, I still do not know what this is about, but I think Mr. Deffew is genuinely worried about his friend."

Deffew gnawed at his lower lip as he waited for the two women to quit the room and shut the door behind them, then pounced forward and nearly got himself punched in the belly before Snowy realized the youth intended to grasp his hand, not to attack him.

Deffew was already talking before he possessed himself of the hand, and he clung to it as he rattled out a long, and not very enlightening, welcome. "Thank you for coming. I did not know who else to turn to. No one cares about him as I do. But I thought, since he is your brother, you might... I know you don't know him. Not really, but he said you're not at all like Uncle Richard said, and so I hoped... He is my best friend in the world. My only real friend, to tell the truth. I'm afraid he will die, and it is all my fault."

"I will help if I can," Snowy said, retrieving his hand and patting the lad on the shoulder. "Come and sit down. Tell me what the trouble is and what you want me to do."

"It was my fault," Deffew repeated, mournfully, but he took a seat. The sullenness was gone. Today, his distinctive dark eyebrows only signaled worry and grief.

Snowy crossed to the window and waved to Blue, who touched his cap in return. He then sat in a chair close to Deffew, but out of easy reach. "Tell me," he said.

It took some doing. The boy had a rambling style of delivery, and a tendency to litter the narrative with self-blame, but eventually, Snowy was in possession of the meat of the story. Lady Charmain was right. Deffew was genuinely worried about his friend, and also about himself.

"Can you keep our meeting here a secret?" Snowy asked.

Deffew nodded. "As long as he doesn't suspect. If he starts to beat me... I don't know how brave I can be, sir. I will try, but..."

"Don't try," Snowy advised. Anyone would break with the right pressure, and this cub had no chance against the villain that faced them. "If you think he is going to hurt you, run if you can. If you can't, tell him everything. Don't defy him."

"You will rescue Ned?" Deffew begged.

"I will. And you, too." Snowy looked up at the mantel clock. "Now go. It is twenty minutes past the hour. Can you be home in time?"

Deffew nodded and repeated his thanks several times even as he hurried to the door.

Lady Charmain appeared from another room as Snowy followed the lad to the stairs. "I suppose you are going to tell me what that was about later, or even soon," she said, her tone both resigned and disapproving.

"I will tell you as soon as I have spoken to one of my men.," Snowy promised.

Deffew was disappearing down the alley to the mews when Snowy emerged from the front door. Good. If the boy was waiting for his horse, Snowy had time to set a follower on his heels.

As Snowy expected, Blue had ignored his orders and remained in place. Snowy waved him over. "I want you to follow that man. He says he is heading home. Let me know if that's what he does. Take Tommy with you and watch the house in turns. Here's some money for a pie or something, for you may be there a while. I'm breaking into that house tonight to bring out an injured man. Look for anything that indicates it might be a trap.

Wait there till I come."

Blue nodded, gestured to Tommy, and hurried into the alley after Deffew.

Snowy returned to the drawing room, where Lady Charmain waited. "I still think you are better keeping out of the whole mess, my lady," he said. "But you are an adult. You are entitled to make your own choices. If you chose to deny all knowledge of what I'm about to do, I will not only accept that I will think you wise."

"Tell me," she said.

Snowy summarized Deffew's rambling tale in one paragraph. "Richard Snowden, my stepfather, was told about my conversation with my brother. He beat Ned to get the details out of him, then beat him some more when Ned accused him of trying to have me killed. Deffew was a witness to the beating, and to Ned's condition afterwards. He was in a bad way and has since succumbed to a fever. Deffew fears for his life. Snowden refuses to fetch a doctor to his son, and told Deffew that, if the boy dies, he'll marry and get another."

One who would not carry the blood of a traitor, Snowden had said. Deffew understood him to be referring to Snowy's and Ned's mother. What sort of a swine thought a mother was a traitor for trying to protect her child?

"You are going to rescue your brother," Lady Charmain concluded.

"I am," he confirmed. "Deffew and Snowden are going out this evening, and Deffew is leaving a door unlatched."

"It's too dangerous," she said. "He could be making it all up."

"Perhaps. I think he honestly fears for his friend. In any case, I mean to take the risk, for if Deffew is speaking the truth, my brother's life is in the balance."

Chapter Thirteen

S NOWDEN EYED THE mirror and the man—the backward world man—within it. The late afternoon sun streaming in through the windows lit one side of his body, elegantly dressed for dinner and a ball.

He stood side on to admire his still-firm figure. Exercise was the key, and a healthy diet. Not for him the self-indulgence that strapped so many men of fashion into corsets.

Where had young Deffew got off to? "That boy is sulking," he told his reflection.

Just because he had to chastise his son. "It is a father's right and his duty to punish treachery and disobedience."

Both boys were weak. Richard blamed the influence of their mothers. He sighed and watched his reflection's chest heave with the effort. "In the case of Chalky, my affection for Madeline was partly to blame," he admitted. "I indulged her and allowed her to indulge him."

He had given the boy the nickname Chalky, taking pride that the child carried the family mark Richard himself had been denied by a cruel fate. The family mark, and the fact that Madeline was his at last and had given him a son, had briefly turned Richard's mind. He could not otherwise account for allowing her to name the baby after his cousin, her first husband, Edmund the Perfect.

When he recovered his senses and forbade the household from referring to the child as Edmund, she had defied him by using the nickname Eddie. "I let it pass. But it was a symptom, Richard. It was a symptom."

The man in the mirror nodded in agreement. It was a small rebellion that became covert warfare after Henry, Edmund's boy, had died. And he *was* dead. He had to be. There was no room for doubt.

Still, Snowden could see the letter on his desk. A very official letter. From the Lord High Chancellor and Lord Keeper of the Great Seal. The hateful words were engraved on his memory. *Evidence that the son of Edmund Snowden still lives.* "Lies! All lies, Richard!"

By an evil chance—evil for Chalky, that was—the letter was waiting for him at home on the very day Chalky spoke to the imposter and was seduced into believing him. "I would still have beaten him for disobeying my direct order," Richard stated firmly.

The mirror man wore a slight smile. It was correct. "Perhaps not as hard," he acknowledged, but who could blame him for losing his temper?

He turned at a knock on the door. "Come!"

His valet looked around the door. "You asked to be told when Master Deffew came in, my lord."

Richard nodded an acknowledgement and a dismissal and turned back to the mirror.

"So much for Chalky being in a bad way. Would Deffew have gone gadding about all afternoon if he was really worried?"

The man returned the cynical twist of his lips. Of course not. Chalky would be up and about soon enough, and far more obedient to his father's rightful authority.

Chapter Fourteen

S NOWY TOLD THE driver to stop around the corner from the Snowden townhouse, and he and Stancroft walked the remainder of the way.

Lady Charmain had insisted someone with social capital should be with him, in case things went wrong. Snowden might hesitate to act against such a person, she argued. She proposed herself, but Snowy absolutely refused to allow her to take the risk, afraid of what a person as volatile as Snowden might do.

Instead, he agreed to her counter proposal, to ask Lord Stancroft and Mr. Ashby for their help. Ashby was in the carriage with Lady Charmain, who would not be left behind.

A lantern burned at the front door and a dim light showed through the window next to the door. Otherwise, the house was in darkness. Snowy came to a halt outside.

Stancroft objected. "I thought the door Deffew was going to leave unlatched let on to the garden. Shouldn't we go around the back?"

"I have a man here somewhere—ah, Blue." The red-headed man loomed out of the darkness as if on cue. "What's the news?"

"No sign of a trap, Mr. White. The geezer what lives 'er 'as gone out and took the young 'un wiv 'im. Tommy's watching the mews, sir. No trouble that side, either."

"Thanks, Blue. Whistle if someone arrives while we're inside."

"I thought I'd come wiv you, Mr. White. Tommy can watch. Mistress Lily'll 'ave my balls if'n anythin' 'appens to you."

"I need the pair of you outside keeping watch, you in the front, and Tommy in the mews. Lord Stancroft and I will let Tommy know on our way to the garden."

Blue opened his mouth to argue but was interrupted when a troop of horsemen came galloping up.

"Snowy!" the leader greeted him, then nodded to Stancroft. "Stancroft."

"Drew? What are you doing here?" Lord Andrew had arrived with four of his father's retainers.

"I've come to bring you this." Drew dropped something out of his hand, and Snowy caught it. A key.

"The key to the front door," Drew explained. "Deffew took me aside at the Redepenning ball, told me what you were about, and asked me to give you this. Apparently, he was afraid the butler would find the unlatched door at the back."

Snowy tossed the key in the air and caught it again. "So, we just walk in the front door?"

"The butler will be asleep, Deffew says. So, yes." Drew swung off his horse and handed the reins to one of the other riders, to whom he spoke in a language Snowy did not understand.

"My men will stay with yours," Drew said. "Let's go."

Inside, Snowy led the way up the stairs.

"The first floor, turn toward the back and it's the second door on the right," Drew said.

The door was locked, but the key was on a side table. His brother was locked in, then.

When Snowy stepped inside the room, his first thought was that the locked door was superfluous. The room reeked of the stale odors of vomit and sweat. A single candle inside a glass chimney gave enough light to show Ned shifting restlessly on the bed, his covers pushed off, the shirt he wore bunched around his waist and sodden with sweat.

He moaned as he tossed his head left and right on the pillow. He was unattended, and a touch to his forehead confirmed he was burning up.

Stancroft brought the candle closer, and the three men stared in pity at the bruises and open wounds on his face, legs, and hips. Someone had made a rough effort to splint one arm, but otherwise, his injuries were untreated. However, the fever was the biggest worry.

"Let's get him out of here," Drew proposed.

Snowy nodded. "I'll take his head." He collected one of the blankets from the floor, pulled the shirt down to cover Ned's modesty, then wrapped the blanket around him, being careful of the arm. Ned whimpered and struggled.

"I'm taking you to safety, Ned," Snowy murmured, but the patient raised his voice in a shout of outrage.

Stancroft hurried to the door to keep watch. Snowy, at a loss for what else to do, began to sing the second verse of his mother's lullaby, keeping his voice low.

Sleep in peace this night my darling;
Gently sleep, you lovely boy.

Ned stopped fighting, and Snowy was able to adjust the burden so Ned's head rested on his shoulder. Drew took the young man's feet. The next two lines took them to the door and out into the hall.

As you sleep, I see you smiling,
What bright visions bring you joy?

"Mama, it hurts," Ned whimpered.

"Keep singing," Drew advised.

Snowy complied.

Do the angels smile upon you,
When they see your peaceful rest,
Are you smiling back and sleeping,
Sleeping gently on my breast?

"Here!" The speaker was a footman by his livery, stumbling from the rear of the entry hall to stop at the bottom of the stairs. "Who are you, and what are you doing?"

Stancroft took over. "I am the Earl of Stancroft. When your master returns, let him know that, as requested, we are taking his son for medical attention."

The footman stood his ground. "I have no orders to let the young master out of his room."

"Nor do you have either orders or the right to stop two peers of the realm and the son of a duke," said Stancroft. "Out of the way, man." He marched past the footman and opened the front door.

Snowy kept singing quietly, his mouth close to Ned's ear.

Do not fear, the sound the breeze makes
brushing leaves against the door;

Drew's men and Blue entered the house. The footman backed away then tried to run, but one of Drew's men spun him against the wall and put a dagger to his throat. "Keep still and silent, and you will come to no harm," the knife wielder said.

"Blue, fetch the carriage that is waiting around the corner," Snowy ordered. Ned began to struggle. Snowy sang, and he relaxed again.

Do not dread the waves that murmur
Lonely waves that wash the shore.

It seemed an age before Snowy was settling into the coach, his brother beside him: Lady Charmain, Stancroft, and Ashby squeezed together on the opposite seat. It must have been only a few minutes, though.

Drew had said goodbye. He was returning to the ball where he would return the key and give Deffew the nod that the rescue had been successful. He would then track down his cousin-in-law, who was a physician.

"Whose place is closest?" Lady Charmain asked. "I need to attend him as soon as possible."

"I have a house only a few streets away," Snowy told her. "The coachman has already been given the direction." Once more, he began to sing to calm his brother.

> Sleep my darling, there is nothing,
> Nothing here to give you fright;
> Holy angels guard your slumber,
> Safe beneath their wings so white.

➤➤➤❰❰❰

SNOWY GAVE ASH his keys. Margaret followed with her sachet of herbals and bandages as he and Peter carried Mr. Snowden to the door and into the house. The place was sparsely furnished, with no ornaments or artworks. "I just got the keys two days ago," Snowy explained. "One bed chamber has a bed and a mattress. We'll take him up there."

Only one bed? Margaret wondered whether there were linen and blankets. And, too, what about servants? At the very least, she would need water to wash her patient.

They would have to make do. She could not countenance a longer carriage ride without first assessing Mr. Snowden's health.

Up the stairs they went, following Ash who was carrying one of the carriage lamps. Past one floor and on to the next. She shouldn't have worried, however; it appeared that Snowy could read her mind.

"It's this first room," Snowy instructed. "Ashby can you take the dust cover off one of the chairs, and lay it over the bed to protect the mattress? I can find some sheets while Lady Charmain is assessing poor Ned's condition."

Once the patient was on the bed, Ash brought the lamp over and Snowy collected two candelabra and several standard candles from around the room. Once they were lit, Margaret was able to get her first good look at poor Mr. Snowden.

He shivered, but at the same time struggled to escape from the blanket. Margaret nodded to Snowy to peel it back, which he did, then attempted to pull down the shirt, the only garment Mr. Snowden was wearing.

"That is going to have to come off, too," Margaret said. "Can someone get the fire going? And I will need warm water. I have soap and cloths to bathe him with in my bag."

"He is not wearing anything except the shirt," Snowy objected. "Perhaps we should wait for the doctor."

"He is far too hot to feel the cold," Margaret retorted. "And if you are concerned about his modesty or mine, then cover his, um, male parts with a handkerchief." She had picked up a candle and was running a hand down one leg.

Some bruising on his upper thighs. A hint of a few cut-like wounds that would show once they turn him over. The rest of his leg was unmarked, though it burned with his fever. The same was true of his other leg, except that one of the cuts was red, puffy, and weeping.

Snowy had the shirt off and placed it over Mr. Snowden's crotch. Margaret moved to the head end of the bed and looked down into the young man's face, marred with multiple bruises and cuts. Both eyes were swollen nearly shut and the mouth and nose were puffy.

She felt the head, moving it from side to side so she could examine as much of his back as possible without rolling him over. She would wait for that until she had examined his torso and the arms.

She found no further injuries, apart from a badly-bruised ear. Now for the arms. She started with the one that was not splinted. Meanwhile, Peter re-entered the room carrying an armload of wood, and Ash brought in a bucket of water. "It's warm," he said. "I begged it from the house next door."

Margaret nodded her thanks and continued her examination, trying to be gentle. Mr. Snowden was becoming more and more restless, and Snowy was trying to hold him still, while murmuring his lullaby. The arms had taken a lot more punishment than the legs; presumably Mr. Snowden had held them up to protect himself.

After that, she checked his broken arm for open wounds, as well as she could without removing the splint. There was nothing beyond the bruises and the break, which had not opened the skin.

The torso had a few bruises, but she didn't think any ribs were broken.

Now she wanted to see the back. "Roll him over, please. Gently."

With Snowy on the shoulders, Peter on the hips, and Ash maneuvering the feet, they eased him over onto his belly, displaying the ruin of the poor man's back.

He had been hit with a thin cane or a whip, which had left thin, bloodied stripes from his neck down to the top of his thighs. Many of them oozed a smelly pus, and were hot, red, and swollen. No wonder he had a fever!

"This is where the trouble lies," Margaret said. "If we can cleanse these sufficiently, we may have a chance of saving him. If the corruption has not spread. If he is strong enough to fight it."

"You will try?" Snowy asked.

Margaret grimaced. "Perhaps I should wait for the doctor."

"I trust you," Snowy told her. "Whatever you decide, I will support you."

Downstairs, there was a knock on the front door. Snowy and Peter went down to see who it was, and Ash stayed to hold the candle for Margaret while she bent closer to the worst of the wounds.

"I would not want to leave this for much longer," she told

Ash.

"I agree," Ash said. "If we don't get the poison out, it will kill him. It might do so anyway."

"Help me roll him to his side, Ash. I'll wash the rest of him, at least, and if Snowy can find us some clean sheets, we can cover him up to wait for the doctor."

Snowy returned to say that Drew's relative and his colleagues had all been called out to a fire in the slums, with dozens of casualties, and that he had sent the men he'd brought with him to fetch supplies from the House of Blossoms.

Margaret bit her lip and summoned her courage. "I will have to do what I can, then."

"Instruct us, Margaret," Peter said. "We will help where we can."

In the end, she needed all three men to hold Mr. Snowden down while she cleaned his wounds with soap and water, breaking open the surface as needed to make sure that no infected fluids remained.

Alcohol came next, drawing a scream from the poor patient. Then an ointment of her own making, a concoction of potted marigold, chamomile and dill from her garden, and honey from her country neighbors' apiary, and more alcohol.

Finally, clean dressings from her basket. Thank goodness she had thought to pack them, since the linen cupboard in this house had been invaded by mice and, she had no doubt, spiders and other creatures.

Mr. Snowden, exhausted, had fallen into an uneasy sleep, and hardly stirred when a messenger arrived from the House of Blossoms with clean linen and blankets to make the bed. There was a bag of clothing for Snowy, too, from which he produced a nightshirt for Mr. Snowden.

Ash and Peter helped to move the patient from one side of the bed to the other so Snowy and Margaret could make it, and then said their farewells.

"I'll have my cook's assistant bring breakfast makings tomorrow morning," Peter said. "She's competent to take over your kitchen until you can hire servants. I'll send some maids, too, Snowy."

"And I shall send a couple of maids, too, Snowy, and some footmen," Ash added. "Are you ready to leave, Margaret?"

"Not yet, Ash. Have my carriage take you home and come back for me."

Peter protested. "We cannot leave you alone with two unmarried men, Margaret."

"I won't tell anyone if you will not," Margaret retorted.

The two men exchanged glances and then inclined their heads in acceptance. When Snowy returned from seeing them out, he protested, too. "You cannot stay alone with me during the night, my lady. Tell me what I must watch for."

"I am staying with my patient, Snowy. It is likely it will take both of us to care for him tonight. If you have paper and ink, I shall write a note for my household and send it with the carriage when it returns."

He opened his mouth to protest, but must have seen the determination in her eyes, for what he said was, "Whatever fate did I offend that independent-minded women beleaguer me at every turn?" But his eyes were warm when he said it.

Margaret wrote to Pauline, telling her what had happened and asking her to stay at home to make sure that Aurelia did not countermand Margaret's instructions for the old woman's departure. Pauline was proving to be the perfect companion. She raised concerns about Margaret's decision to leave her out of the rescue mission, but did not make a fuss when Margaret insisted. She would undoubtedly have concerns about Margaret staying here tonight, but she would do as Margaret asked.

It was a long night. Several times, Margaret and Snowy sponged Mr. Snowden—Ned, as Snowy called him—to bring down his temperature. Snowy sang to him when he was restless, and Margaret soon learned the words and took her turn with the singing.

Every few minutes she dribbled water into his throat, and from time to time she fed the young man willow-bark tea from a spoon.

Toward morning, the fever broke, and he woke with sense in his eyes for the first time. "Hal! You came!" He looked around. "Lady Charmain! You are here, too? Where are we?"

"In a house of my own, Ned," Snowy replied. "One I have only just purchased, so it is a bit bare at the moment. But it has the advantage that no one will know where we are."

"Ah." It was a sigh of satisfaction as Ned's eyes closed again. This time, his sleep was more settled and his breathing regular and deep.

"A natural sleep," Margaret said, pleased.

Snowy took her hand. "You've done it, Lady Charmain. I am forever in your debt."

As he bent forward, she turned her head and the kiss he perhaps intended for her cheek landed on her mouth, tentative and gentle. Margaret closed her eyes and leaned into the kiss. It had been a long time, and never like this. A kiss meant to be quick turned into a leisurely exploration that beckoned and enticed.

It went on forever and yet, was over too soon.

A knock on the front door downstairs broke through the pleasant haze that absorbed Margaret, and Snowy, too, drew back. She was pleased to see he looked as dazed as she felt. He shuddered as he took a deep breath. "I'll see to that," he said.

Chapter Fifteen

THE MAN AT the door announced himself as Lechton, the doctor sent by Drew. He must have come straight from the scene of the fire, for he was rumpled and dirty, and carried a distinct odor of smoke around his person. He was also pale and hard featured with fatigue.

Snowy secured the door again. "Go on up, Dr. Lechton. Lady Charmain is with the patient. She has treated his wounds to eliminate the infection and given him willow-bark tea for the pain and the fever, but she will tell you."

The doctor nodded. "Good. Lady Charmain is a skilled herbalist and an excellent nurse," he commented.

By the time Snowy reached the bed chamber, the doctor was conferring with the lady. "Snowy," she greeted him, as he stepped into the room, "Lord Lechton says that, since Ned is in no particular danger, he will go home and bathe, then return to set the arm." *Lord Lechton. So, another peer, and one who works as a doctor in the slums!* Snowy's disdainful opinion of the upper classes was taking a hammering.

"Perhaps you should take long enough to rest, my lord," Snowy advised. "Ned is not going anywhere, and we can send for you if you are needed in a hurry."

Lechton smiled, and even his smile was tired. "Probably a

good idea. I am not at my best at the moment."

"It was bad." Lady Charmain's statement had a slight upward inflexion but was not truly a question.

Lechton's heartfelt sigh was her answer. "These slum landlords," he said. "Making money off human misery and never a thought to necessary maintenance if they can add a penny to the rentals or shave off a farthing off the cost. It was overcrowded and poorly built. I have no idea how many people were in there, but I do know some did not make it out. As for those who did, and those who were injured fighting the blaze—too many patients and not enough doctors."

He shook his head. "I'm for home."

Snowy showed him downstairs. Several servants were waiting on the doorstep. He handed the house's keys to a man sent by Ashby.

Ashby and Stancroft had followed through on their offer of servants, all to help Ned. A man who had, from what Snowy had heard, conspired to kidnap Ashby's wife last year, probably at his father's instigation. Snowy shook his head in bewildered wonder. He'd believed all the gentry were selfish and shallow, until he met Drew. But one exception did not prove the rule wrong. Then he met Margaret, and after that, her circle of friends, the Duchess of Winshire, Lord Lechton. They were all playing havoc with Snowy's low opinion of the shiftless, careless, selfish nobility.

Snowy went back up to Lady Charmain to tell her he'd sent a footman to fetch them both a pie for breakfast, and that the cook's assistant would make them anything they chose as soon as she had got the fire going in the kitchen.

Lady Charmain rewarded him with a smile. "I am desperate for a cup of tea."

"You won't have to wait long for that," Snowy told her. "Lady Stancroft sent over an urn, tea leaves and cups!"

As if by magic, the next knock at the door—only moments later—heralded a maid and a footman, the footman carrying a copper tea urn and a jug, the maid a basket from which she pulled a canister of tea leaves, a pitcher of milk, a tea pot, and cups and saucers.

They set up on the makings up on the window seat, which was the only flat surface in the room besides the bedside tables and the mantle over the fire. "Do you want me to stay, my lady?" asked the maid.

"No, thank you." Lady Charmain sent both servants on their way, saying that she and Snowy would make their own tea.

"I think she was offering to play propriety," Snowy said.

Lady Charmain raised her eyebrows. "A little late for that, do you not think?"

Ah. She regretted their kiss. "Ought I to apologize?" he asked. He would, though it would be a lie. She had kissed him back, and it had been glorious.

Her brow furrowed. "For what? Oh! You mean the kiss. I was not talking about that, but about the fact we spent the night together."

He wished she meant that the way it sounded, and that it was true, especially when she realized the double meaning of what she'd just said and blushed bright scarlet. "I only meant... Bother. You know what I meant."

"Then you don't regret the kiss, Lady Charmain?" he asked, which was perhaps ungentlemanly, but he wanted to know.

"Under the circumstances," she said, "I think you should call me Margaret."

Was that a yes or a no? Snowy decided to treat it as a *no*, for after all, she was still here *and* had given him the liberty of her Christian name.

"Lord Lechton?" he asked. "I thought he was a doctor."

"He is a physician," Lady Charmain confirmed. "There was a big fuss several years ago. Something of a scandal, so it sticks in my mind. He served an apprenticeship under a doctor in the navy, then completed his degree at the University of Edinburgh. But he is also the Earl of Lechton. His wife is a niece of the Duke of Winshire."

While they were drinking their tea, the pies arrived, and a short time later a note for Margaret. She scanned it quickly and made a sound of disapproval. "Aunt Aurelia is not happy about her travel plans," she said.

"Do you need to see her off?" Snowy asked, keeping his disappointment to himself. It was ridiculous. It was not as if she could stay here indefinitely.

The pleasure he took in her next words was equally foolish. "Not at all. Pauline writes she has it all in hand and will come over to join me when my aunt has gone."

"Miss Turner? Lord Stancroft's sister?" At her nod, he added, "What has Miss Turner... I beg your pardon. It is none of my business."

"Not at all. I do not mind you knowing. I am sending Aunt Aurelia into retirement in the country, and Pauline is to be my companion until I find a new one."

Snowy had been wondering if he should tell Margaret what he had observed. "Good. The sour old besom insults you at every turn, and I would not acquit her of conspiring with your suitors. Or, at least, the ones she favors."

Margaret nodded. "My thoughts exactly."

After that, the traffic increased, though it was still quite early in the morning. Blue returned from the House of Blossoms with messages from Lily, though nothing urgent.

Drew came next, to report that he had spoken briefly to Dickon Deffew. "I advised him to leave Snowden's, Snowy. He's a toothless cub, and the old man will beat his part in the rescue out of him with no trouble at all. He's a brave cub, though. He said he'd go home and take the chance that Snowden wouldn't check on the patient. I told him about the footman, but he doubted that the fellow would stay up to report. Deffew said he'd sneak off in the night. Give any trail we left more time to go cold."

Drew also had a letter for Snowy from the Duchess of Winshire. She listed a number of names, many of them with addresses. Besides each was a note.

Hannah Wilson. Nursemaid. Kept on after your disappearance to care for Edmund and dismissed when he was sent to school.

Sarah Matthewson. Your grandfather's sister. Lives retired in the country. Believed to have been close to your mother and to have complained to friends about her brother's treatment of his daughter-in-law...

The list went on. Servants, friends, and relatives who might be able to cast a light on his disappearance, and on what happened to his mother after he was gone.

Pauline arrived shortly after Drew left, bringing Margaret a change of clothes. She carried her off to one of the spare bed chambers and requisitioned one of the maids to fetch washing water.

They had no sooner returned, Margaret stunning in a fresh gown of pale lemon, when Stancroft arrived to check on the wellbeing of the patient, bringing his wife.

Ned had slept through all the comings and goings, but he was shifting restlessly again, and his temperature was rising. Margaret turned them all out so she could check his wounds, though she allowed Snowy to stay and assist her.

The other guests did not go far. When Lord Lechton arrived a few minutes later, they sent him up, and the half hour that followed was right up there with some of the most unpleasant Snowy had ever known, as Lechton, with Margaret's expert assistance and Snowy's strength applied as instructed, debrided some of the wounds and straightened the broken arm before splinting it again.

Ned was awake for much of it, doing his best to be brave. The arm was the last straw. Everyone was relieved when Ned fainted.

"I'll leave you in charge of dressing the wounds, Lady Charmain," Lechton said when the splint was firmly in place. "Do so every four hours and call me if any of them look to need debriding again. White, I don't believe the boy has internal injuries, not from the way he was moving. And it is a hopeful sign that his fever dropped overnight. I think he'll recover well, in Lady Charmain's care, but I'll call again this evening and every morning until I am confident the danger is past. If, at any time, Lady Charmain judges I am needed, send for me."

Snowy protested. "I cannot ask Lady Charmain to nurse my brother for me."

Lechton raised an eyebrow, whether at his refusal or at the word *brother*, Snowy wasn't sure.

"You do not need to ask," Margaret told him. "You could not pry me out of here with a winkle pin."

Lechton's lips twitched. "There you are, White."

As Snowy walked the doctor downstairs, he asked when it would be safe to shift Ned. "If Lady Charmain is determined to nurse him, and I'll admit it would be a great relief to me if she does, it would be better for her reputation to have him as a guest in her house, rather than to be a guest in mine."

His, temporarily. He had plans to do it up and sell it for a profit, as he had done with a score of other houses.

Lechton stopped at the foot of the stairs, considering. "Not today, White, not with the fever still in the offing. I'll check him again this evening and tomorrow morning. All going well, he should be up to the move then."

So Snowy had another night with Margaret under his roof, for he was certainly not going to leave her to care for Ned on her own. He should not be so delighted.

PAULINE MADE AN excellent companion and chaperone. She was polite, self-effacing, and ever-present. The servants from the Ashby and Stancroft households were competent and busy, turning up all over the house on one task after another. Margaret had no more private moments with Snowy.

Probably just as well, for she yearned to repeat that kiss. When he was present, she kept looking at his lips, wondering how he'd elicited such a powerful physical reaction with such tender and gentle touches. Even when he was not in the room, she thrilled at the memory.

For his part, Snowy was no different toward her than at any time in the past. He was a man. No doubt a relatively innocent kiss was nothing to him.

Over and over again, Margaret reined in her stampeding emotions and reminded herself that, for Snowy, she was nothing more than a means to an end, a way to confront the elder Snowden, a person skilled enough to nurse the younger.

Ned Snowden slept most of the morning and woke without a fever. When she checked his wounds, there was none of the puffiness and seepage that indicated problems.

Treating the wounds and redressing them was easier when he was awake and not fighting her. Indeed, he did his best to move as she needed him to, and to hold himself still against the inevitable pain.

"This is not quite how I imagined having your hands on me, my lady," he joked.

Was that a growl from Snowy? It was, for his words were in the same low rumble. "Manners, Ned."

"You never had the least romantic interest in me, Ned," she countered.

The lad admitted it with a laugh. "I daresay if I was after a leg shackle, you would be a very pretty one." The last few words squeaked up a register as she smoothed her ointment on a particularly raw wound.

Snowy rolled his eyes. "I thought you had a reputation for charm, Ned," he teased.

"Not at my best, Hal."

"Time for the dressings and bandages, Pauline," Margaret said, as she stepped away to wash her hands in the basin of warm water that stood ready. "Ned, do you think you could sit up if

Snowy helped you?"

Ned was exhausted after the redressing and slept away the afternoon. It was the best thing for him, in Margaret's opinion. Her mother had always claimed that sleep was necessary for healing.

Snowy went off about some errands. While Pauline watched Ned, Margaret had a brief sleep on a pallet Snowy had had made up in the next room. She then took the opportunity to deal with some correspondence. At one point, a message came from her house that Lord Snowden had demanded to speak to her and had threatened to come back with constables if he was not admitted. "He said he was looking for his ward, Mr. Deffew, my lady," her butler had written.

She sent a return message, telling him to cooperate with the constables and allow a search of the house. So Dickon Deffew had got away. Good for him. She hoped he had the sense to choose somewhere his guardian would not find him.

Interesting that Snowden was looking for his ward, but not for his son. Could they hope he had wiped his hands of the boy?

Snowy arrived back just as Lord Lechton appeared and came up with him to see the patient. Ned had woken from his afternoon sleep more alert than he'd been since the rescue, and Margaret was keeping him amused by reading aloud from a book Pauline had brought with her.

"I am pleased to see you awake, young man," said the physician. "How are you feeling?"

"As if I have gone three rounds with a tiger," Ned replied, which drew a chuckle from Lechton.

After examining the patient, Lechton agreed that Ned was recovering quickly, and could safely be moved. "He'll still need checking on during the night, and his dressings should be changed once a day, but he no longer needs round-the-clock nursing," he said.

"I can take him to the House of Blossoms," Snowy suggested, after he and Margaret had seen the physician out. "I have imposed on you for long enough, Margaret. Or I could bring in servants to see to him here."

"I will take him to my house in the morning," Margaret insisted. "I do not want to put my patient into anyone else's hands, Snowy. And there has been no imposition. I am a willing volunteer." She chuckled. "Besides, it is probably the last place in London that Snowden will look for him. He brought constables today to search the house because he thought Dickon Deffew might be there."

That diverted the conversation, since Snowy wanted to hear all about the reports from her butler. Snowden had, as threatened, come back with people to search the house, and search it they had, from the attics to the cellars—with respect for Margaret's property, after the butler reminded them that the owner was a peer and assigned a footman to accompany each searcher.

"You should go home tonight," Snowy said, once he'd read the notes and speculated about Snowden's state of mind and Deffew's hiding place. "You've proved his suspicions groundless, but if he has someone watching the house and you do not return home, he will focus his attention on you again."

In the end, Margaret and Pauline returned to Margaret's townhouse. "Promise to call me at any time in the night if you are concerned about Ned, and to bring him to me in the morning," Margaret insisted.

"I promise," Snowy agreed. The warmth in his eyes and the press of his hand said more than his words.

SNOWY WAS DISAPPOINTED that Margaret did not stay another night. Not that he could have sought a repeat of that kiss with Pauline hovering so diligently and not that he wanted to put Margaret at risk in any way. With so many more people in the house, his increasing regard for her was sure to draw comment, whether he was seen kissing her or not.

He was also convinced that the risk from Snowden was real and would only escalate when Snowden found out what Snowy planned next.

He glanced again through Her Grace's list of names. He had been close to discarding legal measures of revenge for lack of evidence, but Her Grace had given him the key to finding that evidence.

He took his dinner on a tray in Ned's room and sat with his brother for a while afterwards, pumping Ned for memories of the Snowden country estate where they had both lived as small children. When Ned's yawns became too frequent to ignore, Snowy cited his own fatigue, and helped his brother prepare for sleep.

Speaking of his tiredness brought it to the surface. After two days and nights of cat naps caught when he could, Snowy was exhausted. He set a footman to check on the patient at regular intervals and took himself off to the pallet on which Margaret had rested for a while that afternoon.

The pillows carried the perfume of her hair and followed him into dreams in which kissing was only the start of what they did together.

In the morning, Snowy took a bath downstairs in the scullery, to save the borrowed footman the task of running buckets of hot water up and down the stairs. He put on a pair of pantaloons and a banyan to go back to the bedroom floor, so as not to embarrass the maids.

His valet must have arrived while he was in the bath, for the man had set out clean clothes and Snowy's shaving tackle in the room where he had slept. This man was a replacement—a cousin of the first man, who had recommended him in a note that explained his mother was ill, and he had to go into the country. The new valet was even more snooty and intrusive than the first.

"I will not finish getting dressed until I have seen to washing my brother and helping him dress," Snowy told the valet. "But I'll start with my shave."

"If you will allow me to do it, sir," the valet said. "I see you have been missing some bits."

Snowy leaned close to the little mirror the valet had brought. Sure enough, the usual morning stubble was thicker in a couple of places he must've missed during his shave the day before. Even so, he'd never allowed anyone else to get near him with a cutthroat razor, and he wasn't about to start now.

"Thank you. I will do it, but I will take more care. You just take the clothes I want to wear through to my brother's room next door and let him know I will be there shortly."

The man's sour expression deepened but he did as he was told. Snowy was slowly coming to terms with the fact that he was going to be a viscount. If a valet went with the position, he was going to have to find one who suited him better. Someone who could manage a bit of cheer. Someone who could serve without looking down his long nose at the very man who paid his wages.

Satisfied he was as smooth as he was going to get, he went through to Ned, who was sitting up in the bed. "How are you this morning, brother?"

"Weak as a kitten," Ned responded, cheerfully.

"Ready to get cleaned up for a bit of an outing?" Snowy asked.

"Perhaps sir would like to change into a shirt first?" said the valet. "It is less bulky than the banyan, and one can roll up the sleeves, thereby suffering less damage."

Snowy decided to ignore the sneer, since the advice was good. He shrugged out of the banyan and bent to allow the valet to fit the shirt over his head. As he felt it settle over his shoulders, the valet suddenly yanked it down so it trapped his arms at his sides. As Snowy tried to turn, he felt a cord tighten around his neck.

Even as he struggled, he heard a thud and the constriction was gone. He turned, stumbling a little as he did, for the valet lay at his feet, the marble paperweight that had felled him a yard or so away.

"Are you all right, Hal?" Ned asked. He was sitting upright, his face white around the bruises.

"Good shot," Snowy said. He bent to check the valet's pulse. The man was still alive, but out cold, with a rising lump on the back of his head.

"Good thing I didn't break my bowling arm," Ned responded. "Hal, he was going to kill you, with me right here in the room."

"He failed," Snowy reminded his brother. "Thanks to you."

Chapter Sixteen

S NOWY HANDED THE would-be assassin over to the footmen and sent to Bow Street for a runner. By the time the man arrived, Snowy and Ned were dressed and ready to be interviewed, but the valet was still unconscious.

"Tried to garrote ye while in the performance of 'is duties," the runner summarized, once he was in possession of the facts. "In front of a witness what was able to knock him out with this 'ere paper weight."

"In a nutshell," Snowy agreed.

"Any notion of motive, Mr. White?" the runner wanted to know.

Snowy had a very clear idea of who had a motive. "Not personal, I should think. I expect he was paid. By whom? We shall have to ask him."

"You have enemies, sir?" the runner asked.

"Evidently," Snowy replied, pointing at the unconscious man. He was not going to accuse Snowden without more evidence, or at least first talking to the solicitors. He had crimes enough to lay to Snowden's account.

The runner sent for a carriage and took the valet away. He'd be put in a cell and given medical attention.

For his part, Snowy thanked the borrowed servants, asking

them to return all the borrowed equipment and furniture and to leave the house in its dust-sheeted original condition.

Blue was going to stay to lock up the townhouse when all was done, then take the keys back to the House of Blossoms.

As for Snowy and Ned, Margaret's carriage had arrived to take them to her house. Ned changed into the clothes the footman in the carriage had brought with him—Margaret's livery.

They planned to sneak Ned in through the mews dressed as a footman, and the original occupant of the carriage would make his own way home later.

It went off without a hitch, and soon a very tired Ned was asleep in a bed chamber at Margaret's. "I have a meeting," Snowy told Margaret, but I hope I may come back later."

"Of course," she replied. "Any time, and you are welcome to stay the night, if you wish. Please, at the very least, join us for dinner."

⟫⟩⟨⟨

NED HAD BEEN exhausted by the move. When they showed him to his room, he settled comfortably against the pillows, and in moments was fast asleep, still fully dressed.

"I have been neglecting my herb garden," Margaret told Pauline. "Would you like to come with me while I check what is ready to be harvested?"

The gardener had kept the beds weed free but had not planted the next succession of culinary and medicinal herbs or clipped back the spent flowering heads. Margaret started in the greenhouse, pricking out herb seedlings into pots.

"May I help?" Pauline asked.

Margaret nodded and found her another pointed stick. "You have done this before," she commented, after watching for a few moments.

"I love gardening," Pauline admitted. "There is something so satisfying about planting a seed or taking a cutting and seeing it sprout and grow into something useful or beautiful."

Margaret knew that Arial had been developing the flower gardens on the Stancroft estate since she and Peter took it over, but as they worked and talked, she discovered Pauline had played a big part in the restoration, particularly of the much-neglected rose garden.

Pauline was excited to hear about the rose breeding program Margaret had set up in the country. Margaret had crossed several varieties, trying to increase the size and quantity of rosehips, which she used to make a beneficial syrup. Pauline shyly admitted that she was trying her hand at cross breeding roses, though for color and form, rather than rosehips.

As they chatted, they moved outside, where they harvested leaves for the stillroom and the kitchen before the sun got too hot. They then clipped the seed heads that were ready to gather, and further pruned the bushes to encourage new growth. In the potting shed they tied the heads in bunches and hung them above trays to catch any dropped seeds.

The sun was getting hot now, but the work had gone very quickly with Pauline's help. Margaret decided she still had time in the day to cut long shoots from the silver willows. If they were left much longer, the bark would be harder to harvest. She was describing which shoots to cut, which to leave for further growth and what she would do with the bark, when they were interrupted by a footman.

"Begging your pardon, my lady, miss, but you asked me to let you know when the young gentleman woke up."

Margaret cast a disappointed gaze at the willows. Still, there was always tomorrow.

"I'll go and see what Mr. Snowden needs," Pauline offered. "You cut your shoots. Perhaps you could bring them inside, and we could strip them together?"

Margaret accepted, gratefully. Pauline went inside, and Margaret fetched her sharp pruning knife from the potting shed.

She had returned to the willows and was bending over to decide which shoot to cut first when she heard a step behind her on the gravel path.

"I thought that other woman would never go inside," a familiar voice complained.

Martin! Margaret straightened and turned, some instinct prompting her to hide the pruning knife in her skirts.

How had she ever found his grin charming? No, not a grin; more of a leer, as he said, "Hello, darling."

Margaret gripped the handle of the knife. "I am *not* your darling, and you are not welcome here." If she yelled, would anyone in the house hear?

"A pity I spoke," Martin said. "Such a lovely, shapely behind. I should have just lifted your skirt and had you. I suppose that would have been ungentlemanly, though given that you have already let me do it, you've no grounds to complain now."

His effrontery and crudeness took Margaret's breath away. All she could do was shake her head, but as he approached closer, she opened her mouth to yell. Before she could make a sound, he was on her, one hand over her mouth and the other clasping her to his body, trapping the hand that held the knife.

"Not yet, sweetheart. You can yell and fetch witnesses once I'm inside you. You were a bit of a disappointment when you were a girl. Let us see if you have learned anything since I initiated you."

Margaret struggled, but that was the wrong move for it only caused him to clasp her more tightly and to push her back against the garden wall so his body could help to hold her in place. She willed herself to become still, even to relax.

"That's better, darling," Martin said approvingly. "Not that I mind a bit of a fight, but it will go easier for you if I don't have to force you."

She glared at him, putting into her gaze everything she could not say with her mouth held shut.

He laughed. "Such a good thing looks cannot kill. Now, now,

Margaret. You seem to forget you promised to marry me. You gave me your virtue. I have only come to claim what is my own."

Margaret held her body still, but her mind rejected his self-serving words. *You seem to forget that you released me when you broke your promise; when you told my father what we had done and offered to go away for a price.*

At last, he dropped his imprisoning arm to begin pulling up her skirts. "Can I trust you not to scream if I let your mouth go?" He thought about it. "No. Probably not."

Her skirts were now above her waist, and she could feel the hard length of his male organ through the coarse fabric of his trousers. His free hand fumbled between them. *Not yet.* A moment more, and he would believe he was about to reach his goal.

He would be distracted and vulnerable. She hoped.

There. Bare flesh against hers. She snatched her hand out of her skirts and drove the pruning knife into his thigh.

With a scream, he staggered backward. Margaret scurried around him and ran toward the house. She did not hear him pursuing her, and when she reached the top of the steps to the terrace, she looked back. He lay writhing on the ground by the willows, his hands over his wound. Even from this distance, she could see blood seeping between his fingers.

She hurried inside the house, shouting for the butler. "There is a man in the garden," she said. "He attacked me, and I stabbed him. Please take some men and detain him."

But by the time Bowen had marshalled several footmen, Martin was gone, leaving only the pruning knife and a trail of blood that led to the gate at the bottom of the garden—a gate that should have been locked, but was not.

AT FORTESCUE'S OFFICE, Snowy was shown straight in.

"My lord," Fortescue greeted him. "Good day."

"And to you, Mr. Fortescue." Snowy supposed he was going to have to get used to being addressed as 'my lord'. "I trust you are keeping well?"

"Indeed, my lord. Indeed." Fortescue got straight to business. "You will be pleased to know that Sir Thomas Brockton has filed your case against Richard Snowden."

Snowy expected the news but he still felt a surge of fierce satisfaction. "What is the next step, Mr. Fortescue? What can I expect?"

"He will be served with a summons to appear before a magistrate to answer the charges. Sir Thomas is confident that, with the information you have collected, the case will go to trial. Can I offer you a cup of tea, my lord?"

"Not for me, thank you. Perhaps another time. I will have to leave for another meeting shortly, but I wanted to give you this." Snowy produced a copy he had made of her Grace's list. "The Duchess of Winshire sent me a list of names of people who might be able to tell us more about my kidnapping and about what happened to my mother. You can have this copy. I have made another for the enquiry agent."

Fortescue read through the list, nodding. "Worth pursuing, Lord Snowden. Worth pursuing. As you know, we need to strengthen the link between the boy in the garden and the boy in the slum alley. This maid who saw you both before and after the abduction would be ideal."

"Wakefield, the enquiry agent, knows how important that could be. Unless there is anything else, Mr. Fortescue, I will give you my thanks and wish you a good day."

Fortescue frowned. "Just a warning, my lord. If we are correct, your cousin is guilty of serious crimes and some of them done to cover up earlier crimes."

Snowy wanted to protest the 'if we are correct' disclaimer, but he understood it was just a solicitor's reluctance to prejudge the case before it went to trial. He nodded in agreement. People who were in Richard Snowden's way or who displeased him had a habit of suffering anonymous assaults and fatal accidents.

"You may expect an attempt on your life, I should think," Fortescue said. "Please take care, Lord Snowden."

"My valet attempted to garrote me this morning," Snowy told him. "I daresay there will be other attempts. Perhaps the Bow Street runners will be able to get out of the valet who hired him. We can add that charge, then, to all the rest."

Fortescue had paled. "You are taking this very calmly, my lord. Please, do be careful."

⇥⟫⟪⇤

SNOWY'S NEXT STOP was the office of Wakefield and Wakefield, where he handed the duchess's list over to Mrs. Wakefield, herself a skilled enquiry agent. He told her about the attempt on his life that morning, and suggested she check on the valet's letters of reference, and the whereabouts of his predecessor.

From there, he went straight to the House of Blossoms. He needed to let Lily know what had happened with the valet, check how Orchid was getting on with the bookkeeping, and persuade Poppy to feed him. Not necessarily in that order.

At this time of day, the house was quiet. He found Poppy alone in the kitchen, kneading dough for the evening's bread.

"Here's trouble," she greeted him, as she had been doing since he was a small boy. "I recognize that sheepish grin. Get a load off your feet, my duck, and I will find you something to eat. Can't have our Snowy going hungry."

He grabbed her for a hug and a kiss on her cheek. "You're the best, Poppy."

She beamed at him even as she scolded. "Get along with you. No hugging the cook. I'll just leave this to rest." She patted the dough into a large, round ball and nudged it off the table into a bowl, which she covered with a cloth.

She then bustled around between kitchen, scullery, and pantry, moving the kettle over the fire, collecting a plate and cutlery to put before him, fetching a pie and some cheese from one place, a loaf of bread from another, a grinder for the aromatic coffee beans, a cake tin, and half a dozen other things.

She talked as she worked, telling him the gossip of the house. Orchid was thriving as the new bookkeeper. Lily had commented on the neatness of her hand and her accuracy, and Orchid was over the moon about the compliment. Jasmine was feeling well, and the girls did much better with her there to monitor their moods and intervene in any scraps.

Snowy knew better than to offer to help. She would soon tell him if there was anything he could do.

Sure enough, she handed him a toasting fork and a couple of thick pieces of bread she sliced off the loaf. "It is yesterday's bread and will be better if you toast it a bit. I have relish or jam to go on it."

The toasting fork was long enough to take both slices. By the time he'd crisped up both sides, so that the inside would be warm, moist, and soft, she had spread a veritable feast around his place at the kitchen table, including a lovely slice of apple pie she said he could have after his toast. "The last of the stored apples, duck, so make the most of it."

Once she was happy he had everything he needed, she sat down across the table from him with a slice of cake and a cup of tea. "Now then," she said. "Tell your Auntie Poppy everything. How is your brother? How is our lady countess? Have you kissed her, yet?"

Before Snowy could answer, Lily spoke from the kitchen door. "Is there more tea in that pot, Poppy?"

She entered the kitchen with Jasmine in her wake; Lily slid onto the bench seat beside Snowy, and Jasmine took the chair at the end of the table.

"Coming up," Poppy said, standing to find two more cups.

"Carry on, Snowy," Lily told him. "We all want to know."

Snowy took another bite of his toast, just to tease them, but didn't fool them for a moment. They simply sat and waited, Poppy grinning, Lily slightly scornful, and Jasmine regarding him with a remote expression and kindly eyes.

"Ned, my brother, is on the mend," Snowy said, at last. "I dropped him off to the countess's house this morning. He is going to stay there for the time being. I saw the countess when I took Ned inside, and I plan to have dinner at her house this evening. She has been marvelous with Ned. I believe she saved his life, she, and Lord Lechton."

He was not going to tell them about the kiss, but he colored slightly at the memory. Poppy's eyes danced merrily while Lily smirked.

He distracted them with another piece of news. "My valet is in custody at the Bow Street Magistrate's court. He attempted to garotte me this morning. He would have succeeded, too, except Ned was there, and threw a stone paperweight at him. Knocked him right out. It turns out that my brother is a champion bowler."

His foster mothers spoke over one another, their responses typical.

"Oh my," said Poppy.

"The scurvy cur," Lily exclaimed. "Was he working for Snowden?"

"Were you hurt, Snowy?" asked Jasmine.

He reassured Jasmine that no, he was not hurt, and told Lily that the valet had still been unconscious when the runners took him away. "They will question him once he wakes, and then we'll see."

"I am disgusted," Lily proclaimed. "I cannot believe a man I employed was involved in a plot to kill you, Snowy."

"No harm done," he reassured her. "I have other news. Fortescue tells me the case against Snowden has been filed. My cousin will receive a summons within the next fortnight." He grinned. "That should take his mind off the disappearance of his son and Dickon Deffew."

"Dickon Deffew?" Jasmine asked. "Is he a relative of David Deffew?"

Snowy nodded. "His son. Apparently, Snowden and the elder Deffew were close friends. So much so, that the boy was named after Snowden, and Snowden was left as his guardian after Deffew died. It was Dickon who told me about Ned. He ran off after the rescue, to avoid Snowden's anger."

"Wise boy," Lily commented. "I hope he is well hidden."

"Deffew and Snowden," Jasmine mused, her brows joined together. "Deffew and Snowden. Something..." Her expression cleared. "Oh, yes. Now I have it. David Deffew and his brother Matthew used to be clients here, Lily, remember? Until one of them roughed up a girl, and we banned them both."

Lily nodded, her face hard at the memory.

"It's just that I remember Matthew Deffew was one who liked to boast in bed. Afterwards, y'know. He said a man could get away with murder, if he knew how. All he had to do was have a friend who wanted someone killed, and they could swap victims."

Snowy stared at her, his mind racing.

"Snowy," she said, "tell your enquiry agent to check where the Deffews were when Snowden had an alibi for one of the crimes you are trying to pin on him. And if the Deffews benefited from crimes, find out where Snowden was."

Chapter Seventeen

NED SNOWDEN BOUNCED back from his beating and fever with the resilience of youth. By the end of his first day under Margaret's roof, he was pacing the bedchamber he had been given, and begging to be allowed out into the garden.

"Tomorrow," Margaret promised. "If you have suffered no relapse from your exertions today."

Not that she thought he would. Her greatest concern was that word of his presence in her house would reach Snowden's ears. Bowen had assured her all the servants knew to keep the secret. That didn't mean they would not let something slip. Accidentally if not on purpose. She could not swear to it that every single person in her employ would resist the opportunity to make a few extra coins by selling information.

She had done what she could to muddy the waters by renaming him for the duration of his stay. Ned suggested he should become Mr. Black, and she went along with that. It was a laughably thin screen over his identity, given how much he looked like Mr. White, and the growing rumors that Snowy was actually Henry Snowden.

They took dinner in Ned's room, four of them at a small gate leg table. She had the servants set all the dishes out for them to serve themselves, so they could talk freely. Margaret mentioned her concerns about Snowden discovering where Ned was.

"I am not going back," Ned declared. "I am of age, and he can't make me."

Snowy nodded, approvingly. "Good for you," he said. "But, because you are of age, you cannot stay in the house of an unmarried woman." He touched his forelock in an ironic salute to Pauline. "Even one with an efficient and diligent chaperone."

Pauline nodded. "A relatively young chaperone. The gossip-mongers would find a way to make a meal of two young unmarried ladies with a gentleman guest. Now that he no longer needs nursing, Margaret, he will have to go."

Ned grimaced. "Two attractive young ladies," he pointed out. "I expect I could bunk with a friend, Margaret."

"You can come and stay with me," Snowy said. "I have rooms on the top floor of the House of Blossoms, and plenty of space." He slid his eyes sideways to gaze at Margaret. "I am thinking of having the townhouse we stayed in for the past few days done up for my own use. I should probably have a more socially accepta-ble address now I've taken steps to claim my title. When it's done, you're welcome to live there too."

"My father is going to spit bullets," Ned observed. He gri-maced again. "I wish I knew where Dickon is. I hope he is safe and well. I know he seems a bit gruff, but he's a good fellow, really. Deep down. And he saved my life, Hal, coming to find you. Could he come to stay, too? If we can find him?"

"Young Deffew?" Snowy asked. "I have a watcher on Snow-den's house. He has seen no sign of your friend, who seems to have made a very efficient disappearance. As to living with us, that is a bit trickier since he is your father's ward. Your father has no right to demand that you return home, but every right to say where his ward will live."

Margaret reflected that convicting Snowden of his crimes would remove that barrier, but any trial would take time to reach a verdict, even if it could be proved that Snowden must be tried as a commoner. More so if he was tried as a peer.

Ned's face fell. "It is nearly a year until Dickon is twenty-one." His thoughts must have tracked with Margaret's, for a light came into his eyes and he added, "Did the valet say who hired him to kill you?"

Margaret's gasp was echoed by Pauline. "Your valet tried to kill you?" Margaret asked.

The two men explained what had happened. Margaret shuddered at the thought of how close it had been. If Snowy had let the valet shave him. If he had dressed in another room. If the paper weight had not been handy, or had been any other shape, or of a lighter material. If Ned was not an expert bowler.

"Unfortunately, we may never know for whom he was working," Snowy said. "I received word from Bow Street that, when he recovered consciousness, he was put into a cell with other prisoners to wait for questioning. When they came to him, he was dead. One of the other prisoners had throttled him."

Ned asked what Margaret was thinking. "Who hired the throttler?"

Snowy shrugged. "The man claims he didn't like the way the valet looked at him. He is up on charges of killing people for the resurrection trade, so I imagine he figures he has nothing to lose. They are investigating whether anyone might have got word to him to kill the valet, but it's hard to see what he would get out of it."

"You will be careful, Snowy, won't you?" Margaret said.

⤜⤜⤜⧓⤛⤛⤛

THE NEXT MORNING, Ned was up bright and early, eager to prove he was well enough to be allowed to move on. Certainly, the cuts that had been infected were now scabbing over and looked clean and healthy, and his bruises had faded to green and yellow.

Margaret invited him downstairs to have breakfast with her and Pauline.

They were still at breakfast when Regina Ashby arrived, following Bowen into the breakfast room without waiting to be announced. She smiled at Ned, who stood at her arrival. "Good morning, Mr. Snowden. I am glad to see you here."

"Fetch another cup, please, Bowen," Margaret said. "Something to eat, as well, Regina?"

Her friend took the chair between Margaret and Ned. "Just a cup of tea, thank you."

"I take it you expected to find Ned here? Are there rumors?"

Regina shook her head. "No, but since Ash and Peter helped with the rescue, and the house they took Mr. Snowden to is now empty, this was my next pick." She addressed the young man directly. "I like *Ned* better than *Chalky*," she said.

"You were looking for him?" Margaret asked.

Regina accepted the cup that Bowen brought with a smile and a thank you. "I will pour for myself," she said. "Please do not let me keep you from your duties."

Bowen exchanged a glance with Margaret, who nodded. He left the room and shut the door firmly behind him.

Regina leaned forward. "I am going to assume that Pauline is in your confidence, Margaret."

Margaret and Pauline both agreed.

Regina turned to Ned. "Ned... May I call you Ned? We have taken on a new footman, by the name of Dickon. Elijah and I are retreating to the country for a few days, and Dickon will be going with us to stay at our estate for as long as needed. I came to see if you would like to go with him."

Ned's eyes were as round as saucers. "Dickon? My friend, Dickon?"

Regina nodded.

"I would never have dreamed he would go to you. After what happened between him and your son. After what I did to you." He shook his head.

"Very smart of him," Margaret acknowledged. "It is the last place anyone would look for him."

"Precisely what Lord Andrew Winderfield thought when he suggested it," Regina said. "Well, Ned? You won't have to actually be a footman, of course. We think it best if you and Dickon use false names during your stay, but you will be at my son's estate as our guests. It is far enough from London to keep you—and more to the point, Dickon—safe from your father."

What Regina and her husband proposed was that Ned, dressed in the footman's livery she had brought with her, should be taken up by the Ashby traveling carriage later this morning.

"Thank you," said Ned, frowning. "But will Geoffrey not mind? We were very unkind to him last year." That was a mild description of their support for a plot to kidnap Regina and forcibly marry her, in order to have control of her fortune and of her stepson's while he was a minor.

"You asked Geoffrey's pardon, and he gave it," Regina pointed out. "The pair of you are in trouble, Ned. I don't want you bringing that trouble on my friend Margaret. Also, I do not think you are a bad man, at heart."

Ned blushed. "I am trying not to be, Mrs. Ashby. I would like to come, but I will need to talk to my brother."

There was a knock on the door, almost as if Ned's words had been a cue. Bowen had come to announce Snowy's arrival. Once the plan was explained to him, he was all for it. "But you can both come and stay with me," he said, "when all the legal matters are sorted out."

Ned had the last word. "It is the best plan," he said, "but I am disappointed, nonetheless. "I was quite looking forward to living in a brothel," he said.

SNOWY'S NEW VALET passed him a cravat, pristine white, perfectly ironed, and with just the right amount of starch. "Rahat is not really a valet," Drew told Snowy when he brought the young man over. "You need someone who can watch your back. Someone you can trust."

Rahat chuckled. "I'll also be able to help you into your boots and press your cravats."

"Good enough," Snowy had agreed.

That had been a week ago, just after Ned and Deffew left for the country with the Ashbys.

Rahat and Drew were understating his skills. The man was one of the Duke of Winshire's foreign retainers, trained as a warrior. He had also served as valet at various times to the duke and several of his sons. He certainly suited Snowy. He lacked any trace of servility and had quickly become almost a friend— certainly a companion.

Which was good, for Snowy was feeling lonely.

Ridiculous of him. His social life had expanded, and he had extended his circle of acquaintances by joining a gentlemen's club, Westruthers, his name put forward by Peter Stancroft. The members were a mixed lot. Retired military officers, professional men, landowners—some of them peers, industrialists, investors.

What they had in common was an interest in innovation, whether in politics, business, or technology. Snowy had several exciting discussions over a meal or the billiards table. He would probably introduce Drew and Gary to the club. They would fit right in.

Joining the club gave him a reputable address to use for invitations and legal letters. Since he'd not looked forward to hiring a lot of strangers to run a house that was much larger than his needs, he'd shelved his plans to move from his rooms.

Unlike the previous valet, Rahat showed no disdain at the location, nor did he avail himself of the services of the residents. At least as far as Snowy knew, and since Rahat accompanied him everywhere, Snowy figured he would know.

"The emerald stick pin, my lord? Or the sapphire?" Rahat asked.

"Both paste," Snowy commented, but pointed to the supposed sapphire, just the color of Margaret's eyes.

There he went again, thinking about Margaret. To be honest—if only to himself—*lonely* was not the right word. He was lovesick, and he didn't know what to do about it.

He stood so Rahat could help him into his coat. She would be at the ball they were attending this evening, or so she had said when they'd met in the Park this afternoon.

Ned's retreat to the country made a lot of sense but left Snowy with no good excuse to keep calling on Margaret. He couldn't even cast himself on her mercy to continue moving into Society, for he'd met enough hostesses to be guaranteed invitations every day—often several times a day.

He was a curiosity and a talking point, of course; the man whose claim to be the rightful Viscount Snowden had been presented to the Lord Chancellor. The Lord Chancellor had sent the competing claims to be decided by the Committee on Privileges. The ton was abuzz with speculation as they waited for it to hold their first hearing.

Snowy's action to prosecute Snowden for attempted murder had also leaked to the papers, which only increased his popularity with those who thought his notoriety would add a sparkle to their entertainments. The magistrate had ruled there was a case to answer, but released Snowden on the principle that the man was a gentleman and could be trusted to present himself for trial.

At least Margaret was at many of the same events Snowy attended, and he always gravitated to her side. If there was dancing, he made certain to be one of the first to ask to partner her. At musicales and lectures, he usually managed to secure a seat in her vicinity.

He took her walking in a maze at a garden party, sadly with other guests too close for him to steal another kiss. He caught up with her walking in the Park one afternoon and had the privilege of escorting her and her companion for close to an hour.

He kept telling himself he could not afford to allow his focus to shift from his battles with his father's cousin to his obsession with one beautiful, dignified, capable, sometimes infuriating, always intriguing countess.

"Perfect, sir," said Rahat, stepping out of the way so Snowy could see himself in the mirror. In all his finery, he had to admit, he looked like a viscount. He still didn't feel like one, and he certainly could not bring himself to believe he should inflict his dark soul on such a pure and innocent lady as Margaret.

Even if she would have him, he should keep his distance, at least until he had resolved the problems with Snowden. His attention was only putting her in danger.

Nonetheless, he kept succumbing to the urge to be near her.

"My lord?"

Rahat's words jerked him back to reality. "I am ready, Rahat," he said, and took the hat and caped coat that the valet handed to him. On the table by his door was a heavy package he had picked up from Miss Clemen's Book Emporium at Lily's request.

The History of England in three volumes by a man called John Lingard. There'd been some discussion about it at the club; he might ask Lily if he could borrow it when she was done.

He put his hat down in order to pick up the book. "I'll take this to Mistress Lily on my way down," he told Rahat.

"I will carry your hat, sir," the valet replied.

The next floor was quiet, it being late enough in the evening that most of the girls were working. Either Lily or Jasmine would be here, however—whichever one of them was not on duty downstairs as primary hostess.

Rahat knocked on Lily's door, then, when there was no reply, on Jasmine's. She took possession of the book, and gave Snowy a kiss on his cheek, for luck, she said.

They took the private stairs that led to the door into the mews, Snowy a little ahead, Rahat still carrying his hat. Daphne met them on a landing part way down, stepping to block Snowy's way. "My," she said. "Don't you look fine? But your hair is a little ruffled, Snowy. Let me..." She reached up a hand.

Snowy, trying to keep the woman's body from pressing

against his from knee to breast, was a second late in recognizing the sudden narrowing of her eyes, the triumphant gleam. But suddenly, Rahat reached past him, grabbing her other hand.

She fought like a she-cat and swore like a dockhand. It took both of them to subdue her. "She had her hand back to strike you, my lord," Rahat said. "Whatever she held, she dropped it."

Rahat held her by her elbows behind her back while Snowy searched the floor till he found a long hair pin, the point discolored. He folded a handkerchief over it to lift it.

By the time that was done, the murderous cat's stream of words had made it clear that the hat pin was poisoned, and that she'd been paid, "by a finer gentleman than you, Moses White."

It was Snowden of course, or someone he had sent, who might be able to give them a lead back to his master.

"Should we send for the runners?" Rahat asked.

"The man who paid her will have her killed, like he did the valet," Snowy pointed out. "We will lock her in the closed room in the cellar and put a footman to guard her overnight. Then tomorrow, I'll take her to Wakefield for questioning."

Daphne spat at him. "The major will not kill me. He loves me. He is going to take me out of here and set me up in a fancy house."

Jasmine must have been drawn by the noise, for she spoke from farther up the stairs. "Daphne has been entertaining a Major Lord Martin Hungerford-Fox," she said.

Snowy had been investigating Hungerford-Fox ever since he found out that the man had been claiming a former acquaintance with Margaret. Stancroft, the former army officer, spoke of the man in the most scathing of terms. His reputation in the army and in civilian life was abysmal. Was Margaret in danger?

As quickly as he could, he arranged for Daphne to be consigned to the cellar. Jasmine was happy to take charge. "I will keep the key, and one of the footmen can stand guard outside. It was Snowden who set Hungerford-Fox to it, I imagine."

Snowy nodded. "Probably." He grinned. "And every time he

does something like this, we are a step closer to catching him. I was wondering whether I would need to take the initiative." He would get his hands on Hungerford-Fox and ask the man directly. If his reputation for cowardice was accurate, he'd talk soon enough.

And then they would have evidence to question Snowden directly.

According to those who had been employed to watch the false viscount, he had given up on searching for his ward. In the week since Dickon and Ned had left London, he met with his—or rather the viscountcy's—solicitor twice, and a new solicitor three times.

He rode most mornings, usually in one of London's parks, but twice to a little house in St. Johns where he stayed for several hours and then rode away again.

He spent his afternoons either in his library or out visiting. He had been to dinner at his club three times, meeting with cronies to play cards.

Each time, he went from the club to the house at St. Johns and stayed the night. An enquiry in the neighborhood confirmed that the current resident was the third mistress Snowden had kept in that particular house.

On other evenings, he attended ton entertainments, often crossing paths with Snowy but never confronting him.

"You are taking this very calmly, Snowy," Jasmine scolded. "Do be careful, dear boy."

Snowy assured her he had never been in any danger, but it wasn't true. "You saved my life, Rahat," he said, once they were in the carriage that had been hired to take them to the ball.

"I did my job, sir," the young guard replied.

SOMETHING WAS WRONG. Margaret stood with Pauline, wondering what was being said behind her back. Her partners arrived, as scheduled, to take her out on the floor, but their conversation was stilted, and they looked at her oddly. Between dances, conversations would stop as she approached. Several of the worst gossipmongers of the ton looked at her over their fans, their eyes malicious.

Her closest friends were not here tonight. Regina had not yet returned from her stepson Geoffrey's country estate. Arial and Cordelia and their husbands were also out of town—a family crisis involving Deerhaven's brother, who was also a close friend of Peter's.

Snowy was late to the ball. He would arrive in time for the two dances he had asked for this afternoon, would he not?

Meanwhile, Martin had had the nerve to ask for a dance, and Margaret was glad to tell him they were all taken. Now he was moving around the room, talking to one person after another then looking at her.

No one said anything to her face, but Margaret was certain that plenty of gossip was being shared about her.

Snowy's first dance—the fourth of the evening—was called, and there was still no sign of him.

Couples began to take their places on the dance floor. Margaret peered around her, hoping that Snowy would appear. Instead, Martin was making his way toward her, a satisfied smirk on his face.

"My dance, I believe," he claimed.

She suppressed her shudder and lifted her chin. She would not allow him to intimidate her. "This dance has already been granted to someone else, Major."

He raised his voice so it could be clearly heard by those nearby. "Your partner has apparently abandoned you, fair lady. But do not despair. I am here to partner you in his stead."

He held out his hand, his stance confident.

Margaret eyed it. She would as soon touch a snake.

Appropriately, Martin dropped his voice to a gravelly hiss.

"Do not make a scene, Margaret. Your reputation hangs by a thread as it is." He snickered, confirming Margaret's impression it was he who had initially been gossiping about her.

"I told you, Lord Hungerford-Fox, I am not available to dance with you." If need be, she would not dance again this evening. In fact, if Snowy was not coming, she did not want to stay.

Martin snickered again. "If you are waiting for your base-born lover, I regret to inform you he has been unavoidably detained."

He was wrong, praise be. He must have seen the relief in her eyes, for he was already turning when Snowy spoke from behind his shoulder.

"I beg your pardon, my lady. I had an encounter with a viper. I am sorry you had to deal with her male counterpart." He evaded Martin's attempt to block his forward motion and held out his hand for hers.

Martin gripped Snowy's other arm. "Leave the lady alone, White. Lord Snowden has told me all about you. You are not fit to kiss the ground on which Lady Charmain walks."

Snowy gave Margaret an apologetic smile as he dropped her hand. "I beg your pardon for one moment, my lady." With that, he took Martin by the wrist, and must have squeezed, for the major paled and let go of Snowy's arm, though he raised his free hand, fisted, and attempted to hit Snowy. Snowy blocked each attempted blow. "Don't make a scene, Hungerford-Fox. Our hostess would not appreciate it."

"Let go of me, you slum rat. You think to court a countess? You're some harlot's get and I am a peer's son and an officer." His sneer deepened. "Besides, I've had her before, you know. She is nothing but my leavings."

Margaret froze, unable to even turn her head to see the reaction of listeners. The gaping maw of social ruin opened in front of her; her head spun, and her entire body tightened as she stood on the edge. If enough people believed Martin—and why shouldn't they when he spoke the truth?—she would fall. Her entire world would be changed forever. She could never come back from this.

And then Snowy pierced the major with a hard, steely-gray gaze. "What you are," he answered coolly, "is a pathetic liar. You were a failure as an officer, with a reputation for cowardice, stupid decisions and lying to blame others for your failings."

He started walking, still holding Martin only by his wrist, but crowding him to force him backward. "You are such a disappointment to your family that your father stopped paying you an allowance years ago. Since your brother inherited the title, he settled on you the income of a single estate and told you that was all you would get. You, fool that you are, insisted on your agents draining the coffers and have refused to pay a penny to keep your land and your tenants in good heart."

Martin sputtered, but Snowy had not finished.

"Your attempts to mortgage the estate have failed, because your brother still owns it; my sources inform me that he has given you a deadline to get your finances in order and begin to look after your tenants. And still you gamble. You sold your commission three weeks ago and have since gambled away all of the cash that brought you. Within six months, you will have nothing."

Margaret followed, fascinated. She had not thought to have Martin investigated. She should have.

She was not the only person to track the pair of men across the floor. Everyone was watching. Even the orchestra had stopped, and the waiting dancers separated to allow the spectacle through.

Martin was sputtering, but Snowy had not finished. "You are too vain and too stupid to find a way to make a living, so you decided to marry a fortune. You thought to leverage off a brief acquaintance with Lady Charmain years ago when she was too young and too naive to recognize you for the scoundrel and liar that you are. When she refused you..."

For the first time, anger heated Snowy's voice and he shook Martin's wrist so vigorously that the other man stumbled; Snowy hauled him back to his feet. "When she refused you, you concocted this scheme to destroy her reputation with lies, to try to remove her choices. Typically, however, you have failed."

They had reached the door out of the ballroom. Several men waited there, including Snowy's new valet, whom Margaret had met several times this week. Snowy shoved Martin in their direction.

Two of them grasped him, one on each arm.

"Get your hands off me!" he screeched. "I am the brother of a marquess! You cannot do this!"

They ignored him, and so did Snowy. He addressed the men. "You know what to do."

Martin darted looks at the spectators, none of whom seemed inclined to intervene. His gaze fell on Margaret. "Who else do you think is going to marry you, bitch? Too plain. Too old. Too bookish. Too damned bossy. You'll spend your life alone. I was glad when your father paid me to go away. You were boring, and a bad—"

He finished with a shriek as the valet gave him a hard cuff before dragging him out.

Snowy saw the alarm on Margaret's paled face. "Lady Charmain, pay him no mind. He lies again. Any man with a modicum of intelligence and decency would be proud to be your choice as husband. Not only do you have great friends of influence who can and will gladly attest to your virtuous ways, but you are beautiful, just the right age, clever and confident. I can imagine no greater joy than a life with you as my viscountess and my wife."

He had arrived late, consumed with fear and anger. Not too late, thank all the powers of Heaven. When he'd found out that Daphne had been Major Lord Hungerford-Fox's harlot of choice for the past week, he'd guessed who have given her the poison, and Daphne had confirmed it.

After that, he and Rahat had driven past the Duke of Winshire's house and borrowed several more of his warriors, who were now preparing to bundle Hungerford-Fox off to be held for questioning. The filthy coward may have been the one to pay Daphne to poison him, but Snowy would be very surprised if the idea did not originate with his stepfather. He thought of the words Lily had shared from one of the Deffew brothers: *All he had to do was have a friend who wanted someone killed, and they could swap victims.*

For now, he had a lady to dance with. One he had all but proposed to in front of a room full of people. He could not help being disappointed that she had not answered him.

"What are you intending to do with Major Lord Hungerford-Fox?" asked a stout matron. Snowy bowed when he recognized her. Tonight's hostess.

"Take him before a magistrate for questioning, my lady. Earlier this evening—even as I went downstairs from my rooms, in fact—a person who lives in the same building attacked me with a hat pin that had been dipped in poison. Thanks to quick action by my valet, her attack failed. She claims that Hungerford-Fox gave her the hat pin and paid her to strike me with it."

Margaret gasped and he smiled to himself when she reached to grab his arm in spite of their audience. She searched his face with wide, startled eyes. "You are unhurt?" she asked.

"She did not touch me," he assured her, placing his free hand over hers.

The hostess nodded, then signaled to the orchestra to start playing. "I congratulate you on your admirer, Lady Charmain," she said. "He is handsome, charming, rich, and likely to be a viscount besides."

Chapter Eighteen

S NOWDEN PACED TO and fro in front of the mirror, too angry to stand in one place.

"That idiot! I *told* him to stay away from the Charmain bitch tonight. I *told* him."

He glared at Richard in the mirror. "Not that he did anything else I told him. *Get the whore to show you where the bastard's rooms are, and lie in wait for him,* I told him. *Or wait for him on the stairs and stick him as he passes.* Or a dozen other ways. *Just get close and jab him.* Simple."

He strode off across the room again, catching himself short before the wall and swinging round to stomp back the same way.

"Just a scratch. All it would take is a scratch. Just enough to put the poison into his blood and then nothing would save him."

He surprised himself with a cackle at the thought of his would-be usurper writhing in agony as the deadly snake venom took hold, first paralyzing its victim then causing every bodily system to break down as the soon-to-be corpse leaked blood from every orifice.

But he had no reason to celebrate. Edmund's bastard was still alive. Alive, at tonight's ball, and brazen enough to have Hungerford-Fox carted off for questioning.

"They will let him go," Snowden assured Richard in the mirror. Hungerford-Fox was the brother of a marquess. he would be released on his own recognizance as soon as he appeared before a magistrate.

Once that happened, Snowden could deal with Hungerford-Fox. He would not allow the man to be questioned. The idiot could tell who had supplied the poison.

Snowden frowned. Not could. Would. The miserable coward would never stand against any questioning. Snowden had no doubt he'd be released when he landed in the custody of a magistrate. But what if he had not been taken to a magistrate?

Snowden had recognized the foreign-looking men who obeyed Moses White's orders last night. It was the Duke of Winshire's men who had taken Hungerford-Fox away.

Richard in the mirror frowned, as if to ask, "Where?"

"I have to find him," Snowden answered. "He deserves to die. He trusted his duty to a woman. Not just a woman; a whore. Fool. Yellow-livered idiot."

If the Duke of Winshire was taking a hand, Snowden would have to be careful, but Snowden had friends, or if not friends, at least tools.

For a moment, as he met the suddenly sad eyes of his reflection, Snowden mourned the loss of Matthew Deffew. His *only* friend. The one man he had always been able to rely on, until the selfish oaf let a woman push him over the edge of common sense and he took the risk that killed him.

"I could have told you, Matthew. No woman is ever worth it. They are all treacherous harlots. Everything I did, I did to win Madeline, and was she grateful? Did she believe in me and trust me?"

Richard in the mirror solemnly shook his head. No. She was not, and she did not. She blamed him for the disappearance of Edmund's brat. She'd refused to believe the little monster was dead. She'd betrayed him, and she'd betrayed the son they had made together.

The reflection winced at the thought of Chalky. Another

traitor. Gone. Run off to be Moses White's lapdog when he might have been Viscount Snowden. After Snowden, of course.

This was all Moses White's fault.

He met his reflection's steady gaze and nodded. Snowden had other tools, and sources of information that the pestilential by-blow and his harlot countess knew nothing about.

Chapter Nineteen

WHEN MARGARET WENT down to breakfast the following morning, Pauline was already in the breakfast room. She had served herself a cup of hot chocolate, and was sitting on the window seat, reading a newspaper. *The Teatime Tattler*, by the look.

Margaret was not fond of the scurrilous rag but had had a subscription for Aunt Aurelia. She'd kept it when she found Pauline was a fan, though she assured Margaret that she knew better than to believe more than one word of three in the gossip and scandal they printed.

As Margaret entered, Pauline gasped, pushed the paper away from her, then pulled it closer to reread whatever had elicited such a reaction.

Margaret went to the sideboard, laden with breakfast selections, to pour her own cup of chocolate and to butter a raisin-laden bun to go with it.

"Something interesting in the *Tattler*, Pauline?" she asked, as she took a seat at the table.

Pauline jumped and flushed. "Margaret. I did not hear you come in."

"You were absorbed in your reading." Which must be something scandalous indeed to cause Pauline to blush.

Pauline looked at the paper on the table, then at Margaret, then back at the table. "Oh, dear. I suppose I need to tell you."

Margaret raised her eyebrows. That sounded ominous.

"The *Tattler* must have had a reporter at the ball," Pauline explained.

Margaret understood her immediately. "There is a report on our confrontation with Martin?"

"Not exactly. Well, yes, I suppose. But it is more what they have implied... wait. You should read it for yourself."

Pauline spread the paper out on the table next to Margaret's place and went to fill her plate from the buffet while Margaret read.

"They have reported what Snowy said to Martin," Margaret said. "Nothing to complain of there." She read on. "Oh dear, they have speculated about my earlier acquaintance with the horrid man." She took a sip of her hot chocolate.

"But, Pauline, they are siding with Snowy. They are calling Martin a known drunkard, an unlucky gambler, and a man who does not pay his debts. That is not so bad." She had been afraid that Martin's accusations about her own virtue might be believed.

"Keep reading," Pauline advised. She had taken the seat opposite Margaret and was sipping her own drink.

Margaret read on to the end of the article, then met Pauline's eyes to repeat Pauline's own words. "Oh, dear."

"What do you think Lord Snowden will say?" asked Pauline. "The *real* one, I mean?"

Margaret looked at the page again.

"Lord H.-F. lost all sympathy from those assembled when he insulted the much-admired Lady C. Mr. W., who might indeed be Lord S., responded by addressing to the lady a stunning and romantic proposal, and sweeping her into the waltz that Lord H.-F. had interrupted.

"So, Lady C. is at last betrothed, and we are to wish her and her gentleman happy. Did they use the waltz or the supper dance to set the date? Will Lady C. insist on waiting until she knows whether her betrothed will be confirmed in his viscountcy? This correspondent will be sure to report all, as soon as possible."

Pauline frowned. "It wasn't exactly a proposal," she said. "Was it?"

Margaret shook her head. "And I do not intend to allow *The Teatime Tattler* to force him into anything he does not want to do."

"He *does* like you," Pauline suggested. "Would you marry him, Margaret? If he asked you?"

Margaret hesitated, taking a moment to suppress the surge of longing. What a fool she was. She had guarded her heart for nearly six years, ever since she imagined herself in love with a man who turned out to be a liar and a cheat. Now she had given it away again, without the least encouragement.

She thought of Snowy's kiss and amended that. With a little encouragement. But men kissed easily, from what she had been told.

He had called her magnificent, in the heat of an argument with Martin. She wasn't. Martin's description was closer to the truth. Snowy must know that.

Pauline was waiting patiently for an answer.

"If he truly wanted me as his wife, I would marry him," she said, honestly. "I won't marry a man who only wants to save face any more than one who wants only my title or my fortune."

Pauline finished her bun and dusted her fingers. "He won't be blamed for refusing to go ahead with the betrothal. He is a man, and probably a viscount. You will be the one to suffer."

Margaret shrugged. "I will be the one to suffer most in an unhappy marriage. If he does not want to marry me..." she grimaced. She had lived through one scandal. She dreaded another.

"You are titled and wealthy, and your friends will stand by you," Pauline soothed. "And even last time, the year of your debut, was largely forgiven by the time you came out of mourning."

Not by her father or brothers. Nor by Aunt Aurelia. But they—and Martin—were the only ones to know the truth of the liberties Martin had taken. Now only her great-aunt and Martin were left. Pauline was correct. His nasty remarks last night could be brushed off as sour grapes. She could live through the disapproval of the cohort of sour old women whose scorn served to keep the ladies of the ton from any show of independence or initiative.

She would have to. For she must tell Snowy the whole, and—for all his fine words—when he knew she wasn't pure, he would not want her.

Poppy, who was a regular reader, sent Snowy *The Teatime Tattler* with his morning coffee, the article circled. "This says I proposed to Lady Charmain last night," he said to Rahat, who was laying out Snowy's clothes for the day.

"I heard what you said about marrying her." Rahat smoothed the cravat he was holding out on the bed, a smooth, snowy field of crisp linen. "Did you mean to propose?" he asked, then changed the question. "Did you *want* to?"

Snowy reread the fateful paragraphs as he considered his answer. Of course, he wanted to. But he'd grown up in a brothel and at the farm belonging to a brothel. He had taken part of his schooling in the rough alleys of one of London's poorest areas. She was a countess! A peer in her own right.

Yes, he'd been born to the manor; was a peer himself, in fact. He had yet to prove it, but he'd thought, maybe after…

But the moment was upon him. Did he dare take advantage of it? "I didn't set out to propose, but yes, I want her for my wife. The real question is, does she want me for her husband?"

"I suppose you are going to have to ask her," Rahat said. "Properly, this time."

So, before he left for the Winshire mansion, Snowy sent Tommy to Margaret's house, with a note asking if he could wait on her at one in the afternoon. "Take the answer to Westruthers," he told Tommy. He planned to head there after visiting Winshire, and then Wakefield and Wakefield, and finally, his solicitor. It would be a busy, but he hoped productive, morning.

≫≫≪≪

HALF AN HOUR later, he was admitted by the Duke of Winshire's butler, and he asked for Lord Andrew. "I have been instructed to show you to the duke's study, Lord Snowden," said the butler.

Drew was there, waiting for him, but so were the duke, his eldest son Lord Sutton, and a tall, bearded retainer.

Snowy bowed. "Your Grace. My lords."

The duke nodded in return. "Snowden, you have met my sons. Allow me to make known to you my aide and dear friend, Yousef ibn Ahmed."

Snowy bowed again. Unsure of the correct way to address the gentleman, he settled for, "Sir."

Yousef ibn Ahmed returned the bow. "Lord Snowden." He glanced at the duke, with one eyebrow raised. The duke nodded.

"I took the liberty of questioning the guest you consigned to Drew Bey's care," the aide said. "He sang like a lark, Lord Snowden. He was apparently under the impression he would have been favored by a certain lady were you out of the way."

He inclined slightly again in another bow. "He complained about his sorrows to the gentleman who is the rival claimant to your viscountcy. This gentleman gave him the poison and instructed him in its use."

"The question is," said the duke, "what is to be done with him?"

Snowy frowned, thinking. "When my valet tried to kill me, I

put him in the hands of the runners. He was murdered in the cells. While I would not weep if Hungerford-Fox suffered the same fate, I cannot in good conscience send him to it. Nor am I willing to let him go, for the same reason."

"Quite apart from the fact that letting him go would be an abuse of justice," Drew pointed out.

Lord Sutton spoke for the first time. "I have a possible solution, if I may."

"Of course."

"Father, would you be willing to keep Lord Hungerford-Fox imprisoned here, and allow the magistrate access to question him?" he asked the duke.

Drew nodded at his brother. "An excellent idea! We could keep him until the case goes to trial, by which time his evidence will be a matter of public record."

The duke and his aide exchanged glances before he looked back at Snowy. "Would that be a solution to your problem?" the duke asked.

It would, of course. Snowy expressed his gratitude and his sense of debt. The duke waved a hand in dismissal. "You are my son's friend, and my wife was fond of your mother. My household will help you in any way that we can. Also, Snowy, before you go my wife wished to have a word. I'll take you to her."

⭬⭬⭬⭬

MARGARET SENT A return note accepting Snowy's suggested visit and inviting him to take refreshments with her and Pauline.

That still left her with hours to wait. Fortunately, the sun was shining, and she had seedlings to prick out from the seedbed into her herb garden. Pauline helped. She was proving to be an apt pupil and a willing helper in the still room, though that work interested her less than the actual gardening.

They were in the still room, finishing the careful peeling of the dried willow bark, when a maid came to find them to let them know that Snowy had arrived. Margaret cast a panicked glance at the watch she carried pinned inside her apron pocket. It was half past noon.

"I had intended to stop at noon, and change," she said to Pauline. "I never thought of him being so early."

Pauline turned to the maid. "Tell Bowen to show Lord Snowden to the small parlor and provide him with his choice of beverage. The message for Lord Snowden is that my lady will be with him as soon as possible."

Margaret nodded, and the maid hurried off with the message.

"Come along," Pauline said to Margaret. "You won't have time for a bath, but we can manage a quick wash and a change of gown. I'll dress for the afternoon after you have gone down. And do not worry about Snowy. Those who arrive early must expect to wait."

Her maid was waiting in her room with a large jug of hot water. Margaret told her which afternoon gown she wanted and accepted Pauline's help to strip down to her petticoat while the maid set out the gown, matching slippers, and a paisley shawl.

In fifteen minutes flat, thanks to Pauline and the maid working side-by-side, she was ready to go downstairs.

"I shall change, and sit in the drawing room," Pauline told her. "Either call me to join you or join me when you and Lord Snowden have had your private conversation."

Margaret descended the stairs alone and nodded to the footman standing outside the door to the small parlor. He opened it, and she entered. Snowy was sitting by the window reading *The Teatime Tattler*, a cup by his elbow. He stood and smiled.

She stopped just inside the door, suddenly nervous. "I am sorry I kept you waiting, Snowy."

"I was impossibly early," he said, "which was rude of me. It is I who owe you an apology, for it is still not the time we agreed."

"I see you have been reading the article about us," she said, nodding at the paper.

"Rereading," he corrected. "My Aunt Poppy is an avid follower and sent it up to me with my morning coffee."

Margaret nibbled at her upper lip, wondering how to phrase the question that had been teasing at her mind all morning. Had Snowy meant the words he had said to Martin? Would he really like to have her as his wife?

His eyes riveted on her mouth, then he blinked and gave his head a swift shake. "Would you like to sit down and discuss our choices?" he asked.

She nodded and led the way to the table in the window, taking the seat beside his.

"May I summarize the situation?" Snowy asked.

She nodded again, and he continued. "Last night I spoke in the heat of the moment, meaning only to express my great regard for you. However, *The Teatime Tattler* report has reinterpreted that as an actual proposal rather than as an expression of my wishes. For, make no mistake, I meant every word. I had not intended to declare myself while my identity and peerage are still in question. I certainly did not mean to embarrass you by stating my intentions in public. I hope you will forgive me."

Tears pricked Margaret's eyes, but she blinked them away. "Of course," she said. "But where do we go from here?"

"A betrothal? I had intended a courtship, but..." He waved at the paper. "I want nothing to touch your reputation, Margaret."

The hollow feeling inside had nothing to do with hunger and everything to do with what she had to say next. She had been so sure his compliments had no substance behind them she had not planned for a real marriage offer. She couldn't accept. Not without telling him the truth, and then he would withdraw his proposal and she would be left to weather the storm.

At least this time, she would be without immediate family to disparage and badger her at every turn.

Snowy looked worried. "If you are set against the idea, we can try to get the paper to print a retraction, or just leave people to think what they will, and go about together as if we were betrothed until some other scandal takes the ton's fickle attention."

He had thought of all possibilities. It would be easy to take the second option. Dishonest, too. For she wanted to marry him, and with all her heart she hoped he would still want her when he knew the truth.

"I am not... I would like to be your wife."

He reached for her hands but she waved him off. "There is something I must tell you first. And if you do not wish to marry me after you hear it, I will understand. In that case, I would be grateful if we can just let things slide, as you suggest."

He inclined his head. "As you wish, but I do not think my heart will be dissuaded, Margaret."

Very well then. She took a breath. "Martin was not lying."

His eyes widened, and then narrowed. "Martin was lying about all sorts of things. May I take it you mean the rotten cad took advantage of you?"

That was it in a nutshell, though it cast all the blame onto Martin. It was true he had persisted even though she said *no*, but she should not have been alone with him, as her father and brothers had repeatedly pointed out. "I am to blame for allowing myself to be alone with him," she said.

"With a man who had promised to marry you. He had promised to marry you, I take it? He is that sort."

Margaret nodded. "But when he approached my father, it was not to make an offer for my hand, but to ask for half my dowry to keep his mouth shut about the fact that I was no longer pure."

"And your father did not shoot him then and there?"

"My father believed the blame was entirely mine," Margaret confessed.

This time, when Snowy reached for her hands, she allowed him to do it. "I cannot claim to be pure either, Margaret. I can promise that, if we marry, there will not be another woman as long as we both live. I will be true to you, and if you will be true to me, that is all I have a right to ask."

She looked at him, assuming she would see deceit in his eyes. Instead, they showed kindness and sincerity. "But how can you not mind?"

"I mind," he said, grimly. "I mind that that unmitigated piece of slime took advantage of you. I mind that your father did not protect you from him. As to what you did—Margaret, Aunt Poppy follows all the Society news, and one of the things she has noticed is that at least a quarter of first children are born within six months of their parents' wedding. If one in four Society brides are with child at the altar, how can you blame the girl you were for believing the lies of a charming and personable man?"

He was right, and she had never seen it before. A number of the girls with whom she came out had had what they called *early babies*. Indeed, her own mother had joked about how honeymoon babies took much less time to arrive than later children.

Snowy lifted first one hand to kiss it, and then the other. "Margaret," he said. "Darling Margaret, will you do me the very great honor of becoming my wife?"

The tears were running freely down her face, but she managed to nod vigorously while choking out a fervent, "Yes".

WHAT COULD SNOWY do but take her into his arms and attempt to kiss away her tears?

He was fairly certain Margaret was no watering pot. He had seen her calm and contained in the direst of circumstances. Her upset was an indication of how worried she had been about the possible scandal, or perhaps about his reaction to her revelation.

He kissed her hair and murmured she need not worry about anything. "Whatever comes, we shall face it together," he assured her, and the thought brought warmth to his own heart.

It did not take her long to bring her tears under control, and he thought she would then insist on leaving his lap, but she stayed snuggled against his chest, allowing him to wipe her eyes one-handedly with his linen handkerchief while he kept his other hand forming circles on her back.

He followed up with a couple of gentle kisses to her temples, hoping she would look up so he could reach her lips.

"Pauline is waiting for us," she said, but she didn't move.

"A few more minutes," he suggested.

She raised her chin to face him. "I have stopped crying," she assured him. "I am truly not the weepy sort."

"I did not think you were," he said, as he lowered his head, stopping when his lips were a few inches from hers, to give her time to turn away or object.

Instead, she stretched up to him. Her experiences with Horrible Hungerford-Fox had demonstrably not included the joys of kissing, but she immediately put into practice what he had taught her last time, opening her mouth immediately for his tongue, and even stroking her own into his mouth.

Having her on his lap for this was not the best of ideas. The kiss was enough to send his blood pumping to his groin. Hell, when it came to Margaret, being in the same room with her was enough.

She was shifting and wriggling on his lap as she squirmed with delight at his kisses and caresses. It was the most delicious torment of his entire life, but he was going to have to end it, or he'd be behaving no better than Hungerford-Fox.

The thought of being compared to that creeping slime ball gave him the strength to gentle the kisses and draw back.

"Sweetheart, if we keep this up, I shall be begging you to take me upstairs to your bed," he told her. Her eyes widened. A flare of interest? Promising indeed! "I hate myself for saying this, but we cannot. Pauline is waiting for us."

She returned his wry smile with one of her own. "I know you are right, Hal. We cannot."

"Hal, is it?" he asked, and gave her a peck of a kiss on the nose.

She blushed. "If you do not mind."

"I like it," he said. "A special name to be used by my brother and my wife. It is what my mother used to call me, my darling."

He helped her to stand and did up the buttons he had undone. Together, they searched for the hairpins he had dislodged while kissing her. They did no talking, but a lot of smiling and touching. She was a dear delight, and he didn't dare kiss her again, or they'd never make it out of this room.

She stood before the window, using the reflection to replace her hairpins, and sneaking glances at him over her shoulder. "May I ask you something?" she said.

"Anything at all," he assured her.

"Can you tell...? That is, Martin is such a liar, I was wondering..."

"Anything," he repeated.

"I like how you kiss, and how you touch me." She hesitated. "Did you like it?"

Snowy nodded. "Very much."

That seemed to make her boulder, for she nodded, decisively. "It made me think. I found Martin's kisses and—er—other things unpleasant. He said it was because I was frigid. He said most Society ladies don't like other things but he didn't mind as long as I let him have..." She trailed off. "Don't be upset, Hal. It was a long time ago."

Snowy had to take several deep breaths before he could speak without the foulest of curses on that boil's excretion. He should have punched Hungerford-Fox when he had the chance. It was not sporting or fair to beat him to a pulp now while he was a prisoner.

"Believe me, Margaret, he lied about that, too. Your kisses are passionate, and when we get to the 'other things', you will enjoy them very much, I promise you."

"And you will?" she asked, hesitantly.

His reply was fervent. "Oh, yes."

A hint of her usual confidence tinted her smile. "Then I look forward to it," she told him.

He almost groaned and he suspected he looked forward to it far more than she did, for he knew what to expect.

Chapter Twenty

P AULINE WAS DELIGHTED to be the first to wish them happy. "When are you thinking of having the wedding?" she asked.

Margaret gave Snowy an uncertain glance. She hoped it would be soon. The gossip Martin had started would not subside until she was wed, and not entirely even then. But all but the most vicious of the gossipmongers would give her the benefit of the doubt once she was married.

However, Snowy had more than enough trouble in his own life, with his challenge to the other Snowden. Perhaps he would want to wait.

He answered, "I told Margaret I wanted to court her but thought to wait until I was confirmed as viscount." He smiled at Margaret. "Circumstances have changed that, and I could not be more pleased."

"You should marry as quickly as possible," Pauline told them. "I know how scandal broth brews. If you delay, it will be hard for Margaret. Those who rejoice in the pain of others will say the betrothal is just for show, and you will jilt her at the end of the Season. If you marry straight away, they will find someone else to torment."

It was what Margaret had been thinking, but she said, "I won't rush you, Snowy. We will wed at a time to suit ourselves."

He took her hand again. "If you do not mind, my dearest, my preference would be to purchase a common license that will allow us to marry without posting the banns. Pauline, I saw the Duchess of Winshire this morning, and she thinks the same as you. She told me that, with a common license, we can marry after seven days."

"Are you sure you don't mind?" Margaret asked.

"I would hate to wait a minute longer," Snowy assured her.

A shadow crossed his face. Margaret had no more decided that he had doubts when he expressed them. "My concern is, by marrying you or even expressing my preference for you, I make you a target for my cousin. But I did that when I spoke out last night, and I cannot change it. If we are married, at least I have the right to protect you."

"You think he will attack Margaret?" Pauline asked.

Snowy shrugged. "Perhaps not. Not now he knows we are wise to him. Better for him to focus on killing me first, since he will have to go through me to get to Margaret." He grimaced. "I'm not a very good bargain, Margaret."

"I will take my chances," she told him.

"Then we get a common license and marry after a week?" he asked.

Margaret nodded.

"I will go to the bishop," he said. "I will need the name of your parish and your own full name and date of birth, Margaret. Also, the name of the church where we will wed. St. George's?"

"I generally attend St. Martin in the Fields," she told him.

"Shall we visit together and arrange a date?"

My goodness. This is really happening. "Yes. That would be best. The Archdeacon knows me, and I can introduce you."

"Today? If we take your carriage, after meeting the vicar you can come home, and I will go on to the bishop."

"Archdeacon Potts is the vicar," Margaret told him.

He squeezed the hand he still held and smiled down at her. "We will have everything arranged before you have to face the ton at whatever entertainment you have planned for tonight. And may I escort you tonight? We will show Society a united face and dare them to make anything of it."

Margaret almost demurred again, but he must be sick of her asking if he was sure. Instead, she gave him the truth. "Yes, I would like that."

⫸⫷

MARGARET HAD ACCEPTED three invitations for the evening: an exhibition by new artists being sponsored by the Duchess of Haverford, Mrs. Worthing's musicale, and an appearance at Lady Mathers' rout.

It was an evening of congratulations, best wishes, and questions, some unspoken but obvious, others direct. All three of them gave the vague answer they had agreed on beforehand. Yes, Snowy and Margaret were betrothed. Yes, they had set a date. It would be a quiet wedding. It would be soon.

Snowy enjoyed the first event, endured the second, and wondered what on earth the purpose of the third was, as he said to Margaret and Pauline on the way back to Margaret's house.

"We came into such a crush of people we could barely move unless everyone in the place cooperated. We greeted the hostess, allowed ourselves to be carried by the current through the rooms, and farewelled the hostess. No food. No music. Nothing but people shouting the most trivial of comments at one another."

"The purpose of a rout is to see and be seen," said Pauline. "Or at least to ensure people know you were there. Tonight, the number of people there made our appearance a rumor to most."

Snowy shook his head in bewilderment. "I will never understand," he declared. "How often do you go to such events?"

"As seldom as possible," Margaret told him. "But Lady Mathers has been a powerful ally in supporting me to the ton. She knew my mother's mother, and I would not offend her for the world."

"That makes sense," he told her. "I can understand doing things for family. The rest of it wasn't so bad. Most people were polite."

"Most people generally are," Pauline commented dryly. "At least to one's face. But truly, Snowy, apart from the man from *The Teatime Tattler*, I thought it went very well."

"You handled him well," Margaret said, and Snowy agreed. Pauline had told the man that he was not getting an exclusive interview; nor would he be told where or when the couple planned to marry. She'd told him, "However, be assured they have set a date. Now go away and leave Lord Snowden and Lady Charmain alone, and they may agree to give you a notice after the wedding."

Snowy and Margaret had nodded. "With a description of the bride's dress and a list of the witnesses?" the man had bargained, with one eye on the footmen approaching to throw him out of the musicale.

They had agreed for, as Pauline said, while Mrs. Worthing's men were quick to chase off the intruder, he might approach them again anywhere, anytime. This way, they could go out with only the harpies of Society and the threat of Snowden to worry about.

➤➤➤◄◄◄

IT WAS PERHAPS three in the morning three days after the betrothal when Snowy and Rahat approached the back of the House of Blossoms. Margaret offered Snowy the carriage to see them home, but Snowy saw no reason to keep Margaret's poor coachman and the two footmen from their beds just to save him and Rahat a fifteen-minute walk.

The front way was more direct, but Snowy seldom used it when the House was open for business, and this time of the morning it was still busy. Successive waves of customers arrived from when they opened at six in the evening through to dawn, as men left ton entertainments, gambling dens, or whatever else amused them and came looking for some female company.

At the back of the building, a door let on to the complex of kitchen, scullery, and pantries. Another, larger door, approached by steps and a ramp, gave access to the cellars. The one they wanted—the door to the private stairs—was less obvious than either, partly masked by a pile of empty barrels waiting for collection and tucked into a shadow cast by the stairwell that stepped out from one corner of the building.

Later, they decided the shooter had not noticed the third door and was not expecting them to turn short of the other two.

Snowy was bending to put his key in the door when Rahat gave a shout and shoved him into the corner behind the barrels. At the same time, he heard the crack of a rifle shot, followed a moment later by another as Rahat landed half on top of him.

He pulled the pocket pistol from his overcoat and wriggled to the edge of the barrels, peering around in time to see a silhouette at the other end of the alley. From the movements, he was reloading his rifle. Snowy took a shot, but his bullet must have missed the man, for he threw the rifle down and ran off.

"He's gone," he told Rahat, then looked back to see Rahat hobbling toward him. "You were hit?"

Rahat's face was a blur in the poor light. His voice was strained. "Just a scratch, I am sure. He caught my thigh."

Snowy dropped his pistol back in his pocket and unlocked the door behind them. "Let's go this way to the kitchen and get that seen to. I'm sure the shooter is gone, but there's no point in putting ourselves out into the open when we don't have to."

Rahat limped inside. "I would not want to run right at this minute," he joked.

It was somewhat more than a scratch—a deep groove, still bleeding when Poppy cut Rahat's trousers short to disclose the damage, but the bullet had continued on its way and Poppy was able to flush out any fibers that had adhered to the flesh.

"There you go, Mr. Rahat," she said, when she had finished dressing the wound. "You should be good as gold in a week or two. Don't let him use that leg for a few days, Snowy my duck. You don't want it to keep bleeding."

"How often should the dressing be changed, Poppy?" Snowy asked. "No, don't get up, Rahat. You heard Poppy. I'll have a couple of the men carry your chair upstairs with you on it."

Rahat grimaced but stayed put.

Poppy shrugged. "Ask Lady Charmain about the dressings," she said. "So, you and the countess are betrothed now, Snowy?"

His smile blossomed at the thought of it. "We are to be wed, and all my foster mothers are invited to the wedding," he said.

"Get along with you, duckie," Poppy jeered. "Your lady won't want the likes of us there."

"She does, Poppy. She said so."

"Poppy, we're nearly out of oysters, and low on frumenty," said Jasmine from the door. "Hello, Snowy." She saw Rahat. "What happened? No. Never mind. Tell me later."

"If I may have a couple of men to carry Rahat upstairs," Snowy said, "we will get out of your way."

"Thank you, Miss Poppy," Rahat said.

꩜

SNOWY ARRIVED WITH breakfast, seeking wound care for his valet. Margaret was horrified to hear of the attack on him. The third! And each one a narrow escape.

She redressed Rahat's wound and agreed with him and Poppy that the wound was relatively minor.

"We can call Lord Lechton to have a look if you wish," she offered, but Rahat thought it was unnecessary.

"I will have beds made up for you both," Margaret told him. "Rahat, you probably need another couple of days of keeping that leg still for the wound to start healing. If you are here, I can keep an eye on things. Hal, I would feel better, and I'm sure Rahat would, too, if you did not go back to the House of Blossoms, at least at night."

"What of your reputation?" Snowy asked.

Margaret looked at Pauline. "I have my companion and my servants. Besides, we shall be wed in a few days. If there is any gossip, marriage will quell it. Please, Hal, I am worried. This is the third attack, and two of them at the House of Blossoms."

Snowy cupped her face with his hand, his smile warming her heart. "I will stay here at night, and I will not go to the House of Blossoms alone or in the dark. Will that ease your mind, dear one?"

She leaned into his hand; the warmth threatened by the chill of the attacks.

"Stopping Snowden will ease my mind." She stepped away from the comfort of his hand and busied herself cleaning up the detritus from redressing the wound.

"He will be stopped if we can prove he is behind any of these attempts," Snowy told her. "Margaret, my biggest worry is that he will try to kill you. Is there any chance I could persuade you to stay within these four walls unless I am available to escort you?"

Pauline gasped, as she tipped the warm water from washing the wounds into the slop bucket.

Margaret didn't blame Snowy for feeling protective. She did not intend to neglect her social responsibilities, but she was willing to compromise. "I will be careful, Hal. I will not go into the slums, or to isolated places. I will not go out without a footman. But I am not going to let fear cage me in."

"At least two guards as well as your footman, even in your garden?" he asked. "And you will let *me* hire the guards?"

Margaret acquiesced. It would make Snowy feel better, and she could not deny that the thought of such virulent hatred worried her.

"Can you have Snowden locked up until his trial?" Pauline

wondered.

Snowy shook his head. "I've spoken to two magistrates as well as my solicitor and a barrister friend. They will not confine him unless we have solid evidence that points directly to him. Especially since they have decided to treat him as a peer until he is proven not to be one. On the upside, they are treating me as a peer, too, until the House of Lords decides which one of us has the title."

"It is very frustrating," Pauline grumbled.

Later, after Rahat had been settled in a comfortable chair, with Pauline reading to him, Snowy told Margaret he had to go out. "I will have Blue with me," he assured her. "I need to consult with Wakefield, the enquiry agent, and I mean to ask him about trustworthy guards."

"I can pay for the guards," she assured Snowy. "We have not discussed such things, but you must know I am a wealthy woman."

He smiled. "And I am a wealthy man. As you probably realized when we discussed the marriage settlements."

Wealthy from what? She knew he invested, but what in? Did he own the brothel in which he lived? She had heard that such establishments were lucrative, but she could not like the idea...

Would he give it up, if she asked? After all, whatever was hers would be his.

Snowy frowned at her silence. "Is there a problem? We should have the documents in the next day or so, but if you have thought of any changes you would like, just let me know."

She forced a smile. He had been more than generous in his suggestions for the settlements, and her failure to find out more about the source of his wealth was not his fault. "I will read them again, Hal, but I am sure everything is more than acceptable."

"You are still worrying," he observed. "Margaret, I am confident there is nothing we cannot solve if we work at it together."

She managed a more convincing smile. "We can talk about it later," she said. "Be careful, Hal."

He bent to give her a gentle kiss—just a brush of lips upon lips, but still her knees weakened. "I will be back in time to take you for a drive at the fashionable hour," he said. "Show the happy couple to the ton."

His second kiss began as sweetly as the first, then deepened into something more passionate, so that, when he broke it off, she was left wanting. "Later," he promised.

WAKEFIELD STILL HADN'T heard back from the agents he'd sent to question those on the duchess's list, nor had questioning Daphne yielded any further information. As for Lord Hungerford-Fox, he had taken heart at not being tortured, had retracted his confession about Snowden, and was now refusing to answer questions.

"I've had a man retracing his steps, and he has been seen visiting Snowden," Wakefield said, "which adds to the circumstantial evidence but, to be honest, with what we currently have, neither of them will be convicted. Hungerford-Fox is linked to the crime by the evidence of a prostitute, and Snowden is not linked at all. Not now that Hungerford-Fox has recanted."

"Then you have nothing for me," Snowy said.

Wakefield shook his head. "I would not say that. I do not have enough for an arrest, but we are building a picture. I appreciated the suggestion to look into Deffew committing crimes for Snowden and Snowden for Deffew."

He shuffled some papers on his desk and picked up a page with three columns. Colored lines circled some of the paragraphs.

"Again, what we have is suggestive rather than compelling, but Deffew was in the village near your childhood home on the day your father was killed. And Snowden provided the corroborating evidence that allowed Deffew to have his wife committed."

He showed Snowy the page. The column headings were Snowden, Possible Crimes, Deffew. "We are filling in their location at the time of events we think one or both had a hand in. More people remember things than one might think, though memories become skewed by time."

"Time is something I may be running out of," Snowy told him. "I am getting married next week."

"Ah. I can see how that might worry your villain. Another possible legitimate heir. Lady Charmain has accepted your gallant proposal, then?"

Snowy raised a brow. *"The Teatime Tattler?"*

Wakefield merely smiled.

"On the topic of the danger to my lady, I am looking to employ guards. Is this something you might be able to help me with? I need men I can trust; men who can't be bought by Snowden and turned into a weapon against us."

Wakefield picked up a quill and wrote a quick note. "Take this to Mrs. Moriarty at the address on the note. She will be able to provide what you need."

Snowy took the note, holding it carefully so as not to smudge the drying ink. "Mrs. Moriarty? It seems an unusual role for a woman."

"She is an unusual woman. Her husband is with the Thames River Police. They both worked with Wellington's forces during the campaign in Spain, under the current Earl of Ruthford, who ran a group of exploring officers," Wakefield explained. "Ruthford has been finding work for ex-soldiers and sailors since he returned to England after he inherited his title. A couple of years ago, he and Mrs. Moriarty set up a formal agency that they call Moriarty Protection. They will only work on the side of the law, and usually require a referral—which you now have. You will find them well-trained and exceptionally loyal. They'll keep your lady safe."

WHEN HE GOT to his next destination, the House of Blossoms, Snowy sent the note to Mrs. Moriarty, enclosed in one requesting a meeting. He then met with his foster mothers, to tell them his plans.

"Good," Lily said, when he explained he was moving into Margaret's townhouse. "You are a viscount, Snowy. You should not be living over a brothel."

Jasmine softened the admonishment. "We want you safe. Being here, where people come and go and everyone is busy with the House's main business, is not safe."

"Don't forget us, ducky," Poppy said. "When that awful man is locked up, come and visit us, if you can."

"I am not about to become a stranger," Snowy reassured her. "For one thing, I want all my foster mothers at my wedding." He gave out the invitations that Margaret had written, one for each of them. "You'll see that theirs go to Lotus, Holly, and Petunia?" he asked.

"Lady Charmain does not want the likes of us at her wedding," Poppy scoffed.

Jasmine nodded, thoughtfully. "It would be embarrassing for her if we met men we know professionally," she said.

Lily's grin was evil. "Amusing, though."

"Lady Charmain wrote the invitations," Snowy pointed out. "It won't be a big Society affair, if that is what you fear. It is important to me you are there. Please say you will come."

From there, he went to Westruthers to collect his correspondence—mostly business of one kind or another, but two messages regarding meetings. The Duke of Winshire had asked him to call when convenient to discuss the fate of his prisoner, and Mrs. Moriarty had written to say she would receive him whenever he cared to arrive.

Another fat package contained the marriage settlements and wills that he and Margaret had had drawn up. Fortescue's covering note said he had worked with Margaret's solicitor and the solicitor who represented the Snowden estate. He suggested a time the day after next for the solicitors to witness him and Margaret signing the documents. Presumably, Margaret would have a similar package.

Snowy glanced over the rest, confirming that he'd have to spend some time today or tomorrow morning looking over reports from his agents and making some decisions. As well as fitting in the discussion of the marriage settlements, being seen in public with Margaret, and whatever else came up.

He checked the time. Visiting Mrs. Moriarty was his priority. He could manage that before he was due to meet Margaret.

Mrs. Moriarty proved to be a surprise. From the name, he had expected an Irish woman, or at least someone with Ireland in their immediate family history. By her appearance, Mrs. Moriarty was eastern Mediterranean, and when she spoke, he narrowed her origins down to Greece or the nearby islands.

She knew her business, too. She subjected him to a grilling on the topic of his cousin and any other enemies he might have. Snowy, more impressed than annoyed, answered all of her questions.

"Very well," she said at last. "I recommend you employ eight of our people. Two women, who will take it in turns to stick like glue to your betrothed, and six men who will stand guard two at a time in shifts. The people I have in mind are all experienced with weapons and unarmed combat, and have stood guard duty many times. We have found that, in the unlikely event an attacker evades male guards and our clients' own protections, female guards are quite unexpected and very effective."

Snowy had no doubt of it. He had grown up with confident women who organized their own lives, and *he* would not expect a woman warrior. How much more unexpected would it be to a man like his cousin, who had little regard for women?

"I accept," he said. "When can they start?"

Mrs. Moriarty arched her eyebrows. "You have not asked me about price," she said.

"David Wakefield recommended you, Mrs. Moriarty. I will

not haggle over the safety of my betrothed. What is your charge?"

She named a daily sum that was higher than he expected, but not by much.

"Paid to you, ma'am? Or individually to your employees?"

"To Moriarty Protection. You will also provide all meals to guards on duty," she said.

"Meals, and accommodation if they choose to live on site," he agreed. "When can they start?"

Chapter Twenty-One

S NOWY ARRIVED AT Margaret's with three new additions to the household, a woman and two men, whom he introduced to Margaret and Pauline as guards from an agency called Moriarty Protection.

A female guard! It was an intriguing idea. Margaret would have picked Miss Trent as a gentlewoman who had been forced into employment by ill fortune, but not as a skilled fighter, both with and without weapons.

"With your permission," Snowy said, "Miss Trent and her colleague, Mrs. O'Brian, will take it in turns to stay here and accompany you on all of your outings, Margaret."

The two men were part of a team of six, who would guard the house and Snowy in pairs. Snowy was taking the danger very seriously. Would Snowden really make an attempt on Margaret's life?

Margaret had believed Snowy when he said Snowden had given the order for Snowy's death, not once but several times, including when Snowy was only a small child. Believed, that is, as she believed a story.

Even after nursing Ned, she had still not truly believed that she was in danger.

Only at this moment, as she met the people who were prepared to put their skills between her and death, did the reality truly sink in. Yes. If he thought she might carry a successor to Snowy's claim on the viscountcy, Snowden really would try to kill her.

"May I have your permission to introduce Miss Trent, Charlie, and Frank to Bowen," Snowy asked Margaret, "and ask Bowen to give them a tour of the house? Then perhaps you and I could catch up on what else I have done today."

While Snowy took the guards to her butler, Margaret spoke to her housekeeper about setting up two rooms, one for Miss Trent and Mrs. O'Brian, and one for whichever of the men were on duty.

They had settled in the drawing room with a cup of tea, and Snowy was telling Margaret and Pauline about his visit to Wakefield and to Moriarty Protection, when Miss Trent knocked on the door and entered, in company with the housekeeper.

"If you will excuse me, my lady," she said. "I have a suggestion to make regarding bedrooms."

"Of course," Margaret said. "If the ones you have been allocated are not adequate..." She trailed off as Miss Trent shook her head and held up a hand.

"Not ours, my lady. It is your rooms, and particularly those of Lord Snowden and Mr. Rahat that we would like to discuss."

Margaret exchanged a glance with Snowy, thinking he might like to take the lead, but he gestured to pass the question to her. "It is your house, my lady," he said.

"Carry on," Margaret told Miss Trent.

Miss Trent gave a brisk nod. "Your rooms are at the end of the passage, where any intruder cannot reach you except by coming up one of the flights of stairs. In either case, they will need to traverse some of the passage. If they come up the main stairs, they will need to pass all the other bedrooms before they get to yours. That makes your room easy to guard. Miss Turner's room is near yours, so no problem, there."

She turned to look at Snowy. "However, Lord Snowden and

Mr. Rahat are on the next floor, which means we would need to split forces to guard both floors. I asked Mrs. Markham to move them to the same floor as you, and she said it was not seemly." Miss Trent's nostrils flared. "Death is not seemly."

Mrs. Markham, the housekeeper, broke into a spate of words. "I would not wish my lady to be in any danger, but I am sure the situation cannot be serious enough to throw all propriety out the window. Unmarried gentlemen on the same floor as unmarried ladies? I have never heard the like. Miss Denning would not have permitted it; you can be sure of that."

"You may be sure that the danger is certain," Snowy told her.

"Because of you," Mrs. Markham spat at him. "Lady Charmain has never set a foot wrong except the once, and there is Lord Hungerford-Fox back to put that wrong right. But you turn up and cozen her into sending poor Miss Denning away, and Lord Hungerford-Fox too. And claiming to be a viscount when you're nothing but a base-born brat from the alleys of Covent Garden. It is wicked. That is what it is. And now you bring—"

"That is quite enough," Margaret said, sternly. "Lord Snowden, I apologize. I am deeply mortified to have a guest so insulted by one of my servants! Mrs. Markham, you will pack your bags. You are dismissed."

Mrs. Markham gaped, then began complaining. "Here. You can't throw me out in the street. I've worked for the Charmains since I was a tweeny. Miss Denning wouldn't—"

"Who has paid your wages these past three years, Mrs. Markham?" Snowy asked, his voice calm and quiet. Just as well, for the repeated reference to her aunt had Margaret ready to shout.

Mrs. Markham stopped in mid-rant and narrowed her eyes at him. "I have worked for the Charmain family woman and girl this past forty years," she said.

"The current holder of the title pays your wages," Snowy said firmly. "In this case, the Countess Charmain. Who no longer trusts you to follow her orders. I wonder, Mrs. Markham, who has been feeding you with tales about your mistress and what you have told that person?"

He turned to Margaret. "I would like to send for Wakefield, Margaret, if that is acceptable to you."

Margaret felt slightly ill. How many of her servants were untrustworthy? She nodded. "Pauline, will you fetch Bowen, please?"

He must have been waiting outside the door, for he came immediately, and Frank came with him. Margaret nodded to Snowy, who took charge again. "Please escort Mrs. Markham to her room and lock her in. She has been dismissed but will not be permitted to leave until she has been questioned."

Bowen swallowed but bowed. "Certainly, my lady." The two men marched Mrs. Markham away.

Miss Trent asked, "Will you allow us to move Mr. Rahat and Lord Snowden to the same floor as you, Lady Charmain?"

"Yes," Margaret said. "Please put Lord Snowden into the room next to mine, and I suggest Rahat could have the room next door."

When Miss Trent was gone, Margaret took a deep breath. "I am going to have to interview all the servants, am I not? And try to find out how deep the rot goes. Will the pair of you help me?"

In the end, they found four other people—two parlor maids, one footman, and one cook's assistant—who had been passing information to Hungerford-Fox, on instructions from Margaret's aunt. The footmen disclosed that Lord Hungerford-Fox had sometimes come with a nameless friend who, for the last few days, had met the footman on his own.

The description was that of Richard Snowden.

AFTER THE INTERVIEWS, Margaret spoke to the assembled servants, and was magnificent. "I am going to tell them what is at stake," she said, and she was right.

She made a thrilling tale of it. The child abandoned in the slums and rescued by a passerby. The frightened mother, suspicious of her second husband, begging the Good Samaritan to keep the child safe. The passing of the years, and with it, the title holder, the child's grandfather.

"A few weeks ago, the man you know as Mr. White was told the truth of his origins and is now waiting for the House of Lords to decide his right to be declared the true Lord Snowden."

There were nods and murmurs. This news was already a matter of gossip. But Margaret's next words brought gasps. "Since he placed his evidence before the House of Lords, there have been three attempts on his life. An attempt to strangle him, one to stab him with a pin dipped in poison, and last night, a shooting."

When the exclamations died down, Margaret said, "You have probably also heard that I am betrothed to Lord Snowden." She put her hand on Snowy's arm. "*This* Lord Snowden; the true one. Some of you may believe, as Mrs. Markham did, that I was promised to Lord Hungerford-Fox. That is what Lord Hungerford-Fox said, but he lied. He cozened me into believing him a suitor six years ago, when I was a girl, but only so he could persuade my father into paying him a large sum of money to go away. As soon as I saw him back again, I knew he was up to his old tricks."

"That is why you have brought in guards?" said Mr. Bowen. "Because of Lord Hungerford-Fox?"

Snowy raised his eyebrows, and Margaret read the message and nodded.

He stepped forward and they all looked at him, eyes wide. "Hungerford-Fox is in custody, because the person who made the attempt to poison me claims to have done so with poison he supplied and on his orders. However, Hungerford-Fox received both poison and the idea of doing away with me from my stepfather, Richard Snowden."

He moved his gaze over them all, waiting until they had time to absorb that piece of truth. "I have brought in guards, and am staying here myself, because Snowden has shown he will kill to win the viscountcy. As my wife, Lady Charmain's first son will not only be heir to the Charmain earldom, but to the Snowden viscountcy."

He leaned forward. "I will protect my betrothed and her household, but I cannot know where danger might come from or who might be at risk. With Lady Charmain's agreement, I am offering everyone who remains in service an increase in wages, proportionate to your position. Mr. Bowen has the amounts for the menservants, and Cook, who has agreed to be acting housekeeper until Lady Charmain can make another appointment, has those for the women."

As if they had rehearsed it, Margaret took over. "This raise will be permanent. However, if you do not wish to remain in a house that may be attacked, you may leave without penalty, with a letter of recommendation and your wages paid to the end of the month."

Snowy's turn: "Provided you have not broken your mistress's confidence by gossiping outside of this house, or by spying on your mistress and her actions. Should we discover you have betrayed Lady Charmain—"

"Or Lord Snowden," Margaret interjected.

"Or me," he conceded, "you will be dismissed without notice and without recommendation."

"Take an hour to think about whether you have a future here," Margaret said, "then tell Mr. Bowen or Cook whether you are remaining. Thank you, Bowen, that will be all."

After that, they went out in the barouche, with Pauline and Miss Trent on the facing seat and Frank up behind with one of the footmen, who had fervently declared his loyalty before Bowen had even had a chance to leave the drawing room. Rahat had stayed reluctantly behind, though he insisted he was recovered enough to resume his duties.

First, they visited the Duke of Winshire, where Margaret and

Pauline were scooped up by Lady Sutton and taken upstairs to visit with the duchess. Miss Trent followed behind the ladies, as silent and inconspicuous as a shadow.

In a locked but clean and tidy room in the cellar, Hungerford-Fox was demanding to be released or taken before a magistrate.

"Snowden killed the man who carried out his first attempt to murder me," Snowy warned him.

Hungerford-Fox sneered. "You would not understand. Gentlemen treat one another with honor, and Snowden is a gentleman."

The duke's smile was almost a smirk. "Since this piece of slime has rescinded his previous confession, Lord Snowden," he said, "The magistrate says we cannot keep him. In his words, the evidence of a loose woman is no evidence at all."

Hungerford-Fox looked triumphant.

The duke took no notice of him, continuing, "I suggest we comply with his request and let him go. We can always have him arrested again later. If he survives. It is not on our heads if the false viscount kills him."

"I shall have you arrested for kidnapping," Hungerford-Fox threatened.

Snowy ignored him as did everyone else in the room. "Agreed. And thank you once again, Your Grace, for keeping him safe for the past few days. I am grateful for your kindness, even if Hungerford-Fox is not."

Two of the duke's men escorted Hungerford-Fox from the cellar and out to the street, while Snowy and the duke joined the ladies. They were discussing the wedding; apparently, the duke and duchess would be in attendance. Snowy wondered if the invitation had originated with the duchess, but since Margaret seemed happy, he said nothing.

They then went for their drive in the Park. It was almost anticlimactic that nothing happened, apart from civil good wishes from some of the ton, and the cut direct from others.

"Friends of Snowden or those who have believed his lies,"

Margaret observed. "We will simply ignore them back."

❧≫≫≪≪❧

MARGARET HAD PLANNED to attend the opera that night, but Snowy and Pauline both agreed when she suggested an early night instead.

"I am very tired, and will make an early night of it," Pauline told them. "Goodnight, Margaret, Snowy."

"I will retire, also," Margaret said. Miss Trent, in her quiet way, stood, prepared to escort Margaret upstairs.

Snowy offered Margaret his arm but left her at the door to his own room. Traditionally, it had been the countess's suite, but Margaret had taken over the earl's suite after her period of mourning for her father, because it had a better view of the herb garden.

Aunt Aurelia had been aghast at the blasphemy; a woman in the earl's suite, even though the suites were mirror images of one another, differing only in their decoration. It was the first time Margaret had openly defied her, ignoring the woman's complaints, and continuing with her plans to refurbish both suites of rooms in shades of brown and blue with identical furnishings, neither overtly feminine nor masculine, but peaceful and welcoming.

Miss Trent saw Margaret to her door, then insisted on coming inside and peering around the sitting room, the bed chamber, and the dressing room. She even tried the door between Margaret's sitting room and Snowy's. If she saw the sudden heat in Margaret's face, she ignored it. "All safe," she reported.

Margaret's maid, who had been laying out her nightwear, watched Miss Trent with wide eyes as she left the room. "Please undo my buttons and my laces," Margaret told her, "And then you may go. I will read for a while before I sleep."

But the words would not come into focus, and when she did

manage to read a paragraph, she had forgotten the first sentence before she got to the end of the last. It was not just that her thoughts were busy with all that had happened—and even more, all that was about to happen.

Snowy was asleep in the very next room.

In a few days, they would be married. He would do what Martin had done. *No. Not that.* Snowy had promised it would not be the same, that she would enjoy it. His kisses argued persuasively that he knew what he was talking about. Of course, he did. He was experienced—he had admitted it.

She smiled at the memory. *I can promise that, if we marry, there will not be another woman as long as we both live.* She trusted him. But then, she had trusted Martin. She had trusted her father and brothers. She had, bother it all, trusted her servants, and look how that had turned out!

She shut the book, put it on her bedside table, and blew out the candles. She was tired, and tomorrow would be another busy day.

Her mind would not stop teeming with thoughts, worries, and memories of Hal's kiss. If only he would kiss her again. All of her doubts melted away when he kissed her.

At last, she fell into a restless sleep to dream she was kissing Hal, only to have him dragged from her arms and replaced by Richard Snowden. He hurled her down and himself on top of her. She woke with her heart pounding and his snarled words in her ears. "You took my son. You owe me another one."

Chapter Twenty-Two

LADY CHARMAIN'S SUBORNED footman had the nerve to come to Snowden's house! Another thing to blame Hungerford-Fox for. The footman should not even have known who Snowden was, when he had met the little group of treacherous servants in disguise, pretending to be acting on Hungerford-Fox's orders.

He sent the man away, of course, and without the payment that the fool demanded. "Hungerford-Fox bribed you to betray your mistress. If you want money, talk to Hungerford-Fox," he said, and had his own footmen throw the man back into the street.

He retreated to his study to consider the news the man had brought. Far more annoying than the footman's impertinence was the fact that Hungerford-Fox's spies had been discovered and dismissed. To add to that, the counterfeit Snowden had moved into Lady Charmain's house already, not waiting for the wedding.

He stopped, as was his habit, in front of the mirror, where reflection Richard gazed back at him, eyes burning, face calm.

"She could already be with child."

Snowden should have expected it. She had shown herself a slut when she let Hungerford-Fox lift her skirts. And the imposter had been raised in a brothel. Why would he hesitate to bed the woman as soon as he could? He had probably had her weeks ago, and that is why she turned away from Chalky. Yes. That must be it. She had already been seduced when Hungerford-Fox put in an appearance.

"I should never have given Hungerford-Fox my support. The man is a failure and fool."

Yet the man had the approval of the tart's great-aunt, a toxic old harridan if Snowden had ever met one. When Chalky had turned to bite the hand that fed him, Hungerford-Fox seemed like a good choice of replacement. He could marry Lady Charmain, and Snowden would get the canal agreement as payment for his help.

Now his plans were in tatters again.

He glared at his reflection, but his mind was still busy, and soon the face before him softened, the lips curving into a smile.

Yes, of course. It was the only way. He would have to kill the false Snowden himself.

Chapter Twenty-Three

M ARGARET LOOKED TIRED, as if she had slept as poorly as Snowy, although Snowy doubted her problem was unrequited lust. Having her one door away was excruciating torture, mitigated only by Rahat's insistence on being moved to a bed in the adjoining dressing room. Much as Snowy would have liked to visit Margaret, he would not risk witnesses, even those he trusted. He would not dishonor Margaret in any way.

Snowy had not been to church services since he graduated from Oxford, but he quite enjoyed St. Martin-in-the-Fields. A visiting vicar gave a sermon on Christianity being about what people did, rather than what they said, which Snowy appreciated, and sharing a hymn book with Margaret gave him the opportunity to stand close to her, their arms touching.

Afterward, it took them some time to make their way to Margaret's carriage, because so many people stopped to wish them well. The Archdeacon nearly let the cat out of the bag when he said cheerfully that he looked forward to seeing them on Wednesday, but fortunately no one seemed to think anything of it.

In the carriage, Pauline announced she was going to visit Arial, who was back in town. "I will leave the pair of you to your marriage settlements and other papers. You will not require an audience for that. After all, you are both adults and will be wed in three days. You have Mrs. O'Brian in the unlikely event you need a chaperone." Mrs. O'Brian had replaced Miss Trent as guard of the day in time to accompany them to church, and her eyes twinkled at Pauline's declaration.

Pauline would not think a chaperone an unlikely requirement if she could read Snowy's thoughts. Or perhaps she could, and that was why she sounded so amused when she bid them farewell.

"We will take our breakfast on trays in the study," Margaret told Bowen, and it was delivered a short time later.

"You will not need me, so I will find a comfortable chair and take out my sewing," said Mrs. O'Brian. I will be keeping watch for any villains who get past the men outside. Never you mind."

Silence fell after Mrs. O'Brian closed the door on her way out. Snowy was reminding himself of the proper behavior of a gentleman. He didn't know for certain what Margaret was thinking, but she was looking at him from under her lashes, a slight crease between her brows.

Best to ask. "You look worried, Margaret," he said. "Is it something I can help with? Something I can answer?"

She lifted her head and colored, then swallowed, hard. "Shall I serve the tea?" she asked.

They were not going to get far if she would not talk to him. Apparently, she was only gathering her thoughts, for as she handed him his cup, she said, "My wealth comes mainly from the estates and other landholdings. I own rows of houses in both London and Brighton. I also have some industrial investments, but I divested myself of the Jamaican plantations when I inherited."

She blushed still brighter. "I freed the slaves and sold the plantation to them, loaning those who wished to stay the money for the purchase. They pay me back from a percentage of the crop."

She elevated her chin higher and glared at him. "My advisers said I charged too little in the purchase price, and that I should be charging a higher interest rate on the loan. They say I could have made far more money keeping the plantation or selling it *with* the slaves. But that was not the point."

"The point being, you do not want to make money from human misery," Snowy said, approvingly. He had heard of a number of men who had sold their plantations so that they no longer owned slaves. He'd always felt that change of ownership, while salving the conscience of the former owner, made no difference to the slaves. He much preferred Margaret's solution.

"That is correct," Margaret agreed. "For the same reason, I will not invest in mills that pay less than a living wage, or that employ children under the age of ten."

He nodded again. "I agree. My friend Drew is part of a mill-owning consortium. He insists on shortened hours for those aged between eleven and fourteen and provides schools at the mill for any children of mill workers, whether the children are also employed there or not."

Her face had softened. "Do you invest in any mills?" she asked.

Snowy shook his head. "Not mills, no. Houses, yes. Mostly I buy them, do them up, and sell them again, but I do have a row of rental terraces in Manchester and another in Birmingham. I also have part ownership of a ship, and I am an investor in several canal projects." He grinned. "Drew is trying to talk me into funding the development of a steam engine to pull railway carriages, but I am not convinced."

"What of..." she avoided his eyes, looking up at the top of the curtains as if they were of profound interest. "Do you own the House of Blossoms, Hal?" Her eyes met his. This was the real question, and one he was about to pass with flying colors. He hoped.

"I do not now, nor have I ever owned the House of Blossoms or any other brothel," he said. "Lily and my other foster mothers founded the House and still own it, and the farm, too."

He had been right. Her face cleared and the strain left her. The story was a bit more complicated than that, though. Perhaps she didn't need to know? Or perhaps she would find out on her own, and better by far it came from him.

Besides, she had shown the way, courageously questioning the source of his wealth.

"I am glad. I do not mean to criticize your foster mothers, Hal. I am sure they have their reasons."

"They do. They each had their own reasons for being in the trade, the one common factor being that other choices were worse. Working in a house that they jointly owned offered my foster mothers much greater safety and security than working alone or in a house belonging to others. When the opportunity arose, they took it. They do their best to look after those who work for them, more so than others in the trade. But I do not invest in it. I do not judge others for what they choose to do, but I do not, myself, benefit."

He hesitated, wondering where to begin.

"I am glad," she said again. "I suppose you have heard and seen many sad stories."

"I have been one of those sad stories," he told her, then spoke quickly to counter her dawning horror. "As an adult, and by my choice, and in truth, I was not much harmed." Not entirely true, but how to explain the aching void in his self-esteem, largely scabbed over but still painful?

After that, he had to tell her. "I was at university when my friend Gary and I were offered an opportunity to invest; one of our other friends was a son of a man who was trying to raise money for a canal. He was selling shares for fifty guineas each, a sum Gary and I could only dream about."

He paused, remembering the moment when he set out to make that dream into reality.

"There was a woman. A wealthy widow. We had met her at an assembly, and she had—cast out lures, I suppose you could say. I had flirted back, but not with any intent. To me, at eighteen, she seemed old. I suppose she was nearing forty, though she was still an attractive woman."

Margaret's eyes were wide. "My goodness," she said.

"Goodness had nothing to do with it," Snowy assured her. "And yes, you have guessed it. I told her I needed the money and what I needed it for and offered my—um—bedroom skills for fifty guineas."

The widow had laughed and told him he valued himself rather high. He gave her a demonstration of some of what he had learned as a randy youth surrounded by highly skilled girls keen to be his tutors.

She gave him the fifty guineas in return for a private contract, drawn up between the two of them. His services in a place and at a time of her choosing four times a week. He bargained her down from six months to three, and had made it clear that the times and places must not interfere with his commitments to lectures and tutorials.

The contract was unenforceable, Gary pointed out. If their arrangement came to light, Snowy would be hurled from the university, probably with some force. But Mrs. Below would face an even bigger scandal.

Snowy hadn't cared. He had the fifty guineas, and he intended to keep his word, so the contract was nothing more than a record of the agreement. He bought one share, in his name and Gary's. "You shall be my attorney," he said, "and you can pay me twenty-five guineas back out of the money we earn." Which Gary did. They partnered on that investment and those that followed, until Gary was as rich a man as Snowy.

"It was an easy way to make money," he told Margaret. "When the three months were up, she offered me another fifty guineas, but she had told some of her closest friends I knew the ways of pleasure, and they entered into a bidding war."

He grimaced. "I prefer to gloss over the next two years. It was lucrative, but I soon realized I was merely an object to be awarded to whichever one of them won the games they were always playing. Mrs. Bedlow won a week of my time at cards. Mrs. Furness beat the others at croquet and had me for two nights. Mrs. Chalmers picked the winning team in a boat race and carried me off to her husband's hunting lodge. The whole thing gave me a disgust of well-bred women and their morals, which I've come to realize., in the past few weeks, was quite unbalanced and unfair."

Margaret appeared as revolted as he had expected her to be. With him?

"So, in a sense, the flesh trade is the foundation of my wealth, Margaret. Lily and the other Blossoms paid for my education with their earnings. I paid for my first investments with mine. I vowed never to be used in that way again, and never to use another human being."

Especially after his last Oxford affair, forced on him by the neglected mistress of the Warden of his college. She threatened to expose his activities to her lover if he did not give her what she wanted. Her aberrant tastes had nearly broken him. And Margaret did not need to hear about that.

She still said nothing, sitting quietly within reach, thinking over his story.

He couldn't bear to wait for her judgement. "I hope… I have no right to expect… Can you overlook my past, Margaret?"

With hesitation, he reached for her hands, expecting her to turn him away; instead, she launched herself into his lap. "Dear Hal, how awful they all were, taking advantage of a boy in that way."

Her comment startled a laugh out of him. Not because she was wrong, but because no one else who knew had ever seen it that way. "Gary thought I was the luckiest creature on earth, to have so many women fighting to get me into bed," he told her. To be fair, Gary changed his mind over the two years of Snowy's venture into commercial copulation and had even put his lawyerly mind to a scheme to extract Snowy from the clutches of the warden's mistress.

"They did not fight over you. You were just the medal they passed around between them," she replied, firmly, kissing the corner of his lips. "Horrid. No one deserves to be treated as less than a person."

"You are an amazing woman, Margaret Lady Charmain," Snowy told her. "I am finding it hard to believe you have promised to be mine." He captured her lips with his, and she returned his kiss with such enthusiasm that his head spun. Or perhaps it was just all his blood leaving his brain for parts south.

"We have to stop," he gasped, although his dazed brain could not quite articulate why.

"I suppose we must," Margaret mourned, sounding so reluctant that he had to kiss her again. This time, it was she who stopped, drawing away just enough to say, "We ought to read the papers before Pauline comes home."

Yes. That was the reason. "You are right," he acknowledged. "In that case, dearest Margaret, will you please sit in your own chair? Having you in my arms is too tempting by far, and I can think of nothing except touching you." He kissed her again, a quick peck on the corner of her lips, but released her as she took him at his word and moved away.

He took comfort at the way her hand lingered in his before she picked up the packages of documents and carried them to the desk.

"Pull up a chair, dearest. Let us finish this, and then kiss again," she proposed.

>>><<<

THE SOLICITORS HAD followed Margaret's and Snowy's instructions meticulously. Margaret couldn't find anything in either the settlements or the wills that she needed to question.

The settlements were thorough and generous. Some of the provisions were dictated by the earldom, of course. The entailed lands and their incomes would remain in Margaret's control if Snowy died before her and pass to their eldest son upon her death. In addition, Hal had insisted that her generous dowry should be set aside to provide her with income not connected to the title if she was widowed. If she died before Snowy, he would be trustee and guardian of the Charmain estates during their son's minority, and the dowry would be split amongst their children.

Further dowry amounts were set aside for their daughters, and Snowy proposed that their second son should inherit the lands associated with his viscountcy if his claim was successful.

"Our eldest son will inherit my title as well as yours, of course," Snowy had told her. "The Snowden solicitor says that Snowden and Ned renewed the entail on Ned's birthday last year, but if Snowden is not the viscount, then the renewal is invalid. We can leave the lands where we wish, and I propose to entail them on our second son when he is old enough to make the agreement."

They both had minor estates that could be given to younger sons, and these had been listed in the settlements, though the precise distribution would be established in their wills, as amended over the years. Meanwhile, they had each written a will to apply from the date of their wedding, providing for each possible scenario: all the possible combinations of dying together or one dying and the other surviving, and dying childless or leaving a daughter or a son.

"I see you did decide to leave the Snowden estates to Ned if you die without a son," Margaret observed. "Which is fair. He is next in line after you and his father. I hope it will not be necessary, however."

"Likewise," Snowy agreed. Margaret had seen no need to make any special provision for the distant cousin who was her own heir, should she die without a son. The entailed properties would allow him to keep up the title; she could leave her private wealth how she liked.

Like Snowy, she made small bequests to servants. If she died childless, several charities that provided medical care to the poor would benefit. Snowy was of a similar mind, dividing the bulk of his estate between an orphanage, the place that he called *the farm*, and a charity that provided rescue services and retraining to prostitutes who were being kept in the trade against their will.

They set the documents aside to be signed in front of witnesses.

"Now," said Snowy, invitingly. The single word was the only warning she had before his mouth claimed hers.

He had edged his chair closer and closer to hers as the afternoon progressed, claiming that it made more sense for both of them to read from the same copy at the same time, so that they could discuss any point that arose.

It had been an excuse to touch her, of course, and to drive her mad with wanting. He was just as affected, which had severely tested their determination to finish their reading before they kissed again.

She gladly gave herself over to his kisses, and to the caresses that grew more urgent and more intimate as they moved to a nearby sofa, still kissing.

A knock on the door had Margaret pushing down her skirts while urgently refastening the line of buttons down the front of her bodice. Snowy leapt to his feet and strode to another chair, while attempting to tidy his cravat and then shrug back into the coat she had managed to half-remove.

"One moment, please," she called out, to give themselves time to set themselves at least partly to rights. Though anyone with eyes would be able to guess what they had been doing.

Pauline certainly did, when she entered a few minutes later. The affectionate amusement in her eyes made her knowing smirk tolerable. "I trust you have had a good afternoon," she said.

"Excellent, thank you," Hal told her, showing no embarrassment at all, whereas Margaret was blushing like a peony. "How was your afternoon?"

"Arial and Peter send their love," Pauline said. "They would like to call tomorrow and wonder if you are attending the Cushing Ball in the evening. I told them I was not certain but would ask."

Margaret agreed they had accepted that invitation. "How are the children?" she asked.

Pauline's eyes lit up, and soon she and Margaret were in a detailed discussion about what each of the little tribe of girls had said and was doing, and how much the Stancroft heir had grown in the short time he had been out of London.

Snowy went off to find Bowen and order refreshments and must have taken the time to comb his hair and retie his cravat, for he returned to the study as the tea tray was being delivered.

Margaret was pouring the tea when Mr. Wakefield was announced. "I have news," he announced without preamble, "and it requires us to act quickly."

Chapter Twenty-Four

"MAY I SPEAK freely in front of her ladyship and Miss Turner?" Wakefield asked.

"My betrothed is fully in my confidence," Snowy said, "and we trust Miss Turner implicitly."

Wakefield inclined his head. "Lord Snowden, I have an affidavit from your grandfather's sister and from the maid your mother sent to verify your identity after your rescue. The maid is still in your great aunt's employ. However, we also found that your great aunt knew where your mother was sent."

"Does she live?" Snowy asked.

Wakefield shook his head. "I am sorry, my lord. She died some eight years ago." Snowy had not realized he had reached for Margaret's hand until she gave his hand a gentle squeeze.

"She was incarcerated in an asylum—a small, private establishment with only a handful of patients. I went there myself to interview the governing physician, who is also the proprietor. It may set your mind at rest to know that the place appears to be kindly run and the patients well treated."

"Yet my mother died," Snowy pointed out.

"A bad case of influenza that went to the lungs, apparently. When Doctor Chapman knew I was representing her son, he was happy to show me his records, and also a box of items your mother asked him to keep for you. Apparently, she knew and believed you had been abducted, rescued, and were growing up safely somewhere."

He reached into his pocket and handed Snowy a small notebook; the kind printers made up with surplus paper. Snowy's hand shook as he received it reverently in his palm. *This belonged to my mother.* Carefully, as if it might crumble to dust with rough treatment, he opened the cloth-bound cover—pink linen, a little stained and fading with age. Inside, the pages were closely written.

"This is one of her diaries," Wakefield explained.

Snowy could not bring his eyes to focus on the words. *My mother.* He didn't remember her. Not really. Just snippets. The lullaby she sang. Violet-scented perfume. Soft skin. Beyond that, he had no idea what memories came from before the abduction, and what after. Did she write about him? Did she blame him for her incarceration? If he had died, as Snowden intended, she would have been safe.

Margaret sat on the sofa beside him and slipped a supporting arm around his waist. Her warm comfort eased his trembling, and he was able to swallow the threatening tears.

"The box," he asked. His voice came out as a croak.

"Doctor Chapman says he will give you the box if you come in person to collect it."

"He did not let you have it?" Snowy asked, his voice steadier. Why not?

"He says he swore to put it into your hands, Lord Snowden, and yours alone. I suspect you might find support for your petition to the Lord Chancellor and perhaps for the case against the false viscount within its contents."

Snowy turned the notebook over in his hands, then remembered what Wakefield said when he came in. "This is important," he agreed, "but how is it urgent?"

Wakefield nodded. "Quite right. My concern is that Dr. Chapman and his wife are very afraid of Snowden. I believe they might run, and I think that you need to talk to them first. You, and young Mr. Deffew."

"Dicken Deffew? What has he to do with it?" Margaret asked.

Snowy had been about to ask the same question. His future wife was smart as well as beautiful. He was being blessed in many ways.

"I think Chapman will trust Lady Snowden's son more than he trusts me," Wakefield answered, "And, if what I suspect is true, I believe Mrs. Chapman will tell us everything she knows if Dickon Deffew asks her."

Snowy could make no sense of it. "What is that you suspect, Wakefield?"

"I believe that Mrs. Chapman is the former Mrs. Deffew, Dickon Deffew's mother." He counted points by raising fingers, one at a time. "One. Mrs. Deffew is in the asylum records, admitted as a patient six months before Lady Snowden. Two. She disappears from the records shortly after Lady Snowden dies. There is no record of her death, or her release. Three. The time that Doctor Chapman's wife begins to be mentioned in the asylum's day books follows directly on from the time that comments about Mrs. Deffew cease. No overlap. No time lapse."

Snowy nodded. "Suggestive."

"Then try this. When they spoke of Snowden, his reach, his spies, and his vicious retribution toward those who disobey him, they mentioned Deffew as his chief enforcer. I told them Deffew had been dead for a year, and Mrs. Chapman burst into tears. Chapman ended the interview. But here's the thing. They were both overcome with feeling—Chapman was just better at hiding it. But I would swear on a stack of Bibles that the predominant emotions were joy and triumph."

Snowy and Margaret exchanged glances. He lifted his eyebrows in question, and she nodded. They would go. "Dickon Deffew and Snowy's brother Ned are not in Town, but we know where they are," she said, cautiously.

Wakefield replied, "Staying at the Paddimore estate, Three

Gables." He shrugged at their looks of surprise. "It is my job to know things. The asylum is probably about halfway between here and Three Gables. Perhaps Mr. Deffew can meet you there?"

Pauline objected. "Lord Snowden and Lady Charmain are to wed on Wednesday," she said.

Wakefield inclined his head. "If we leave in the morning, perhaps by eight o'clock, you should be able to do the whole journey there and back in a day. I suggest you send a rider tonight with a message to the Ashbys. If the messenger rode until dark, then proceeded on his way at first light, Deffew will be able to reach the village at about the same time as you do." He frowned. "It would be best if Snowden does not realize you've gone."

Margaret penned a letter to Regina and Ash, asking them to bring both young men to the asylum to meet her and Snowy, and Snowy ordered a horse and groom to take the message and a carriage for the morning for him and Margaret.

"I'll stay here while you are gone," Pauline offered. "I can maintain the fiction that you are both still in town but lying low until after your wedding."

⋙⋘

IN PREPARATION FOR the journey, they went early to bed. Margaret changed and dismissed her maid, then lay in the dark, thinking about Hal's caresses.

It was funny how when they were with others, she thought of Hal as Snowy, as if he was a different person. And perhaps he was—for her, and for himself. Hal was his private name, just within the family. His mother's name for him, and his brothers', and now hers. It wasn't a name to share with others.

Hal had made her ache, and yet the ache was also a pleasure. He had made her restless for something wonderful that remained just out of reach.

She had been frustrated when they had to stop, and she had

caught some warm glances from him during the evening that hinted he felt the same.

She tried to reassure herself that she did not have long to wait. *Not tomorrow and not the next day, but the day after that, we will be wed, and he will make me his.* It didn't help. She was almost certain Martin had been a bad lover as well as a liar, but his jeers echoed in the back of her mind and now she was frightened of her wedding night and of letting Hal down, as well as filled with desire for Hal's touch and the mindless pleasure that melted away her worries.

She tried to turn her mind to another topic, but it kept drifting back, heating and chilling her alternately, as first desire then worry came uppermost. What if Martin was right, and she could never give Hal pleasure in bed?

She had not meant to trap him into marriage, and he was putting a very good face on it, but men could not be expected to ignore their appetites. Her father had told her that when he berated her for trusting Martin. If she did not please Hal, someone else would. She would not be a compliant wife. She could not. And he would first resent and later hate her for it.

Finally, she threw back the sheet and sat up, swinging her legs over the side of the bed, and reached for a shawl to cover her night rail.

Her eyes had adjusted enough to the dim light that she could cross the familiar suite to the door that connected her rooms with Hal's. She turned the key to unlock it. Then, she hesitated. Perhaps he was asleep?

After what seemed like a long time, she knocked, a light rat-a-tat-tat that would alert Hal if he was as sleepless as her but not, she hoped, wake him if he slumbered.

Still silence.

She was about to turn away when the door suddenly opened. It was Hal. "Margaret? Is something wrong?"

Looking past him into his sitting room, she could see the valet, Rahat, rising to his feet from one of a pair of chairs by the window. From the looks of the glass in his hand and the one near the matching chair, he and Hal had been sharing a nightcap.

Margaret looked helplessly at Rahat. "No. Nothing."

"I am going to bed, Snowy," Rahat said. "Goodnight, Lady Charmain." He put down his half-full glass and walked away through the door into the bedroom, a slight hitch in his walk the only sign of his recent injury.

Of course. He was still sleeping in Hal's dressing room. Margaret blushed.

"Nothing?" Snowy prompted.

The heat in her face deepened. "I just..." She could not find the words.

Snowy cast a glance over her shoulder. "Just a minute. Stay there."

He lit a spill from a wall sconce, then used it to light a candle before taking her hand and leading her back through her door into her own sitting room, shutting the door firmly behind him. He led her to the matching pair of chairs by her window. "You just...?"

"I can't stop thinking about this afternoon," she confessed.

"Our kisses?" he asked. "Do you want a goodnight kiss, my love?"

It was time to be brave. She dropped the shawl. "I want more," she told him. "I want you to bed me, Hal. Would you?"

Desire flamed in his eyes, and he leaned toward her, then jerked himself back. "You are to be my wife, darling. We should wait until after our wedding."

"Why?" she demanded. "We are to be wed in three days, and it is not as if I can be ruined again. You mentioned learning the ways of pleasure, Hal. Tonight, I want you to show me."

She could see his hesitation. "Please, Hal. The closer the time comes, the more nervous I am. Your kisses and caresses promise so much more than I ever thought I could have, but I am so afraid that when the time comes, I shall let you down. I cannot stop thinking about it."

He lifted her to his feet and took her into his arms. "You will not let me down, Margaret. I'm afraid I will let you down. I long for you so much that I fear going off too soon, like an untried boy."

"I don't know what you mean," Margaret admitted. "I am almost sure that you could do nothing I disliked."

Hal's chuckle was wry. "It is better explained by demonstration. But if I do, and if you forgive me for making an idiot of myself, I shall make it up to you." He scooped her up and carried her to the bed. "Are you sure, my love?"

She nodded, vigorously. *Very sure. And very nervous.*

"We can stop at any time," he said. "If I do anything you do not like, or if you decide you have had enough, just tell me."

She nodded, and then her mouth went dry as he removed the banyan he was wearing, for he wore nothing underneath. He was naked. And magnificent. He knelt on the side of the bed, looking down at her splayed on her pillows.

"You have a tattoo!" she exclaimed. It was a bird. A magnificent fantasy of a bird in red, orange, and yellow, its wings outspread across his chest, its talons outstretched toward his left nipple, its long tail sweeping down the center of his torso and across to the right, reaching almost to his waist.

"A phoenix," she decided, touching the crown. He shuddered but stood still. She traced it, feeling him quiver as her finger glided over his skin. "It is beautiful, Hal." She smiled into his eyes. "You are beautiful."

"May I..." his voice was hoarse. He coughed, and started again, in a low growl that she felt to her bones. "May I remove your night rail?"

Margaret's nervousness, forgotten in her exploration of Hal's skin, returned, but she nodded, and knelt so he could lift the garment over her head. He did so slowly, his hands brushing against her thighs, then her hips, then up her torso to her breasts before he pulled it over her head and tossed it behind him.

She went to lie down again, but he put out a hand to stop her.

"Let me look," he begged.

The part of him that would breach her, the part she had been trying not to look at, lengthened and thickened as she watched. She would not have thought it possible.

"*You* are beautiful," he told her.

"Shall I lie down so you can..." she offered.

"Enter you? You are not ready for me, my love." He reclined on one elbow and tugged her down to face him. "First, we shall kiss and caress. You will learn my body and I will learn yours. I will prepare your body to receive me, and you will know only pleasure when I do."

Margaret had her doubts, but her only previous experience had been with someone who did not want her to touch him and who had barely touched her, beyond a few hard gropes, some punishing kisses, and a rude and uncomfortable invasion.

She put Martin from her mind. This was Hal. She loved him and she trusted him. "Show me," she said.

And so, he did.

⋙⋘

IT WAS JUST as well, Snowy reflected, that Miss Trent and Wakefield shared the carriage with them. Margaret was most likely tired and was probably a little sore, and he could not be in her presence after their night together without wanting her again.

He had remained in her bed until dawn, and they had come together three times.

The first was careful, sweet, and over too soon, though at least he made sure she found her peak before he reached his. The second, half an hour later, was altogether more vigorous. She had lost her apprehension and was eager to meet him in his enthusiasm.

The third time was in the early morning light, a slow, long loving that twined her even more fully around his heart. He had been irrevocably hers before their night together. After it, he could not imagine life without her and didn't want to try.

She sat beside him and slipped her hand into his; instantly, he was as hard as a rock, with no relief in sight. They would be stuck in this carriage for four hours, except for a single stop half-way to change horses. If railway passenger travel could be made commercial, he mused, then they might be able to shorten the travel time.

There. A topic of conversation to take his mind off his desire. "If a feasible steam locomotive could be produced to pull the carriages, would you be willing to try railway travel?" he asked.

Railways provided them with a lively discussion for the first half of the journey. Miss Trent knew little about them and asked a number of intelligent questions. Margaret showed she'd heard his previous comments on the subject by answering some of them with his own words. Wakefield had investigated a couple of nasty accidents and had views about what could make such travel safer.

At the change of horses, Wakefield fetched drinks and food, including for the driver, the footmen, and the guards on the roof, and they all visited the privies. Even so, the stop was no more than twenty minutes.

This time, Margaret started the conversation by asking about steamships. They were common on rivers and lakes, but experiments had begun with ocean-going ships. One that was about to attempt the Atlantic crossing they disqualified by agreement, because its main propulsion was wind in its sails.

"Still," Miss Trent pointed out, "the extra maneuverability inshore, and being able to proceed in a dead calm must be an advantage."

By the time they arrived in the village that was their destination, they had moved on to balloon travel, which was fascinating but, they all agreed, of little possible use, since the wind direction was so variable and it was impossible to navigate with any precision.

They stopped at the inn, where their horses would be rested,

SNOWY AND THE SEVEN DOVES

and where they would wait for the Ashbys to arrive with Deffew.

Snowy was assisting Margaret from the carriage when Wakefield, who had descended first, shouted, "Dr. Chapman," and hurried off across the courtyard. Snowy and Margaret followed.

A grey-haired gentleman stopped in the act of helping a matronly lady into one of those chaises for hire known as a *yellow bounder.* Both turned to look at Wakefield with dread that turned to resignation.

"Mr. Wakefield," said the gentleman. "If you have more questions, they will have to wait, sir. Mrs. Chapman and I are about to leave for a journey."

Snowy followed Wakefield, Margaret on his arm. *Wakefield was right about the urgency. Another ten minutes, and they would have been gone.*

"I am sorry to detain you, Dr. Chapman," Wakefield said. "I brought Lady Snowden's son, the true Lord Snowden, to meet you both. We are expecting Lady Snowden's younger son at any moment. Also, another young gentleman, whom I expect Mrs. Chapman will be pleased to see."

Mrs. Chapman gazed nervously at Wakefield, while Chapman looked anxiously around the courtyard. "I am sorry you have had this journey for nothing," he said. "You should have made an appointment. We must go. Come along, my dear."

He took his wife's arm to help her to the carriage. Snowy stepped in front of them, and Frank hurried to the lead horse to have a few words with the post boy. The Chapmans stopped and the doctor stepped partly in front of his wife, his fists clenched and his chin set. Snowy sought for words to reassure him, but Margaret spoke first.

"Please, I am Lady Charmain, Lord Snowden's betrothed. We are to be married on Wednesday, but we have made the trip today because Hal was so anxious to see you. Will you not spare us an hour before you begin your trip?"

"You have no right to stop us," Dr. Chapman began, but Mrs. Chapman tugged at his arm and addressed Margaret. "His mother called him Hal."

Margaret smiled at her. "He remembers. He was young, of course, but he has a few memories of his mother. He and Ned remember the lullaby she sang to them."

"The Welsh one." Mrs. Chapman returned Margaret's smile. "Anthony, let us give them their hour. We owe Madeline that much."

"It could be a trick, dearest," Chapman told her. "They could be sending for a magistrate, or that villain Snowden. How do we know this man is even Madeline's son?"

"Anthony, look at him. He is the image of the portrait in her locket. And if he is who he says he is, Snowden is his enemy as much as ours."

At that moment, a group of four riders arrived in the coach-yard. They must have seen Snowy and his group because the lead rider led the others toward them, through the jumble of horses and carriages.

"Snowy," called Elijah Ashby, even as the rider at his elbow called, "Hal!"

Mrs. Chapman turned white and then flushed red, her eyes shining as she stepped away from her husband and toward the third rider, who was ignoring everyone else, his gaze fixed on her.

"Dickon?" Mrs. Chapman answered her own whispered question. "Dickon!" She flung herself forward, even as the rider swung from his horse and opened both his arms, and they embraced, laughing with delight even as tears ran down their cheeks.

"Correct again," Snowy said to Wakefield, though he could not help grinning at the happy pair.

"Is that Richard Deffew?" Chapman asked. "It must be." His smile dawned and grew to a beam. "This is a happy day, gentlemen! Why did you not tell us that he was coming? Of course, we do not mind a delay for such a reunion! It has been a wound in Mrs. Chapman's heart, and one I feared we would never see healed."

The ostler interrupted. "Doctor, do you and the missus want

the carriage or not?"

Chapman considered that with a slight frown. "A family emergency. Let me have a word with Mrs. Chapman, but I think we will have to put the journey off until tomorrow."

The ostler shrugged. "I 'spect old Ferblowe," he hooked a thumb in the direction of the inn, "will want you to pay for the post chaise, since you booked it. But no skin off my nose."

At this point, Ned walked up to Snowy. "So, you are to marry Lady Charmain," he said to Snowy. "Congratulations, Hal." He gave Margaret a hug and a buss on the cheek. "My best wishes on your nuptials. I think you will be a wonderful sister."

Ash, too, had congratulations to offer. "Regina is following in the carriage, but we rode ahead. Dickon was anxious to see his mother."

He turned to smile at the family reunion. The young man had Mrs. Chapman tucked into his side and was shaking hands with Chapman. All three were smiling.

Dr. Chapman said something to Wakefield who came back toward Snowy and those with him. "Ash," he said in greeting, "Mr. Snowden."

"Call me Ned," the young man suggested. "Less confusing."

"The Chapmans are putting off their trip until tomorrow. Mrs. Chapman has invited the three of you to lunch. She wants her son to meet his little brother and his sisters, and she knows you two Snowdens will have some questions about your mother. Miss Trent and Frank should go with you, just in case. Ash, I thought we could treat everyone else to lunch here while we wait for your wife."

THE ASYLUM WAS a pleasant manor house set in a couple of acres of garden. Apart from the high gate and walls, it looked like any other substantial residence. More than a dozen people were at leisure in the garden, enjoying the sunshine; on second look, Snowy realized that at least half of them wore some sort of uniform.

Patients, presumably, and their keepers. When he asked Chapman, the doctor confirmed the assumption, but corrected his choice of words. "We prefer to call them our guests, who are with their attendants," he said.

Smiles and waves reassured Snowy that Chapman was liked by "guests" and "attendants" alike. Wakefield had said the asylum was a kindly place, but Snowy had heard too many horror stories not to have been afraid for his mother. From Ned's expression, he had felt the same way.

His opinion of the doctor was confirmed when an elderly woman with flyaway white hair and eyes of faded blue launched herself at the doctor and latched onto his arm.

"Dr. Chapman! You are back! Has it been seven days? Mrs. Pullman said you were going away for seven days. I wanted you to help me find Fluffy. I think he has gone into the village. Mrs. Pullman says I cannot go into the village. Will you take me to find Fluffy, Dr. Chapman?"

Chapman exchanged glances with his wife before leading the old lady off down a passage, talking quietly to her. He and the woman were joined by a flustered-looking woman in the uniform of an attendant; she patted the woman's shoulder and tilted her head close to listen to her.

"Lady Barlow's cat died three years ago," Mrs. Chapman explained. "We thought she might forget when we got her another kitten of the same coloring, but unfortunately it turned out to be a short hair, and every now and again she goes looking for her Fluffy. Anthony will get her settled and come back to us. If you just follow me down here, I will take you to our private family quarters."

THEY SAT DOWN to a magnificent spread, courtesy of the former Mrs. Deffew, where they were joined by the Chapman's three children, ranging in ages from seven to two.

Dickon was soon absorbed in getting to know his brother and two sisters. The little boy had the same fearsome eyebrows as Dickon, and his face fell into the same glower on those rare occasions when it was not bright with laughter. The children's antics absorbed Dickon; Margaret conversed with Chapman, who had arrived shortly after them.

Which left Ned and Snowy to talk to Mrs. Chapman. If she was Mrs. Chapman at all. Snowy remembered Wakefield commenting that Deffew's death had come as a surprise to her.

But focused on Mrs. Chapman's stories about his mother, and the little box of keepsakes she had produced for him and Ned to share, he thought no more about it.

"I want you to believe that she was happy here," Mrs. Chapman assured them, "though she missed you both. She had reports about your good health and your accomplishments, Ned. Lord Snowden, she believed her friends were keeping you safe."

Ned surreptitiously wiped away a tear, and Snowy had to swallow hard. *It would have been worse if she had been abused*, he told himself. All the lost years! All the years stolen from the three of them, him, Ned, and his mother. But at least she had been safe, and she died among friends. Grief clawed at his heart, and his gaze turned unerringly to his heart's peace, where she sat, talking to Chapman.

"I want to stay with my family," Dickon announced. "To get to know them." He turned his glower on Chapman, but his voice was both humble and pleading. "May I, sir?"

Chapman exchanged a glance with his wife. "We have to make that trip," he reminded her. "It *is* urgent."

"Hal and I are to be wed tomorrow," Margaret commented. "We applied for a common license." The others appeared as nonplussed as Snowy, but Snowy caught on when Margaret added, "It allowed us to be wed after seven days, without the banns being read."

The Chapman's important errand was obvious when Snowy thought about it, as was Margaret's purpose in introducing the topic of their license. The pair had been eloping to Scotland to regularize their union out of sight of local gossip.

Snowy added his mite. "One can apply for a common license to a local bishop, to the archdeacons of some parishes, or to the vicar of a Royal Peculiar," he informed the group.

"Our bishop lives in Oxford," Mrs. Chapman commented. "Dearest?"

"Would you excuse us for a moment?" Chapman said politely to the company. A hurried consultation with Mrs. Chapman and then with her eldest son, had him firmly stating his intention to use his post chaise after all. "I will be able to return by evening," he declared.

So, when Snowy's party walked back to the inn, Chapman went too. They left Dickon Deffew with his mother and newly-discovered sisters and brother. "I will stay here at least long enough to go with mother and her husband next week," he said, his jaw jutted as if he expected someone to deny him. Nobody did.

While Margaret's carriage and the post-chaise Chapman was going to use after all were being readied, he showed Ned and Snowy their mother's grave in the little churchyard. They stood over it in silence for several minutes. Ned gripped Snowy's shoulder hard, and Snowy returned the grip.

"Rest in peace, Mama," Snowy said, and Ned's voice shook on the *Amen*.

Wakefield must have guessed Chapman's secret, for when he heard that the doctor was now making a day trip, he mentioned he knew the vicar at Dorchester Abbey, just out of Oxford, and that the parish was a Royal Peculiar—beholden to the Crown and not in any diocese.

Dorchester was closer—less than two hours. Wakefield offered to go with Chapman to talk to the Dorchester Abbey vicar.

"I'll catch the mail coach from there and still be home in London tonight," he said.

Then Chapman and Wakefield departed for Dorchester Abbey, and Snowy, Margaret, the Ashbys and their parties for London.

Snowy, Margaret and Ned arrived back at Margaret's townhouse in the twilight, weary and stiff after the journey. "No need to tell me anything tonight," Pauline said, when she greeted them. "I've had water on the boil for the past hour, and the footmen are carrying it upstairs to pour into your baths even as we speak."

"I need to see Ned settled," Margaret told her.

"If someone will just point me at that bath and then bed," Ned said, "I will be more than happy."

"I can do that," Pauline assured him. "A little supper as well, Mr. Snowden? I've arranged trays for Lady Charmain, Lord Snowden, and Miss Trent."

"Miss Turner, you are an angel," Ned declared, and followed her and the maids she summoned up the stairs to the guest chambers.

Margaret was nearly asleep in the bath when Hal let himself in through the connecting door, still damp from his own bath and carrying his tray.

He held her towel for her, then used it to dab her dry, managing a few caresses and kisses before Margaret's maid walked into the dressing room without knocking and shrieked in shock.

"Her ladyship will not need you," Hal told the maid. "I will serve as my lady's maid tonight."

The servant blushed and giggled.

"Shall we go through to your sitting room for supper, my love?" Hal asked. "So the footmen can empty your bath?"

Margaret managed a few bites but gave up after a particularly jaw-cracking yawn.

"Time for bed," Snowy decided, and Margaret agreed.

She stumbled through the necessary pre-bedtime routines in a haze of fatigue, and when her head was on the pillow, she barely had the energy to mumble, "I don't think I can manage to stay awake for... Hal?"

His eyes were closed and his breathing had slowed.

"Hal? Are you asleep?"

No response. *I'll take that as a yes.* It was her last thought of the night.

Chapter Twenty-Five

MARGARET'S FIRST THOUGHT on waking was there could be no better way to start a busy day than waking in Hal's arms, but then he proved her wrong and also showed her that he was no longer fatigued.

After a very satisfying interlude, he retreated to his room to wash and dress, grumbling as he left that he supposed they should put in an appearance.

"Since the day is about us, we should," she retorted. "And may I remind you that the compromise was your idea? I was all for having your foster mothers at the breakfast the Stancrofts are hosting for us tomorrow."

Lily had been adamant that it would just not do for her and her friends to mix with Margaret's friends. "We will come to the church, since Snowy insists," she had conceded. "We will not set the whole of the ton talking by inserting our sinful selves into your wedding breakfast. The focus of the day is you and Snowy."

She shook her head when Margaret opened her mouth to argue. "If we are there, we'll have half the young bucks speculating about whether their friendship with the pair of you will get them a discount in the sack, and half of their fathers avoiding the eyes of any of us they've bedded. And all the ladies tearing great holes in your reputation and that of your children to the sixth generation."

Margaret assured Lily that she and Hal did not care about small-minded gossips, but Lily would not budge.

Hal's suggested compromise was that his foster mothers come to lunch at Margaret's townhouse on the day before the wedding. Delighted, Poppy had offered to provide the lunch, and Margaret had suggested that all six ladies stay the night so they could travel to the church together in the morning.

Ned and Pauline were tucking into breakfast when she and Hal arrived downstairs. "Is it true the Cyprians from the brothel are all coming to lunch today?" Ned asked, almost before they had had a chance to say good morning.

"Hal's family are joining us for lunch in a pre-wedding celebration," Margaret informed him, "and I will thank you to treat them all as ladies, and not to use those words in their presence or mine."

"Sorry," said Ned cheerfully. "So how many of them are coming? Are they pretty? I hear the House of Blossoms is very exclusive—entry by invitation only! Could you get me an invitation, Hal?"

"We will not be discussing this at breakfast with two ladies," Hal growled. His brow furrowed. "Or at all," he added.

Lily was apparently right, at least about the young bucks.

So re-educating Ned was going to be Hal's first task of the day, after breakfast. Margaret's was ensuring that the remaining six guest chambers had been made ready for visitors while she was away yesterday.

After that, Margaret visited the kitchens, to be assured by Cook that everything was under control. Cook had eyed Poppy with suspicion and thinly veiled contempt at first, but, as the two of them had worked out the lunch menu, trailing and sampling each dish, they had formed a firm friendship and were now attempting to outdo one another in professional courtesies.

"Mrs. Poppy's dishes have already started to arrive, my lady, and they look wonderful. Relax and enjoy yourself," Cook said.

"We will do you proud."

Relaxing was easier said than done. Margaret had met three of Hal's foster mothers. What of the three from the farm? What would they think of her? She would not have believed three months ago that she would crave approval from six retired prostitutes.

Then she had met Lily, Jasmine, and Poppy, and found them to be women of courage and strength. Women she respected. Women who were responsible for raising the man she loved. They were important to him, and so they mattered to her.

Holly, Lotus, and Petunia were expected at any time, coming straight from the country. They would be meeting Margaret for the first time. She hoped she would make a good impression! Meanwhile, she had nothing to do to keep herself occupied, so she worried.

She was grateful for the knock on the door. If they were here at last, she could get the initial introduction over and stop fretting. Her butler did not open the door to the group from the farm, however, but to Mrs. Wakefield, Mr. Wakefield's wife and business partner.

"I have news, my lady," she said. "Would you summon Lord Snowden so I might tell you both together?"

"I'll take you to him," Margaret decided. Hal and Ned were in the study, keeping out of the way of the bustle.

Mrs. Wakefield got straight to the point after Margaret closed the door. "Two things happened yesterday while you were out of town. My husband and I thought you ought to know. You still have the Moriarty guards?"

"We do," Hal replied. "What do I need to tell them?"

"My first piece of news is that Lord Hungerford-Fox was knifed in the street yesterday. The assailant got away. Lord Hungerford-Fox is not expected to live."

Margaret had been about to sit down. Her knees failed and she dropped into the chair.

Concern showed in Mrs. Wakefield's eyes. "I beg your pardon, Lady Charmain. I did not intend to upset you."

"No, not at all," Margaret protested. "I was just surprised." She took a deep breath. "Lord Snowden warned him of the danger," she remembered. "He refused to believe it." Hal came to stand behind her and put a comforting hand on her shoulder. She covered his hand with her own.

"A waste," he said. "If he had stayed in protective custody for a few more days, he would have been safe. With the work your agency has done, and particularly with what we found out at the asylum, we have enough to put Snowden away for his crimes."

Mrs. Wakefield gave a sharp nod. "Which brings me to the more important matter. Richard Snowden has disappeared. He has not been home for two nights. He has slipped the attention of those set to watch him and has gone to ground somewhere."

⟫⟫⟪⟪

MRS. WAKEFIELD LEFT, after advising them to increase the guard when they went to the church tomorrow, and otherwise, to stay at home until Snowden was apprehended.

Snowy forced down his jealousy over Margaret's reaction to Hungerford-Fox's death and took her aside to comfort her. "How are you, Margaret?" he said. "What do you need?"

Her smile seemed cheerful enough. "I am not such a frail creature as to be frightened just because Snowden has run away, Hal. With the provisions you have made for my protection, I could not be safer."

"Not that," he said. "You seemed upset about Hungerford-Fox."

Her reply was tart. "One does not expect to hear that a person one knows has been knifed in the street."

That was all very well, but he had not imagined the tremor in her muscles as she sucked in a couple of deep breaths, as if suppressing tears.

228

She grimaced. "If you must know, I was ashamed of my first reaction. Not the involuntary one. The thought that came after. What sort of person am I, if I can hear of a person's untimely death and think, *at least he will not spread stories about me anymore!*"

Snowy kissed her forehead, cheered by the confession. "A human one, my love."

Their private conversation was interrupted when the butler came to announce the ladies from the farm, and the other three arrived shortly after.

After that, Snowy had his work cut out to keep an eye on everyone to make sure that his foster mothers were respected. Ned had clearly taken the lecture he had received to heart. He was being his usual charming self, flirting madly, but with all the over-the-top sincerity of a nephew with a maiden aunt. Not by a word or an expression did he treat them any differently than he would a mature lady of the ton.

Pauline was a known quantity. She behaved as she did with everyone, polite and self-effacing.

Snowy had had no doubts about his beloved, and he'd been right. She was everywhere at once, talking herbs and vegetables with Holly, recipes with Poppy, the management of staff with Jasmine, crop rotation with Lotus, kittens with Petunia, investment with Lily, and—to his embarrassment—Snowy. with them all.

The servants and guards, too, behaved impeccably, as if the six visitors had come from a fine country estate, and not from one of the most exclusive brothels in London.

Then the food started to arrive. Poppy and Margaret's Cook had outdone themselves. Dish after dish was set out on the sideboard for them to help themselves. Snowy loaded Margaret's plate and went back to fill his own. They must have cooked all of Snowy's favorites and all of Margaret's. He noticed only one lack. No apple pie, sadly. He remembered Poppy saying she had used all of the stored apples from the last harvest.

When he'd eaten his plate empty, he would come back for a

slice of raspberry pie, instead.

Maids and footmen trotted in and out of the room, removing empty dishes and bringing full ones. The drink was as plentiful as the food: punch, light on the alcohol given the time of day, lemonade, tea for those who preferred it.

Conversation flowed as freely as the food. Of course, pleasing conversation was part of his foster mothers' stock in trade, and it was taught to Society ladies, too, from the cradle. Everyone seemed to be truly enjoying themselves, however.

Maids brought around coupe glasses, followed by footmen with bottles of champagne. Lily stood up. "As stand-in for the mother of the groom, Lady Charmain, my sisters and I would like to thank you. Nineteen years ago, we took on the job of raising Henry Snowden, and we have done our best to make a man of him. It has had its moments." She shared several stories from his youth, setting off Snowy's other foster mothers, until he wanted to crawl from the room in mortification.

"We think he has turned out rather well," Lily concluded, embarrassing Snowy still further. "Apparently you do, too, or you would not be taking him on. It is, I am told, traditional to congratulate the groom and wish the bride every blessing. We do, Lady Charmain. May the pair of you enjoy the best of life and avoid the worst. Ladies and gentlemen, please raise your glasses in a toast to the bride and groom."

Snowy took his turn, thanking each of his foster-mothers for their part in his life, and for embarrassing him in front of his betrothed and his brother. He made it short, and finished with a toast to families, especially those present.

The flow of dishes from the kitchen had paused for the speeches, but after Snowy had finished, it began again, with sweet cakes, cut fruit, cheese, nuts and the like. A maid brought Snowy a large slice of pie. "Apple, sir," she said. "I am told it is your favorite."

Snowy smiled at Poppy. She must have saved just enough to make him the treat. A pity he was so full, but he could surely eat some of it to show his appreciation. He took a large spoon full. It smelt a bit odd. Musty. Old apples, clearly.

In the mouth, it tasted bitter. He washed it down with a gulp of his wine. Would Poppy notice if he put it to one side? She wasn't watching. He put the plate behind him on a handy side table, and turned to Ned, who had just come to sit beside him.

"They are formidable women," Ned said, quietly. "I can see why Margaret doesn't frighten you."

Margaret frightened Ned? "They are," Snowy agreed. "And so is Margaret."

"My father despises women," Ned admitted. "He says they are weak, driven by their emotions, in need of direction."

"Our mother survived him," Snowy pointed out. "I'd say that makes her strong. My foster mothers and Margaret? They are capable, intelligent, and willing to work hard. If they had been men, that would have been enough for them to succeed. But they are women, so they meet with obstacles, barriers, and abuses that a man cannot comprehend. And they succeed anyway, on their own terms. Formidable? Yes. They had to be."

"Is it true that Mistress Lily was left an inheritance by her protector, and used it to start the House of Blossoms? Why wouldn't she find another protector? She is lovely enough, even now."

An inheritance of a sort, but not from her protector. Now was not the time, but perhaps he would ask Lily for permission to tell Ned the story. How their mother had given Lily all of her jewelry, and Lily had used it to have paste copies made to return to their mother and sold the originals to fund a life that would allow Lily to keep Snowy with her, as well as to protect her sisters and friends.

"You should ask her to tell the story." There had definitely been something wrong with that apple. His mouth felt odd—both numb and burning at the same time, and his stomach heaved.

Ned said something, but he seemed a long way away, and Snowy could not hear him. "Ned. The apple." He found it hard to move his chest to breathe. He had to do it; had to stop Ned from eating the pie. He flung out an arm toward it, or so he intended, but it was more of a jerk with his shoulder. "Something's wrong," he choked out.

"Hal? What is it?" Ned's voice was shrill with concern.

Snowy saw the darkness coming for him, turned his head with the last of his strength to see his lady. In the narrowing tunnel that was left of his vision, she hurried toward him, her eyes wide with alarm. *Love you.* He didn't have the strength to say it. He hoped she knew.

He was glad she was the last thing he saw as the darkness consumed him.

⇒⇒⇒⧫⇐⇐⇐

MARGARET PUSHED BACK the panic that was clouding her mind as she fell to her knees beside Hal. He had stopped breathing, though he still had a pulse. "What happened, Ned? Did he choke?"

She rolled Hal to the floor, on his side so that she could thump his back.

Ned dropped to his knees beside her. "I don't think so. He wasn't eating, Margaret. We were talking. He started mumbling. Then he said, 'The apple' and 'Something's wrong'."

"Apple?" Poppy said. "We had no apple today. We finished the last of the dried apples and have to wait for the harvest."

Margaret arranged Snowy on his back and began breathing into his mouth. Mouth-to-mouth expired-air breathing had been known to keep people alive after drowning or suffocation in the mines. Perhaps it would help.

"Snowy had apple pie," said Petunia. "The girl gave it to him."

"She's right," Pauline said. "See? On the side table behind where Snowy was sitting."

"Don't touch it," Miss Trent warned. "Which girl, Miss Petunia? One of the maids?"

Margaret listened to them talk, hoping they would happen upon something that would let her help Hal. She would not remove her focus from him, taking every moment between breaths to check his pulse—thready but there—his color, and anything else she could think of.

"I didn't make it," Poppy insisted, and I'll be bound Cook Bronson did not, either. She told me she had no apples."

"It smells musty," Ned reported.

Musty? "Use a napkin to pick up the plate and bring it to where I can smell it," Margaret insisted.

A moment later, a piece of pie, with a large chunk out of one end, was lowered in front of her. She gave Snowy another breath, then put her nose near the pie. One sniff confirmed her suspicion. "Hemlock," she said.

After that, Lily took over, sending for the maids and questioning the one that Petunia identified. Margaret stopped listening. There was no antidote for hemlock, but if she could just keep pushing breath into his lungs, if his heart kept beating, if she could keep him alive until the paralysis wore off...

She was not going to consider the alternative. "Live, Hal. You promised to marry me. I need you. Don't leave me."

She continued breathing, continued muttering, continued checking his pulse. Around her, people came and went. She gathered they'd tracked the pie to a delivery that purported to come from the brothel—a small box with a label saying it was just for Henry Snowden.

They'd sent out searchers for the old woman who had made the delivery.

None of that mattered. What mattered was another breath, and then another, as the minutes crawled by and Snowy's pulse slowed and weakened but never quite failed.

Someone must have sent for Lord Lechton, for an interminable eon later he was there, gently putting her to one side and telling her to rest as he took over. "You have done everything right, Lady Charmain. Now it will be down to how much of the poison he ingested, and how strong he is."

She refused to leave Snowy's side, holding his hand as Poppy fed her sips of tea and each of the other foster mothers in turn came to hold her other hand or squeeze her shoulder. She kept talking to him, calling him back to her, heedless of who was listening.

Then Lechton stopped his ministrations.

"No!" Margaret protested. "We can't stop! Here. Move out of the way. I will do it."

Lord Lechton put a hand out to stop her. "He is breathing on his own, my lady."

He was. Light breaths, barely moving his chest, but she could feel the puff of warm air on her palm as she held it over his mouth.

She looked up at Hal's family, smiling. "He is breathing," she repeated. She did not realize tears were running down her cheeks until Ned knelt in front of her and dried them with his handkerchief. "He'll be all right now," he assured her. "Won't he, Lord Lechton?"

Lord Lechton smiled. "We will have to watch him, Snowden, but yes. I think we have cause to be optimistic."

They moved Hal to a couch. Margaret sat with his head on her lap, watching every breath, holding his wrist so she could feel every beat of his heart. Both were strengthening, and his color was returning.

Meanwhile, Pauline had ordered tea and coffee, and those who had not eaten enough lunch were snacking on leftovers. To Margaret's surprise, only a little over half an hour had passed since Hal's collapse.

"Thank you for coming so quickly," she said to Lord Lechton. He was staying until Hal woke up and had the pie in a box to take with him to a chemist friend. Apparently, her footman had found him on the point of leaving his house, for an errand that could wait, he insisted.

Margaret lapsed into silence again, until she thought of something else. "Did they find the old woman who brought the pie?" Margaret asked. Ned shook his head.

"Miss Trent has sent to let Mrs. Moriarty know, and Wakefield," he said. "If she can be found, they will find her."

Margaret didn't care, except she wanted Snowden to be brought to justice so that she and Hal would be out of danger.

"Margaret, do you want me to send a message to the Archdeacon?" Pauline asked.

Margaret could not make sense of the question. "What for?"

"If Snowy is not going to be well enough for the wedding..." Pauline began.

Margaret caught her breath. Her eyes caught Lily's concerned gaze. "Stop the wedding?" she asked.

The husky voice from her lap stopped all talk and movement in the room. "No," said Snowy.

⟫⟫⟪⟪

SNOWY WAS WALKING in a garden. He was not sure where the garden was or how he got there, but somehow, his ignorance didn't worry him. Surrounded by peace, he was certain that, in this place, at this time, nothing could harm him.

Through an arched opening in a hedge of fragrant roses, he could see the glint of water. A lake, ruffled by the gentle breeze that, closer at hand, played with the long heads of the wildflowers in the meadow that sloped down from the hedge to the water's edge.

A mown path led through the meadow and into a grove of trees. Willows, probably, since they grew with their feet in the lake. Beyond them, he could see a roof. A house? He strolled toward it along the path, stopping every few feet to admire another flower.

They were subtly different from the wildflowers he had known as a boy on the farm. This one was a corncockle, but the flowers came in a rainbow of colors instead of just magenta. There was columbine, but with larger flowers. The daisies were pink and purple, the harebells white and pink as well as powder blue. Lady's smock eschewed its pastel colors for bright magenta and vibrant cerise.

Chicory, cornflower, lady's bedstraw, everywhere he looked he saw old favorites, made anew with some magic paintbrush and endowed with a scent that surpassed any he remembered.

It was the same under the trees. Who had ever heard of red bluebells? Or orange forget-me-nots? Or pink and purple wood anemones?

By the time he came out of the woods, he had realized another anomaly. Flowers of spring, summer, autumn—even winter—all out at the same time.

Later, he would wonder that he felt no disquiet. Perhaps the sight of the pavilion in the gardens beyond the woods drove any other thoughts from his head.

The lake curved into a bay just in front of him, and the pavilion rose from the center of the bay, three stories high, with a delicate spiral staircase climbing as far as the third level. Bridges crossed the bay in a series of gentle arches, linked by platforms, and on one of those platforms sat the first people he had seen since he found himself in the garden.

Something about them teased at his mind, and as he grew closer, he realized what it was. The woman was his mother. The man with her—surely that was the man he saw whenever he looked in the mirror?

As he reached the first bridge, they saw him, and his mother gave a glad cry and started forward. The man followed her more slowly, so when Snowy met his mother on a bridge part way across to the pavilion, the man was still a bridge and a platform behind.

"Hal, my darling." His mother flung her arms around him,

and he hugged her back for a long moment. "But why are you here?" his mother asked. "Surely it is too early?"

Without letting go of Snowy, she turned to the other man who was suddenly beside her. "Edmund, I think he has done it. I think Richard has killed Hal."

I am dead? That explains the flowers. Snowy thought he should probably care, but it didn't seem important. Not when the man who looked like him was clasping his hand and smiling at him. Close up, Hal could see that his father's jaw was slightly squarer, his nose more humped than straight, his hair darker. In dozens of tiny ways, they were different, but to the casual eye, they could be the same man.

"Not dead yet," Papa said to Mama.

Mama narrowed her eyes and seemed to look inwards. "Ah. Yes. I see. Hal, darling, you need to go back. Before it is too late."

How could he go back when he didn't know where he was or how he got there? Besides, why should he? He liked it here. He smiled at his father. "I would like to get to know you," he said, and then, to his mother, "I missed you."

"You can choose to stay," his father said. "You need to know, though, that Margaret and Ned will grieve."

"Listen," said Mama, and she held up a hand.

Snowy heard birdsong, the lap of water against the supports of the bridge, the movement of grass and flowers in the wind, and then, beyond them all, as if a huge distance away, a voice. "Live, Hal. You promised to marry me. I need you. Don't leave me."

"Margaret! I have to go. But how?"

"Go with our blessing, my son," said Papa. "Live long and well. We will be waiting."

"Just breath, Hal," his mother said. "Breath in. That's it. Now out. And again. In. Out." As she repeated the words, her voice faded, and the blackness returned.

He hurt. Everything was sore. His chest. His stomach. His throat. His head felt as if he'd been banging it into a brick wall. His eyelids were too heavy to lift.

Then he heard Margaret's beloved voice again. "...stop the wedding?"

That was the impetus he needed. His eyes shot open, and he said, "No!"

Chapter Twenty-Six

T HE SMILE OF the reflection in the mirror spoke of both pride and glee, which was fair, for Snowden had been very clever.

"Did they think I would not expect watchers on my house?" he gloated. He'd known they must be there and had searched until he found them. A street sweeper who lingered overlong on a little used corner. A lamplighter still out after all the lamps were lit. A schoolboy loitering around a boring square of townhouses.

Snowden spotted more than a dozen suspicious people, and if some of them were innocently about their own business, some were in the employ of the false Snowden. Snowden was sure of it, and Richard thought so, too.

Snowden giggled. "I hope they were paid up front, for that interloper will not be able to pay them now that he is dead!"

He had left the house early yesterday morning, two days after he'd found out Lady Charmain's wedding plans, and about the gathering today. He passed the watchers dressed as one of his own footmen, hurrying in that swift stiff walk that footmen perfected. He still had the keys to the rooms his ward Deffew had once lived in, and there he opened the large basket he carried.

When he left, he was someone else. An anonymous merchant, bearded and portly just prosperous enough to be out for the day in London, seeing the sights, his arms full of shopping.

Snowden had not played at theatricals for years, but he had always enjoyed it in his youth. "It was fun to be someone else," he told Richard in the mirror.

His merchant alter ego took a room in a nice comfortable hotel, selected from those suitable for such a gentleman according to two criteria. The hotel had to be close to Lady Charmain's townhouse. And it had to have an outside staircase that would allow his next character to leave the hotel without being seen and to return the same way.

"It was the best disguise yet," he gloated. "No one suspected." If they went looking for the old woman, anyone who noticed her would mention her bent shoulders, her straggly white hair, her wrinkled cheeks, her long nose, her shapeless brown gown, and large black shawl, some of which was now buried in a rubbish heap at the back of the hotel.

"Edmund is dead at last." No. That was wrong. *Henry* was dead. Deffew killed Edmund long ago, so that Richard could have Madeline, the way it was meant to be.

And he had won her, for a short time. All he had ever wanted was Madeline as his wife and the title to go with the estate he had cared for as steward.

Madeline was long dead, and Richard had been betrayed by the son she had given him. Winning the victory was dust and ashes, but it was still a victory. Edmund's son would not have his title.

"He is dead. Bastard or true heir, he is gone." He cackled, startling himself and the reflection, which jerked so that brandy slopped from its glass.

Hungerford-Fox's whore had promised that White could not resist apple pie. The old lady he had become assured the maid this was a special delivery from the House of Blossoms. "I told her to take it directly to the groom and tell him it had been made with love." He cackled.

Snowden had not been able to see the job done, more's the pity, but he'd put so much of the poison in with the apple, a mere mouthful should kill White or whatever his name was. And if he ate the whole thing, he'd be dead ten times over.

If Lady Charmain did not share the pie, she could live. Snowden did not like killing women, and any child she might be carrying would be illegitimate, and therefore not a threat to his title. He didn't need her land anymore, either. He was mining under her land without her knowledge and had dropped the canal project. Young Deffew had suggested looking at the improvements to railways, and that allowed him another route. The boy was also a traitor, but the idea was good.

To escape from the scene of the murder, he made the transformations in reverse, throwing away each costume as he abandoned it. He had returned to his townhouse dressed as himself. Let the watchers on the street see him. He had nothing to hide.

Richard in the mirror grinned at him, and he chuckled. "It wasn't me. It was an old lady," he said.

"This old lady," said a voice from the door.

It was that foreign guard who followed around after the false Snowden, pretending to be a valet. The one who had thwarted both the lightskirt and the sniper. He was holding up the garments the old lady had worn, and her wig.

For a moment, Snowden felt a frisson of fear, but he drowned it in indignation. "How dare you walk into a viscount's house? I'll have you arrested!"

"We also have the merchant," the valet said, his tone steady. Worse, amusement flickered in his eyes.

A thundering knock on the door changed that to a hawk-like alertness. "That will be the runners," he announced.

It was, and they had the nerve to announce he was under arrest on a charge of murder and attempted murder. Attempted? He damned well had murdered the imposter! "You cannot arrest me," he sneered. "I am a peer."

"You are not," said the woman who had accompanied the runners. "You are an imposter and a murderer. The magistrate has seen the evidence of your crimes and has ordered your arrest."

Snowden took a step back, then rallied. "Thompson!" he shouted. He would have his butler throw these fools from his house. But no one came to his call.

"Your servants are being detained in the servant's hall." The foreign guard was now openly wearing a smile. "It is over, Snowden. You have lost."

Snowden looked around. Burly men by the door. The window? It was his only chance. His eye passed over the mirror. He barely recognized the man he saw there. Trepidation? Even panic? Shoulders hunching against fate? That was not Richard. He snarled and saw welcome anger leap to the features in the mirror.

Escape. Now.

He hurled himself toward the window, and the room devolved into chaos as the runners threw themselves after him. Even when they pulled him away from his goal, he continued to struggle, anger and fear fueling his strength. Furniture broke under falling bodies, ornaments fell from shelves and side tables.

It had been a desperate attempt, and it failed.

Snowden finished up on the floor, a burly runner sitting on his back to hold him down. He closed his eyes as despair filled him. He had failed. He would hang; choke to death at the end of the rope, jerking, struggling, voiding waste.

The image consumed his mind and his eyes shot open to find something else on which to focus.

Before him, scattered across the floor, were the remains of his mirror, a multitude of shards. His friend Richard looked back at him from a dozen angles.

Cheat the hangman. You know what to do.

He would have to be quick, or they would stop him. He thought about where to cut. Now. Fast and hard.

He grabbed the nearest large shard and jammed it into his throat, just below the angle of his right jaw bone. Someone shouted, and his captor shifted his weight, forcing his head down. With his last thought, he wished he had never met Madeline.

Chapter Twenty-Seven

S NOWY KEPT TELLING everyone he was perfectly well. His looks
must have belied his words, for they kept asking. He would
have to feel a great deal sicker if he was to delay his wedding.
True, he was as weak as a kitten and his head still felt somewhat
detached from the rest of him, in addition to which, staying
upright when standing was problematic.

His attention, too, floated, which had nothing to do with
hemlock poisoning and everything to do with his bride. He had
not seen her since she had crept from his room at dawn, after
instructing Rahat to monitor his breathing and his pulse, as she
had been doing all night.

Her friends had arrived early and closed themselves up with
her in her chambers. According to Rahat, his foster-mothers had
been invited to join the bridal preparations. From the occasional
burst of laughter loud enough to penetrate the walls, a good time
was being had by all.

Meanwhile their husbands, his own friends, and his brother
gathered in his rooms, ignoring the fact that he was fresh from his
bath and still in his smalls. They took over from Rahat to get him
dressed, refusing to allow him to lift a finger. The married men
passed on facetious advice and the single men tossed about
farcical commiserations. Everyone told jokes, even Rahat.

The ladies may have heard a few bursts of laughter from his room, too.

No one, not even Ned, mentioned the news that had been delivered last night—that Snowden was dead. "My father's death, and what it means, is a matter for later," Ned had said. "Tomorrow is about you and my new sister."

When Snowy's supporters deemed him sufficiently brushed, buffed, polished, and primped, they escorted him downstairs, Gary on one side and Ned on the other, no one commenting on his slightly random foot placement that made the support necessary.

He was loaded into a carriage with Gary, Drew, Rahat, and Ned. The other men were going to wait for their wives.

At the church, a man showed them to the vestry to wait, and Gary produced a chair from somewhere for Snowy to sit on. She would be here soon if nothing prevented her. Perhaps Snowden had left another trap?

Snowy knew the guards were alert to such a possibility, but still his heart pounded, and his breath came short. He would not be at ease until she was beside him, and they were wed. Ned sensed some of his turmoil, for he said, "She is coming."

At that moment, the door to the vestry opened and Stancroft looked inside. "We are here, Snowden. Our wives are out in the vestibule awaiting the bride. Time to take your place."

"We can put the chair out for you to sit on," Gary suggested.

"I'll stand," Snowy told them. "I've been saving my strength."

The congregation was small, as expected, and mostly known to him. On the groom's side of the church, his foster-mothers sat close to the front, all in their most demure day gowns, looking as respectable as any matron of the ton. Farther back, a cluster of girls from the house had also made a special effort to blend in, as had Blue and Tommy. In the intermediate pews, Forsythe, his solicitor, sat with a couple of people unknown to him, and he was pleased to also see Mr. and Mrs. Wakefield.

On the bride's side, Stancroft, Deerhaven, and Ashby sat in

the front pew.

Behind them sat the Duke and Duchess of Winshire, and behind them again, most of the servants from Margaret's townhouse.

Snowy took his place and stood, locking his knees, keeping his back straight. When a stir in the church hinted it was time to turn to see his bride, he grabbed his brother's arm for support. Ned, without a word, turned with him.

The cluster of attendants was first: Pauline, Lady Deerhaven, Mrs. Ashby.

They took their seats in the front pew on the bride's side of the church.

Then came Margaret, on the arm of an older gentleman who must have been her uncle. Good. She had been uncertain whether he would make the effort to attend, but the man looked down at her with a warm smile and every sign of regard.

Snowy dismissed the man from his mind, giving all his attention to the beautiful woman who was about to join her life to his. She was wearing something blue and flowing. It gleamed and shimmered as she walked. He could not have described it to save his life. All he could see clearly was her lovely face, her beaming smile, the eyes that met his and softened with love.

He was vaguely aware of disentangling his hand from Ned's arm and holding both hands out for hers.

>>>><<<<

HAL WAS CLEARLY determined to stand, and Margaret had no intention of embarrassing him by insisting that he sit. She wasn't sure, though, if she could hold him up, and was glad to see Ned hovering, ready to provide support if it was needed.

By halfway through the Archdeacon's description of the purpose of marriage, she had realized that Hal could hold up his own weight, but his balance was unreliable. Still, her two hands in his were enough to keep him steady.

She clung on throughout the ceremony.

Even when it came time for him to place the ring on her finger, she kept tight hold with her other hand, and Ned, after passing the ring to the Archdeacon, took Hal unobtrusively by one elbow.

It was a relief, though, when it was time to kneel at the kneelers placed ready for them.

"Don't look so worried," he whispered, out of the corner of his mouth, as the Archdeacon prayed for blessings, for children, for long life, and for love. "I am not about to keel over."

He didn't, either. Not then, not while they stood for the Archdeacon's closing remarks. Not while they signed the register, with Arial and Ned as witnesses. And not on the walk down the aisle, though her arm curved through his took more and more of his weight as they approached the doors.

Those who had come to support them frothed out of the doors behind them, but Hal was nearly through his strength. "Ned," Margaret said, "fetch our carriage, please. Arial, Snowy and I are going home. Would you give our apologies?"

Arial, with a swift assessing glance at Hal, nodded. "Of course. Go and put your husband to bed, dearest. Do not tell anyone. They will assume you are heading for my house for the breakfast. We will tell them otherwise when they arrive."

Hal didn't object, which was evidence enough he was near the end of his endurance. And here came Ned, with the carriage. *Thank goodness.*

With the help of the guards from Moriarty Protection, they were soon in the carriage and away. Margaret leaned forward to wave. Hal leaned back with his eyes shut. "Sorry," he said. "Not the wedding of your dreams."

Margaret squeezed his hand. "Yes, it was. It was my wedding to the man I love and who loves me. That was my dream wedding, Hal."

He tipped his head toward her, opening his eyes. "Mine, too.

And the start of my dream life."

She bent closer for his kiss, achingly tender and sweet.

Even so, she was pleased when the carriage stopped. Hal needed to be in bed. She must have said that out loud, for he chuckled. "The words I hoped to hear on my wedding day, but alas, not when my body is betraying me so."

"There will be other nights," she promised.

"And mornings, and afternoons, and evenings," he added, with a wicked glint in his eye.

Most of the servants had gone to the wedding and had not yet returned. The guards fetched a chair for Hal to sit on and carried it and Hal inside and up the stairs to her bedchamber.

He raised an eyebrow but said nothing until Margaret had sent the guard away to find a servant and ask for hot washing water.

"Your bed, my love?" he asked. "It would be my preference, though I am not up to much beyond sleeping. And you must be sleepy, too, for you were up all night, and not for the reasons I'd hoped."

Margaret could feel herself blushing. "You and I have not talked about it, Hal, but I know my friends all share a bed with their husbands. I hoped we might—"

He didn't allow her to finish. "Yes," he said. "I would like that, too. For better, for worse."

"For richer, for poorer," she repeated.

"In sickness and in health."

"To love and to cherish." She leaned over to kiss him. "I love you, Hal."

They went to sleep in one another's arms and when they woke, Hal was feeling much more himself, as he soon proved.

In the years to come, Lord Snowden's tribulations became a well-known and oft repeated story (though never where he or his wife could hear). Duchesses and dressmakers alike told of how his wicked stepfather stole his title and nearly his life, and how, after many years, he defeated the evil man and convinced Parliament and the Crown to recognize his right to the title.

In the ballrooms and clubs, the ton insisted that the story of the seven soiled doves was just salacious nonsense. No one as true and noble as Snowy (a nickname he carried with good humor) could have been raised in a brothel, not even one as well run as the House of Blossoms.

In the slums, they knew it was not nonsense. Many of them remembered the boy from the House of Blossoms. Those who sent their children to the schools that Snowy funded, or received medical care at the clinics to which the countess gave her support knew Lord and Lady Snowden to be the truest and the best of the aristocracy, but Snowy was also one of their own.

As for Hal and Margaret, some days were better and some worse. They had disagreements and troubles, misunderstandings, and sorrows. Also, many joys. Their children were welcomed into a large extended family, with six grandmothers, their Uncle Ned and later his wife and cousins, and a circle of honorary aunts and uncles.

Still, life throws up challenges for all people. Not every day was wonderful. But as long as Margaret and Hal lived, for richer, for poorer, in sickness and in health, they kept their promise to love and to cherish, and year by year their love grew.

AUTHOR'S NOTE

CYPRIANS AND THE SEX TRADE IN LONDON

In Georgian England, according to Dan Cruickshank's *The Secret History of Georgian London*, one in five women in London earned income from the sale of sex.

Cyprians were high-class prostitutes. They needed to be not only sexually active, but also pleasant company and entertaining. The regency era had a multitude of names for commercial sex workers, most of which showed both the general contempt in which they were held and how ubiquitous they were.

Cyprians, soiled doves, Covent Garden nun, Drury Lane vestal, lady of easy virtue, impure, fashionable impure, left-handed wife, short-heeled wench, three-penny upright, woman of pleasure. And more, even less repeatable in polite company.

Sex workers—defined as those who made some or part of their living by selling sex—ranged from those offering a quick bang up against a wall in a slum alley to those accepting gifts from hopeful admirers while mixing on the fringes of Society. And everything in between.

Most prostitutes seem to have been working class girls who, having surrendered their virtue to a man of their own class, sought some profit from their lapse.

Many worked for a year or two, then took their savings home, and married or set up in business. Prostitution might also be a way to supplement income from another job; seamstresses and milliners, in particular, were so poorly paid that many of them sold their bodies as well. So much so, that many took it for granted that all seamstresses and milliners offered sexual services on request, which must have made walking home after work a fraught exercise for those who didn't.

The risks of conception and disease were great. Even those with wildly successful careers seldom came to good ends. Many—probably most—died young. Some married. Some set up in business for themselves and retired rich. And some, like Harriet Wilson, became penniless as their appeal faded.

Since I needed a refuge where Snowy could grow to adulthood, I made my Blossoms both clever and lucky. Even so, Iris died young.

HEMLOCK AND EXPIRED–AIR VENTILATION

I needed a commonly available poison that would put my Snow-White character into a death-like state. The internet came to my rescue, telling me that even small doses of hemlock caused paralysis. Even today, the treatment for hemlock poisoning is artificial support for breathing and heart until the paralysis wears off.

So, then I had to find out about what we in my youth called *mouth-to-mouth* resuscitation, and (as it turned out) the Georgian era called *expired-air ventilation* (EAV). Medical history reports the use in 1732, when a surgeon at Alloa, Scotland, successfully used mouth-to-mouth to resuscitate a miner who was, to all appearances, dead.

There are other intriguing references going back over millennia that might have been mouth-to-mouth, but certainly, the practice became better known in the 18th century after the Alloa surgeon wrote his account.

The first humane society to promote artificial respiration was established in Amsterdam, and was followed by others, first promoting EAV, and later the use of inflating bellows. Mouth-to-mouth, however, continued to be something any bystander could do.

LOCOMOTIVES

One of the joys of the regency era is the rapid changes in

technology. Locomotives were a case in point, revolutionizing at first the movement of materials from mines and then public transport. All the advances I mention in the story were being discussed in the year of this story, and the first passenger train ran in 1825 (the incident also being the occasion of the first death of a person hit by a passenger train). By 1830, the first fully timetabled railway service was running scheduled freight and passenger traffic. From 1840, the canals began to decline, because the railways were more efficient.

THE WELSH LULLABY

The lyrics of the lullaby that Hal and Ned remember are an English version of *Suo Gên*, a very beautiful traditional Welsh lullaby, which first appeared in print in the early nineteenth century but has been sung by Welsh mothers and nursemaids for centuries. The song was a feature of three crucial scenes in the movie *Empire of the Sun*.

The words are not a direct translation. As the story says, Mrs. Snowden rewrote them in English from the Welsh lullaby her own nurse used to sing to her when she was little. Or, rather, I wrote an English version on her behalf. Here are the full three verses.

Suo Gân (which simply means lullaby)

Sleep my baby, warm and cozy;
In your mother's loving arms.
Nestle close and safely slumber
Where my love is, there's no harm.
No one will disturb your resting;
Hurt will ever pass you by.
Child beloved, on my bosom
Sleep to mother's lullaby.

    Sleep in peace this night my darling;
Gently sleep, you lovely boy.

As you sleep, I see you smile,
What bright visions bring you joy?
Do the angels smile upon you,
When they see your peaceful rest,
Are you smiling back and sleeping,
Sleeping gently on my breast?
    Do not fear, the sound the breeze makes
brushing leaves against the door;
Do not dread the waves that murmur
Lonely waves that wash the shore.
Sleep my darling, there is nothing,
Nothing here to give you fright;
Holy angels guard your slumber,
Safe beneath their wings so white.

TATTOOS IN REGENCY ENGLAND

It is a common perception that only sailors and criminals had tattoos back in the Regency era, and that they were crude affairs, little better than body scribbles.

When I researched body art, I found little specifically about the Regency era, and it is, of course, too early for photos.

However, artistic and complex tattoos have been part of the European story for thousands of years. The Romans, who used tattoos to mark criminals and who therefore saw them as a sign of shame, were amazed by the men and women of England, who had themselves covered in images. As with many peoples, in Pictish culture, a tattoo was a sign of honor, showing that a person had courage and fortitude. People marked significant events by marking them permanently on their bodies.

Vikings, too, had a tattoo tradition, and some researchers think the Germanic tribes did, also.

In the Middle Ages, those going to the Holy Land would have crosses and other symbols tattooed to show their piety. And probably for the practical reason of body identification if something happened to them along the way.

Essentially, the way to get a complex tattoo was to have the design carved into a wooded block, and then printed onto the skin by dipping the block into ink. Then tattooists would use a single needle and puncture by hand with blank ink of various colors into the skin.

In the Georgian and Regency era, soldiers and sailors—both rank and file—marked their bodies to help their comrades recover them for burial if they were killed in a way that rendered them unrecognizable.

Since the technology existed to make those tattoos both meaningful and beautiful, it is not too much of a jump to suggest that wealthy young men would hire a master tattooist to create a personal mark that was a work of art. In my imagined back story, my hero and his friends very likely submitted to the needle of such an artist as a bit of teenage bravado—and my hero chose the phoenix because of his scorched earth beginnings.

Certainly, tattooing was very sophisticated in the Victorian age, not too many years after this story. Several members of the British Royal family are known to have been tattooed in the 1860s and beyond, starting a fashion trend that lasted for a hundred years.

ABOUT THE AUTHOR

Have you ever wanted something so much you were afraid to even try? That was Jude ten years ago.

For as long as she can remember, she's wanted to be a novelist. She even started dozens of stories, over the years.

But life kept getting in the way. A seriously ill child who required years of therapy; a rising mortgage that led to a full-time job; six children, her own chronic illness... the writing took a back seat.

As the years passed, the fear grew. If she didn't put her stories out there in the market, she wouldn't risk making a fool of herself. She could keep the dream alive if she never put it to the test.

Then her mother died. That great lady had waited her whole life to read a novel of Jude's, and now it would never happen.

So Jude faced her fear and changed it—told everyone she knew she was writing a novel. Now she'd make a fool of herself for certain if she didn't finish.

Her first book came out to excellent reviews in December 2014, and the rest is history. Many books, lots of positive reviews, and a few awards later, she feels foolish for not starting earlier.

Jude write historical fiction with a large helping of romance, a splash of Regency, and a twist of suspense. She then tries to figure out how to slot the story into a genre category. She's mad keen on history, enjoys what happens to people in the crucible of a passionate relationship, and loves to use a good mystery and some real danger as mechanisms to torture her characters.

Dip your toe into her world with one of her lunch-time reads collections or a novella, or dive into a novel. And let her know what you think.

Website and blog:
judeknightauthor.com

Subscribe to newsletter:
judeknightauthor.com/newsletter

Bookshop:
judeknight.selz.com

Facebook:
facebook.com/JudeKnightAuthor

Twitter:
twitter.com/JudeKnightBooks

Pinterest:
nz.pinterest.com/jknight1033

Bookbub:
bookbub.com/profile/jude-knight

Books + Main Bites:
bookandmainbites.com/JudeKnightAuthor

Amazon author page:
amazon.com/Jude-Knight/e/B00RG3SG7I

Goodreads:
goodreads.com/author/show/8603586.Jude_Knight

LinkedIn:
linkedin.com/in/jude-knight-465557166

Printed in the USA
CPSIA information can be obtained
at www.ICGtesting.com
CBHW070402260724
12186CB00053B/677